Running Home

2nd in the Beachside Romance Series

Carrie Thorne

Also by Carrie Thorne

A Demon Hunter Romance

Six

Wildest

Changed

Echo

Fury (TBD)

Foothills

All the Days After

The Next Day

A Day Late

A New Day

About Yesterday

280 Days (2025)

Day Dreaming (2026)

Again Tomorrow (TBD)

Days of Summer (TBD)

A Beachside Romance Series

Chasing Forever

Running Home

Hiding Away

Standalones

The Christmas Bet: A Double Feature Christmas Standalone.

Enjoy free books, first looks,

review team access,

and occasional hellos from Carrie?

Let's do this: carriethorne.com/newsletter

1

Frigid white flakes fell from the dreary London sky, each clinging to the dark sidewalks only for a brief moment before melting away. Tonight, Ronan didn't mind the bitter cold. He'd been waiting months for this moment.

Cracking his neck with a shrug, Ronan worked out the stiffness that had taken hold. He'd held his position in the dark alley for hours, leaned against the grimy brick wall. Disguised as a vagrant, his beard was long and matted, his chestnut hair a tangled mass.

Nearly imperceptible footsteps approached. Only the soft squeak of the mercenary's left boot gave him away. "Target approaching," Ronan whispered covertly into his earpiece. Walking carelessly as he rounded the corner, the merc's face was shielded by the gray watchman's cap and thick scarf. Squeak, step, squeak, step… Ronan waited for the sound to pass the green door before making his move.

Squeak, step… The click from the staged dress shop sounded the opening of the metal backdoor. A rumbling Scottish accent boomed, "Here lass, I'll give ya a hand with that."

The sweet-as-pudding cockney accent of his partner trilled down the sidewalk. Trap engaged. "Thank ya', sir. Afraid of tearin' the bag; litt'ring rubbish all o'er the sidewalk."

Pushing off from the wall, Ronan pulled the loaded syringe from his pocket. Quiet as a murmur, he closed the distance to the merc in a matter of seconds. Foot reaching out to tap the merc's leg in misdirection, the merc reacted, shifting away from the invading foot as Ronan reached around with the syringe and swiftly, skillfully injected the tranquilizer into the merc's arm.

Tossing her trash bag back into the open doorway, Rose took one of the merc's arm's while Ronan gripped the other, catching the limp, sedated body before he crumbled. On cue, a black taxi van arrived at the curb. Laughing as if they'd imbibed too heavily at the nearby pub, the odd trio slid into the cab.

Running his hand over his filthy hair, Ronan peered through the tinted windows at their surroundings. To the driver, he inquired in his adopted East London accent, "Any tails?"

From the front, Jim responded, "Not a soul in sight. It's a sound plan. We should be at the safehouse in under twenty minutes." As promised, the cab pulled through the quiet pre-dawn streets before reaching a deserted warehouse on the outskirts of the city.

Ronan wasn't convinced the plan was sound. Something still wasn't right. Maybe he was a control freak, but he found that planning around someone else's parameters carried inherently an increased risk. He'd anticipated any eventuality and knew the timing was perfect, but the capture had been too damned easy.

For nine long years, Ronan had served as an operative for the CIA. Intense, terrifying, lonely, rigid. The work had always come to him as easy as breathing. Like he'd been born to it. Over the years, he'd learned to trust his instincts, and right now they were screaming. But, there wasn't a damn thing he could do about it.

Nodding to Ronan, Rose whispered, her brow wrinkled in an unrestrained scowl, "What's the plan? Sharpe wouldn't tell me anything."

Clenching his jaw, Ronan shook his head. "Me neither. All I know is that we're not to ask a thing. Merc knows too much; eyes only, top secret material that we're not cleared for. Bollocks if you ask me."

Six months he'd been following Peter Young. Since he'd stumbled upon the pile of mutilated carcasses outside a rural Syrian village. He'd been following a lead on a small band of mercenaries spotted crossing the border, in possession of cargo suspected to be biologic weaponry. Seller unidentified, buyer a known terrorist group.

He'd flown under the radar, strictly collecting intel with no authority to take any action... then he'd found the disfigured families, but no sign of the mercs or the terrorists. They'd flown the coop before the weapons test. It hadn't been easy, but he'd managed to track down the mercenary leader, Peter Young.

When he'd found Young in London, Sharpe had intervened, having been tracking Young for another case. Ronan had worked with Sharpe before. A reputation for ruthlessness, the asshole was a fucking narcissist. Cold, precise, and a don't-ask leadership style. He'd only seriously listened to Ronan when he had a solid lead on Peter Young.

Pulling into the open bay door of the seemingly abandoned warehouse, Jim looked back and motioned that the area was secure. The three dragged an unconscious Peter Young out of the backseat and upstairs to a break room in the back of the warehouse. Dark and desolate, it was a fitting place for an interrogation. Sharpe was waiting and had Young cuffed to the chair before he started to stir.

"Out," Sharpe directed, without acknowledging the team that had brought him his quarry.

Although he knew Sharpe would refuse, Ronan had to try anyway, "I've been after Young for months. I need intel about where those damn biologics came from, and where they are now."

With a curt nod, Sharpe responded, "I want those weapons as much as you do. We only have three hours before Interpol arrives to arrest him." Ronan tried to object, but Sharpe continued, "It was the best I could do. We're not the only ones after him. Get the hell out of here, and stay out of sight." Sharpe stood still as a hawk, looking hungrily at Young as if he were a plump, juicy field mouse.

Ronan bit his tongue to keep quiet. Fuck. Once Interpol had him, he wouldn't be able to get close. If he wanted to continue the investigation, with or without the support of his government, he'd need to stay off the grid. Young was wanted all over the world and had yet to even be linked to the weapons through any legitimate channels.

Ronan stalked out to the car, Jim and Rose following close behind. Jim hopped back in the driver's seat and tore out of the building, as furious as Ronan. None of them spoke as they returned to the city. Rose loved a good interrogation, was better at it than most. Had an innocent face, big doey eyes few could resist, with the bite of a viper veiled behind the sweet façade.

Dropping them at the nearest Underground station, Jim tore off into the distance. Ronan didn't even glance over at Rose, avoiding their being seen together. He worked his way to the Underground line and headed home to his flat. Stepping onto the deserted subway car, he was grateful the morning rush of commuters hadn't started yet. He stood and gripped the subway pole, despite the plethora of available seats, for fear the gentle rocking of the train would lull him to sleep.

Long night, but he was dead on his feet after taking the long way home. Despite the fatigue, he still needed to shake anyone who might be following him. Six weeks he'd been in London. Six weeks of Sharpe's constant interference. Yeah, Sharpe outranked him, but that was just on paper. If it hadn't been for Sara, Ronan's contact and mentor at CIA, breathing down Sharpe's neck and insisting on Ronan's inclusion, Sharpe would have run the entire mission solo.

"Gregory Stevens, age 32, height 5 feet 10 inches tall. Gainfully employed as a neurologist, and enjoys poker, golf, and travel," Payson nodded with a satisfied smile.

Payson Roberts was convinced true love was just around the corner, currently hoping to find him via this latest online dating program. She'd been trying the online thing for a while, but this new app was promising. Not to mention the Adonis currently on her screen, a candid shot of him wearing a tailored suit in the middle of an elegant dinner party.

Maddy, her best friend - and half-hearted online dating supporter - responded, "Is he handsome?"

Payson flashed her phone to her friend with a grin, "Not bad, eh?"

From the jewelry counter across the shop, her soon-to-be-former-assistant chuckled without looking up, "Of course he is. Have you ever seen her date anyone that wasn't model material?" Natalie finished polishing a sterling silver necklace that Payson had picked up at an estate sale a few weeks back.

A gust of wind rattled the front door of Flotsam Antiques, announcing that winter had officially arrived. About time, too. They were well into January, and the weather had been mild so far.

The three were attempting to entertain themselves on the dull day, as town was deathly quiet due to the foul turn in the weather. Payson walked over to Maddy and leaned across the old-fashioned buffet she'd converted into her checkout counter.

Nodding appreciatively at the photo on Payson's screen, Maddy agreed, "Wow, yeah. Nice looking guy. Did you set up a date yet?"

Gazing at her phone, Payson sighed wistfully, "Next Saturday night. Normally, I'd arrange for a coffee meet-and-greet first, but I have a good feeling about this one. He's rated at a 98% likelihood of a successful match for me. And, I've had way too much coffee lately. I'm in the mood for a fancy dinner." She set her phone down and stood up straight to stretch out her body, stiff from a long day of processing online orders and rearranging stock.

"Just keep telling yourself that. You just like his resume and his staged '*I'm not posing, I naturally look this good*' glamour shot." Natalie finished up the last of the polishing and carried the cleaning materials to the cupboard.

"Lucky for you, this is your last official day, or I'd fire you for your insubordination." Payson winked.

Maddy made herself comfortable on the stool behind the checkout counter as her friends razzed each other. Hollering to Natalie, she defended her friend, "She is fond of a good resume and a pretty face, but she's a sucker for a good heart. Don't let her fool you."

Natalie shook her head, her short blond waves bouncing in agreement, "I suppose there isn't much to choose from locally. Where'd you find this one?"

Plenty of eligible bachelors passed through her shop during tourist season in the small, coastal town of Seaview, Maine, but Payson wasn't interested in a quick fling. Not her style. Nor was there much happening in the dead of winter. "I've expanded my circle as far as Portland. Not too terrible of a commute for the right man."

Payson didn't think she was exactly model-material herself, but knew she was easy on the eyes with her long, pin-straight auburn hair, fair skin with a dusting of freckles across her nose, and a body on the curvier side of slim. She'd had no trouble finding dates when she lived in Boston. There just wasn't much selection of permanent residents in the little fishing-slash-tourist town. Plenty of fishermen, but most were married or not her type. Or, she'd already dated them.

Not her fault she was picky. Her weakness was the type staring back from her screen: strikingly handsome, successful, the sort of man that could pull off a sharp tuxedo as naturally as James Bond. But, one that had a great sense of humor. And humility. And was amazing in bed.

Nothing too specific. *Ha.* She laughed at her own naivete. When she had ignored her pickiness, she'd wound up in an incredibly dull engagement.

"I'm not sure you've *got a good feeling* about this guy, or if it's that you just haven't seen much action lately." Maddy grabbed the phone back and started scrolling through the new beau's bio.

Payson opened her mouth to object, finger raised in the air and eyes wide with resolve, but Maddy interjected, "I get it. You are due for a fun date. Chase took me out to The Schooner last weekend in Portland; it was phenomenal. Didn't hurt that the fish was freshly caught by McAllister Fisheries that morning, a deal that Chase had recently negotiated with some of the high-end Portland restaurants, so dinner was on the house. Otherwise, that place is absurdly pricey."

Maddy shook her head in disbelief as she described the extravagant meal.

Pacing around her antique shop, Payson wistfully dreamed of finding the right guy. Her shop was exactly the way she wanted it. Holding up a mirrored platter, she wiped off a subtle smudge, catching her reflection in the glass. Although she was satisfied with her life, she was overwhelmed with the need to find *the one*. Why couldn't she just be happy with what she had?

Walking back to the register, she pouted as she grabbed the phone back, yet again, "See, I want that. You didn't even want to fall in love, yet you and Chase... I'm so ridiculously happy for you. Honestly, I am also incredibly jealous." She quickly amended, "In a good way."

She stared at the photo for a few more minutes. Gregory was incredibly handsome. Dark hair, dark features, rich chocolate brown eyes, chiseled jaw. Her heart took a bit of a dive, fantasizing how he might just be the one. She sure hoped so; she was tired of searching. After the all-too-easily broken engagement with Clive, she was not settling for anything less than perfect.

"Maybe you should stop looking for your soulmate, and you might just stumble upon him by accident." A few inches shorter, Natalie wrapped her arms around Payson for a farewell hug. "I'm out of here. I live a block away and will be working a block down from that, so don't hesitate to call me if you need any help around the shop."

As Natalie left, Payson couldn't help but feel teary. As her first - and only - employee, Payson felt torn. Happy her friend was living her dream working at the local art gallery, but sad she wouldn't be working with her anymore. End of an era, she supposed.

Settled in the latter half of her twenties, her dismal love life was starting to get her down. Not to mention the constant nagging by her older sister, Jen. *Time to settle down. You're not getting any younger.*

Since their mother had died, Jen filled the empty role a bit too strongly sometimes. Actually, Jen had set her up with Clive in the first place.

She loved her sisters and her niece and nephew, but it was nice to have the geographical barrier sometimes. It was a constant struggle to keep her younger sister, Cara, on track. The girl was so terrified of disappointing everyone, especially herself. Last summer she'd had to drive all the way down to Boston to convince Cara that the world wasn't over just because she got a D in an elective. Crazy girl went straight into grad school this past Fall and, so far, was doing great.

After their parents died, Payson had run away to Ireland as an exchange student for a year to escape the grief that she'd been drowning in at the loss of her parents, and the stress of supporting her sisters. Out of guilt, she'd moved back to Boston, found a job that she hated, but was stable, and a fiancé that was just as stable, but bored her to tears. Finally, she'd had enough and found her balance by moving up to Seaview and opening her own shop. Close enough to see them often, but enough distance to let her younger sister find some independence, and to escape her older sister's bossiness.

She'd met Maddy shortly after moving from Boston, and they'd become fast friends - the antique shop owner and the cop. Maddy's brother, Aiden, and her boyfriend, Chase, had quickly become part of their little circle as well. Now that Natalie was going to be working at the renovated art gallery full time, she was afraid she wouldn't see her much anymore. Natalie was so shy; she'd have to drag her out now and again.

Yeah, she had it pretty good. Just needed to be swept off her feet like something in her favored romance novels. Was that too much to ask?

Maddy nudged her from her thoughts, "I am now officially off duty. I'm going to head home before this weather gets too intense. Chase should be home from work soon anyway." Grabbing her heavy police jacket and winter cap, Maddy made her way to the front door. "You closing up for the night?"

Payson nodded, "Yeah, I'm calling it a night. I'll head upstairs to my apartment to relax with a glass of wine in front of the fire and watch the snow fall. My favorite time of year."

Freezing wind added an extra oomph as Maddy opened the door. Gripping the handle against the gust, she managed to turn back and shake her head at her friend with a smile, "Does anything ever get you down?"

Head held high, Payson flipped the sign to *Closed*. "Lots, but there's nothing I'll let keep me down. Not for long anyway. Have a good night. Big hug to Chase for me." Closing the door behind her friend, Payson sighed to herself. She'd worked damn hard to be sure nothing kept her down. After her parents died in the car crash, she had hit a real low point. Wasn't sure she'd recover.

When that opportunity had arisen to study abroad her senior year of high school, she hadn't even checked with her sisters before accepting. She'd known, even then, what it was. She had been running away. It worked. Throwing herself into the trip, she learned how to forge a new path, to carry herself forward when everything around her collapsed.

2

Long night. Long year, really, without the relief of closure. Ronan was exhausted. Mentally, physically, emotionally. He dragged his feet as he walked back to his flat. Not that he'd lived there long, but he'd made it a safe space.

Nothing personal, as he wouldn't risk blowing his cover. None of his London team knew his real identity, not even Sharpe. Hell, no one at CIA, besides Sara, knew the real him. Sharpe, those with high enough clearance at Langley, and even payroll, knew him as Max Kennedy, a kid from Vermont that had been recruited out of school by the CIA.

It was partially true. He had been hired before he even finished college to join the CIA. Was from Maine rather than Vermont. When he'd joined up, he'd insisted on anonymity from the start. Didn't ever want his job to follow him home; not even his family knew what he was doing.

Nine years. He'd hardly spoken to his family, and had given his time, his energy, and his damned soul to the CIA. Had one more painfully long year left in his *agreement.* He was the best at what he did, but his job satisfaction was rapidly declining. The ever-changing political landscape was sucking the life out of him. Every time he'd made a real difference, his higher-ups made an enemy out of old friends, going behind the backs of allies to accomplish a pointless mission driven by money and power.

Those biologic weapons sure hadn't magically appeared in Young's control, but Ronan had been assigned to tracking down Young himself. Sharpe had assigned others to finding out where the weapons had come from, and where they had gone.

Now that Young was captured, Ronan was out. Reassigned. Back to Langley to debrief and be assigned to a new region, a new mission.

Not that he minded; he was sick of the Sharpe's dictatorial leadership style already. Maybe he'd call Sara and see what she could do. She always had his back, since he'd been the smartass college kid she'd taken under her wing.

Aside from the street-sweepers and earliest of the morning commuters, the last of the trek home had been quiet. Uneventful. Too cold out for wanderers.

Wind picking up, the snow was blessedly starting to accumulate. Shouldn't be more than an inch, but the fresh white coat always brought him a sense of peace, a sense of renewal. Maybe in his new assignment, Eastern Europe in all likelihood, he would feel refreshed with new ground, interesting new ops... no more biologics. Letting himself breathe a small sigh of relief, he felt the knot between his shoulder blades loosen at the prospect. Maybe one day the nightmares and the flashbacks of mutilated bodies would stop.

Reaching his building at last, an old brick structure that was older than his hometown of Seaview, Ronan unlocked the shared front entrance of the building and closed the door tightly behind him, trudging up the four flights of stairs to his flat. Checking the hall first, he unlocked the front door, walked into the dark, silent apartment, and checked his alarms.

As always, he ensured that the fishing line was taught across the entry hall, ensuring no intruders had unwittingly nudged it. Rudimentary, but a damn effective system he'd devised himself. *Good. Line intact.* Not that anyone had traced him back to his lodgings before, but that was a result of his uncompromising vigilance.

He shed his warm coat and tossed it onto the entry table. Too tired to even think about dinner, which he should have eaten hours ago, Ronan headed straight toward his tiny bedroom. A few steps into the living room, he stripped off his shirt, crumpling the grimy piece of fabric and pitching it onto the arm of the threadbare couch.

Bending over to peel off his boots, a sudden loud crack and the unmistakable burning, piercing, aching pain of a bullet embedding into his shoulder rattled through him.

What the fuck? As if in slow motion, another sharp hit pushed him backwards as second shot nailed him low in the abdomen, then a third struck his hip on the way down.

He knew immediately; his position was absolutely compromised. Maybe more. Before losing consciousness, he saw movement from the flat across the street. "Bloody snipers," he muttered as he collapsed, and the world went dark.

"Thanks for stopping in today. You're going to love the settee. We'll deliver it Friday morning," Payson grinned from ear to ear as she escorted out the stylishly dressed young woman, and new owner of her favorite blue velvet settee, circa 1924. Not many truly loved their jobs. She knew she was lucky.

Most had thought her foolish, leaving her prestigious position at an international trade firm in Boston. But, after she'd called off the engagement to Clive, realizing she'd never loved him, she also realized that she didn't love her job either. Nor did she have anyone she would call a close friend. Rather, she had accumulated a collection of snooty financiers as dull as Clive.

Uprooting and starting fresh had made sense, or her hard-earned optimism would've died a woeful death. Opening her own shop had been risky, but she dove in with everything she had – financially and emotionally. Fortunately, the investment was paying off. Flotsam Antiques was now a hallmark of the prominent Beachfront Street shops in Seaview.

Although much quieter in the winter months, she still ran a good business. She kept a unique and predictable stock to keep up with demand from her online and in-person sales. Every transaction was a personal triumph, each antique she sold had been hand-selected and displayed. Not the cold negotiations to get the cheapest price on crappy trinkets that were sold for pennies at tourist shops all over the world, as she'd been stuck negotiating in Boston.

A total shot in the dark, she'd opened Flotsam about three years ago now, but she'd been smart about it. Stylishly decorated and marketed to a variety of customers, from fun pirate-themed treasures for the kids to ornate furniture for the discriminating investor. In posting many of the antiques online, she found that she earned more from online sales, but it wasn't as fun as seeing the smiling faces of her happy customers.

She found joy in her day-to-day routine and was totally hands-on in running her business. Initially, she hadn't been able to afford any help, so she'd had to run the store alone. Now, she found even the most menial tasks satisfying.

Smile still pasted onto her face from a satisfying sale, she turned at the sound of her cell phone chirping to announce an incoming text. Must be Gregory confirming their date. She flipped the shop sign to *Closed*, so she could head to her upstairs apartment and get ready.

Digging out her phone from her purse on her way to the back, she frowned at the message. *Sorry, work emergency. Can we reschedule?*

Well, at least he didn't stand her up. Always a plus. When one suffered so many first dates, the stand-up risk was no joking matter.

No worries, she responded.

Leave it simple. Of course, she was disappointed, but wanted to appear nonchalant. One never should to sound too keen. Let him fall in love with her before he got to witness her potentially insurmountable flaws.

Her phone chirped again. *Can we reschedule for the 22nd? Same time, same place?*

And a reschedule. If he was as handsome as his profile picture, he just might be worth the wait. She knew he had a crazy work schedule. He'd mentioned he puts in a lot of hours on-call at the hospital.

Sounds great. See you then. She decided to forego the exclamation point and happy face she would have added in a text to her friends.

Dammit. Now what? She reconsidered her plans for evening. Maddy had already told her she was surprising Chase with a romantic dinner at home tonight. Aiden, Maddy's brother, was in Boston for the weekend visiting some of his law school buddies.

Aiden had offered to take her with him so she could visit her family, but she had no one else to watch the shop these days. Natalie had said she she'd be willing to lend a hand. However, Natalie was working long hours at the gallery for the upcoming grand opening, so Payson didn't feel right asking her.

Not that Payson minded, Natalie was a budding artist and a hard worker and deserved her own success. Nor did she want to take advantage of Natalie's generosity, not unless she was desperate anyway. She still hadn't found Natalie's replacement, so no time off was foreseeable in the near future.

She could run the shop alone quite comfortably, but she finally recognized that she needed a break now and again. Not to mention, she offered fair-priced delivery of large items within a thirty-mile radius and would need someone to help with deliveries. Come spring, she'd desperately need some assistance. Maybe she'd find a high school or college student needing some extra cash.

Looks like she was spending the evening alone. As usual. Not that she minded too much; she enjoyed her own company. Although, she admitted, it got a little lonely sometimes. Payson took a few motivating deep breaths and walked through to the back, skillfully dodging the boxes cluttering the small hallway and storeroom on her way out the rear exit. She pushed open the heavy steel door, setting the alarm on her way out.

Living upstairs was handy, as it made for a convenient commute. Forgoing a coat for the quick dash up the stairs, she rubbed her arms to stay warm against the chill wind. Shivering violently in the icy, thirty-five mile-an-hour gusts, she barely managed to get the door unlocked.

Just as she settled in with a glass of wine, curled up in front of the blazing fire with a favorite book, her phone chirped again. *Can you come down to Boston next week? I screwed up.*

Double dammit, Cara. Payson had been called down for bad grades, broken hearts, food poisoning... you name it, Cara didn't hesitate to call for help. She was glad her little sister felt she could turn to her for support, but she also wondered if she and Jen were overly enabling of her during the tough years, rather than empowering.

Rather than texting, she went straight for the direct approach. Cara could dance around the topic for hours. She tapped the send button. As soon as the call connected, she started, "I'm sure you didn't screw anything up. What's going on?"

Sniffling on the other end. She could hear Cara trying to breathe slowly so she could speak. "I broke a ten-thousand-dollar piece of equipment." And more blubbering.

Yikes. Let's hope she didn't expect Payson to pay for it. "Back up a few steps for me, sis. What did you break?" She sat up and marked the page of her book. This would take a while.

"It was my turn to check on the weather station in Rockport. It's been buggy lately, so I knew some repairs were needed. I took up a few undergrads to do the grunt work, as usual. Total rooky mistake, but a huge gust of wind rushed through, right as I had the panel open and exposed. One of the undergrads was messing around and knocked into me..." Uncontrollable sobbing.

Payson could just make out words like "I... bruised butt... the computer..." Not knowing a darn thing about meteorology, she had no idea what she was talking about, but it didn't sound good. "Cara, I am sure no one would blame you; it sounds like an accident. Are you ok?"

· "I'm sore, but I'm ok. Mistakes like that shouldn't happen."

"Did anyone say that you need to pay for it?"

"No." Sniffle.

"Do you know how to fix it?"

Goose-like honking sound of dramatic nose blowing. "Sort of."

"Do you have a professor you can ask to help you fix it?"

Hiccup. "Yeah; Moser would help if I asked."

Calmly, Payson helped her sister troubleshoot. "Do you still need me to come down? Since Natalie left, I don't have anyone else to run the shop."

"I forgot she was leaving. No. No. I'll be fine. I can handle it."

"You can do this. You're going to be Dr. Cara Roberts in a few short years. Teach your own class or even run your own research or meteorology department. You won't have been the first one to break an expensive piece of equipment, nor will you be the last. Most importantly, you are taking the initiative to fix it."

Cara agreed to update her with her progress or to call again if she just couldn't make it work. "Love you, sis."

"Love you too. Go relax for the rest of the evening. Nothing you can do tonight."

"Pace?" She could hear the relief lifting from her sister's shoulders, her voice less watery and more perky.

"Yeah?"

"You're so much like Dad. I love Jen, and I loved Mom, of course. But you've got that steadiness like he did." Payson was touched. It had been years since they'd done it, but she and her sisters used to stay up late, recollecting their parent's strengths, their idiosyncrasies. Somehow, it helped them to feel their parents were still with them.

She knew she had quite a bit of their mother's perfectionism in her, but it felt so good to hear herself compared to their dad. Her mother's dreaminess, but her father's patience and perseverance. Her favorite inherited trait, however, was her exuberance for even the little things - that came from Granny, their dad's Irish mother. "Thanks. I like to think so."

Another sniffle. Dammit. "Where do I fit in?"

Payson sighed, wondering how to answer. Honesty was likely the best policy. "You're right, you're neither. You're Grandma. Not Granny, but Mom's mom. You have Grandma's anxiety and fear of making mistakes, but you also have her determination to do it all, and do it right. I'm sure you don't remember her very well, but you even look like her."

"I like that. Thanks."

"Goodnight. Get some rest and don't worry, you'll figure it out. Like you always do. Have some faith in yourself."

One more fire extinguished, Payson picked her wine and her book back up and relaxed into her favorite chair. Cara was going to be just fine; she just needed a little reassurance. It had taken her long enough to figure that out for herself.

3

Putrid, fleshy odor filled Ronan's nostrils; mangled bodies reached out to pull him into their decaying pile of limbs.

The scene changed, and the sharp report of three shots ricocheted in his skull.

Ronan's eyes opened in a flash, breath coming fast and sweat dripping from everywhere. Damn nightmares were worse than ever. Getting shot wasn't good for a body or a mind.

Stretching out his legs in the cramped hospital bed, Ronan groaned. He still hurt. Everywhere. Asshole had shot him three fucking times; left thigh, right abdomen, right shoulder. Several surgeries later, he was damn lucky to be alive. He just didn't feel particularly pleased by the miracle at the moment.

Skin pinched where his wounds were still healing; Ronan guarded his movements as he lowered himself out of the hospital bed. He winced as his feet touched the ice-cold floor. Where were those grippy socks they'd given him? Nowhere in sight.

Whatever. Hobbling across the yellow linoleum floor, he made it to the bathroom before his bladder exploded. Felt like he was still peeing out IV fluids even though he'd been hydrating orally for days now.

In the small mirror over the sink, he cringed when he saw the state of his gnarly beard and knotted long hair. Bandages long gone, strength returning, he managed to take a slow, cautious shower without assistance. Hot steam soothed his cramped muscles.

As he had awoken every night since he'd come across the mangled corpses, he felt overwhelmingly devastated, disgusted, his soul shredded to pieces. Failing as he did every morning, he tried to scour the images from his memory.

Struggling to lift his arm high enough to scrub his mangey locks, he debated asking for help. Not that he'd get any help around here, even in this rehabilitative nursing facility. The techs had refused to help him bathe after they'd gotten sick of his piss-poor attitude.

His own damn fault. In his frustration, he'd growled at the simpering candy striper that he could wash his own balls. Poor thing had only been trying to help, but he was sick of being waited on, of being pitied.

With difficulty, he dried off the bulk of his body and long hair with the crusty institutional towel that was supplied fresh daily. He pulled on some cargo pants and a black t-shirt, forgoing socks and underwear. Too much effort.

A knock at the door was a welcome distraction from his mental diatribe. "Hey Cole, ready to get out of here?" Dr. Singh asked as she calmly sauntered in, attired in her typical white coat with her stethoscope tucked in the pocket.

"About bloody time," Ronan grunted back.

"I'm going to miss your cheerful banter," she teased. He attempted to crack a smile. After he'd recovered in the hospital and was sent here for rehab, he'd been ready to crumble. Career over.

Although he'd disconnected months ago, now it was official. No friends to speak of. A family who loved him, but he had never made much of an effort to connect where his family was concerned. Mistakes. A lot of them.

He wasn't suicidal, just fucking *done*. When Dr. Singh, the physician assigned to his care at the rehab facility, had first walked into his room and looked over his injuries, he'd asked her why the fuck he was still here. Why couldn't that asshole have had decent aim?

Ronan would have had better aim; he hated the job, but he was a damn good sniper when the mission called for it. Unofficially and extremely judiciously of course; murder was murder no matter how much of a threat the target may be.

Dr. Singh had stuck with him. She'd challenged him, saying, "Well, you're either really lucky or really unlucky. I guess you'll have to stick around to find out which." He still wasn't sure which it was.

"Get me out of here, doc," he asked in his perfect West Country accent, maintaining his current ruse as a struggling writer named Cole from Devon.

"I'm processing your discharge paperwork now; I'll have you out of here first thing tomorrow morning." She smiled as she performed her final exam. His bandages were gone, scars healing, body sore. "Keep up with your home exercises. You ok on pain management?"

"I got it. Thanks for not pushing any of those bloody pain pills." They'd had him pretty drugged up initially. As soon as he was coherent enough, he'd put a stop to the damn pain pills. Muddled his brain, and he was still in deep cover.

He had no doubt he could maintain his cover even in the drugged delirium, but he still wanted to keep a clear head. Max Kennedy had been declared killed in action by the CIA. Sara's attempts to convince the anyone interested, particularly the assassin, that he was dead.

"You're very welcome. Not being nagged for pain meds was a welcome request compared to the norm. Stay out of trouble, ok?"

He nodded with a crooked half-smile. She shook his hand and left him to his dark thoughts.

At sunrise the next morning, Ronan grabbed his only belongings from his dresser and walked straight out the front door. Sara had been thorough enough to have his new identification, a few changes of clothes, and toiletries delivered in a nondescript, worn-looking backpack by "a neighbor." Inside was a note and a drop phone. *Call me. I have instructions for you.*

As soon as the rehab facility door closed behind him, he placed an outgoing call to the only number saved in the phone's memory. "What's the plan?"

"How are you feeling? You were lucky to make it out alive," Sarah answered back. Her sympathy was obvious; he was miserable enough, he didn't want any pity.

"Feel like I've been shot, but I'm walking and talking. All my parts are still attached." He was exhausted after just the walk through the facility and out to the loading zone toward the waiting taxi. "Am I heading to Heathrow?"

"That's right, come on home."

Hopping in the cab, he asked the driver to take him to Paddington Station, continuing with his meticulous accent. Complimenting the song on the radio, he asked the driver to please turn up the volume. Hated the damn song, but it would prevent the driver from hearing Sara's voice through the phone. "Am I to see you again soon?"

Sara's pause on the other end was heavy. "Only briefly. Take a look at your passport. John Clayborn will be picked up from Dulles by a hired car service. You'll spend a few days wrapping up final reports at Langley, then you're retired."

"But my contractual agreement…" Ronan objected. What was wrong with him? He'd been mentally finished with the damn CIA for months, since he'd obtained the permanent worst-nightmare mental images of civilians dead and rotting. Yet here he was, fighting to get back in the action. Didn't make any sense.

Guess he just didn't know what else to do with himself. He'd wanted to be a CIA operative since he turned eleven. Maybe if he could at least get a sense of closure on the weapons, some vengeance for those families, he could retire in peace.

"You've done your service. It's going to take a while before you've recovered enough to work again, if ever. And… all your covers are blown; Young confirmed what we had already suspected. He was on to you for months. Pissed that you blew his big deal. We now know the attack on you was tied to him. Blames you for extinguishing a 14 million dollar deal he'd bartered. You're not safe."

Ronan felt a black hole forming in the pit of his stomach. "Did he say where they went, the biologics?"

He waited for Sara to respond. "No, so far he is sticking with his story that they were lost in transit. We'll get it out of him. We managed to keep you safe in London for now, but you need to get out quick.

"We think we know the identity of the shooter: Connor Young, Peter's right-hand man and very pissed-off brother. We've called for a manhunt to find him and the rest of Young's team, but they've gone to ground. Young knew way too much about you; you're not safe in the field anymore. We can only hope they believe our story that you're dead. You'll be safest back home."

Thankfully, the cab driver was listening to his own music, ignoring him completely. Still, he didn't want to say too much and maintained a pleasant face, as if chatting with an old friend. Sara continued, "You'll be fully compensated for your full term, plus disability pay-"

"Bollocks. I don't need any bloody money; I'm perfectly capable-" he argued.

"Do you want to keep working? I know you; you've been ready to get out for months now."

Ronan didn't say anything, but he gritted his teeth so tight he could feel the building pressure threatening to crack his molars.

"You went through a hell of an ordeal. Take the money. That's what it's there for. You got us Young, which is a huge break for our continued operations in Syria. Trust me, you earned it."

Ronan couldn't think on it now. Voice clipped, he ended the call, "I'm about at my stop. Talk to you later." He paid the driver with cash from his backpack; his to keep, plus a nice wad for the trip, courtesy of Sara.

After a long trek from the cab to the Underground to the long international flight, and an incessant debriefing at Langley, Ronan McAllister was finally home. As he landed, a burning, hard lump in his throat formed. His fellow passengers were happily chatting as they de-planed.

Ronan grabbed his backpack and leather motorcycle jacket, both of which were brand new; he'd traded out his attire several times since leaving the rehab facility. Didn't bother shaving his beard or hair, but he'd added a ball cap once he switched to his American persona.

At Langley, Sara handed him documents with an identity he hadn't seen in almost 9 years: Ronan James McAllister. His own name. It felt foreign, almost like another assumed, undercover disguise.

Trudging along at the back of the bubbling crowd as they made their way through the airport, Ronan was glad to find his parents waiting for him. His mother's eyes were misty as she struggled to hold back the tears, knowing he would hate the fuss. Emotional displays had always made him uncomfortable. Today, he was good with the tears; he was fighting a few of his own.

Last summer, he'd managed to meet his parents in Rome for dinner, and it had been hard to leave them. Even well before college, he'd pushed them away, adopting the secretive life of a spy long before it became necessary. Now, he knew he'd been an idiot. His parents had always been there for him, even when he hadn't asked it of them. Even when he'd pushed everyone away, his family most of all. But, his distance had kept them safe.

As soon as Ronan crossed the line signifying that he was now outside of the secured area, Frank, his gentle giant of a father, stood back as his slender mother, Laura, rushed across the sunlit waiting area and threw her arms around him. Crashing right into his injured shoulder and abdomen. With a guarded wince, he adjusted the hug, but held her just as tightly.

Eyes filled with tears, she looked up at him, "Ronan, honey, are you ok? You didn't say much, just than you're coming home. For good... right?" Hearing his own name out loud felt like coming home, almost as much as his mother's weepy hug, his father's proud grin.

"Yeah, Mom, I'm home for good. I'll fill you in when we're in the car." He'd gotten the ok to tell his family where he'd been the past 9 years, but was still restricted in how much he could tell them, what details he could share. He held her at his side and walked out of the airport, Frank trailing close behind.

"I'm still having trouble believing you're really home, like I'm holding onto a mirage," her watery voice shook with a gentle chuckle. As they walked, she continued to stare up at him, as if afraid he'd disappear the moment she looked away. She gently tugged on his scraggly beard, "This is a lot longer than when I saw you last."

From behind, Frank grabbed Ronan's backpack off his shoulder. "This all you got?"

"Yeah, I travel pretty light," he shrugged, the movement causing a zap through his shoulder.

"Are you shipping the rest of your belongings home?" Laura asked as they reached his dad's massive 4-door pick-up. Before waiting for his answer, Laura opened the door for him, motioning him to sit up front.

"Ah, no…" he gritted his teeth as he pulled himself into the truck with his good arm, his injured arm bracing his abdominal wound. Once they were all securely in the cab of the truck, with his parents both staring at him in anticipation, he struggled to find the right words. "I, uh… have no other belongings… This is all I own." They eyed his uneasy expression intently, waiting to hear him reveal the mystery of where he had been and why he was suddenly home.

He continued hesitantly, anxious to see their response. "This is all completely confidential. I'll tell Maddy and Aiden, but this cannot leave our immediate family." He studied their confused faces, pleading for their agreement. Their heads bobbled as they nodded, brows drawn with worry. "I… I'm being discharged from the CIA. For medical reasons. I'm a CIA operative… or, I was a… a spy. For the US government."

From their seats, his parents stared at him, eyes wide, bodies frozen, not yet able to speak. He continued, "I was shot by the brother of the guy that blew my cover... all my covers, so I've been put out to pasture."

There was a long silence. His parents just stared at him, unable to answer.

Frank spoke first, patting him on the good shoulder, clearly not knowing exactly how to respond. "Son, I'm real proud of you." Frank paused, searching for more to say, but gave up and put the truck in gear.

As they pulled onto the expressway, Frank shook his head with a smile, having found his words, "I always knew you wouldn't do anything ordinary with your life. Computer programmer. Didn't believe that one for a damn minute. Guess I should have expected you'd only have dropped out of college for that sort of opportunity. Don't rush yourself into deciding what you want to do next. Take your time. Gonna be a hell of an adjustment."

Sitting in the middle seat behind them, his mother reached forward and patted his arm affectionately. "You're welcome to stay with us, but we figured you'd want to have your own space. Chase is moving in with Maddy, into her beach house, so he's arranged for you to take over his lease. If you want it. It's paid up for the next 3 months. Some of the furniture he's leaving there for you, but the rest we've rounded up so that you'll have a furnished place of your own."

Ronan was relieved to hear that. He loved his parents, and greatly appreciated they knew him well enough to make sure he had his own space. On the drive home, his mom filled him in on everyday updates about the family, changes in town since he left, what the weather had been doing. It was nice to hear her voice... and not be expected to respond. His dad was right, this was already a major adjustment.

Melting into the plush leather seat, he managed to stay awake... only just barely.

4

"And that's why I was promoted to Chief of Neurology for our medical group," Gregory finished his dreadfully long work story as he gazed adoringly at Payson across the table.

Ok, maybe he was not *the one*. Maybe he was just nervous? First dates could make one ramble. She looked down at her empty plate, her lobster and arugula salad long since consumed.

The man did wear his suit well; sleek black with crisp gray starched shirt and coordinating tie; he may pull off a tuxedo as well as James Bond. Sean Connery version of course, although Pierce Brosnan was sexy too. She'd heard that the next Bond would be a woman. Payson was ridiculously excited. About time.

"Payson?" Crap, she forgot to pay attention again. Gregory was looking at her, awaiting her response to his question. What did he ask her?

Decked out in her favorite olive-green sweater dress, snug enough to pique interest, but without any come-hither slutty-ness, Payson didn't deny that a big part of why she enjoyed dating was the excuse to wear her favorite dresses. Even if the date was a total flop.

"I'm sorry, Gregory, neurology and the healthcare system in general are just way beyond me. What were you asking?" Puff up his ego a bit so he wouldn't be offended that she'd tuned him out. They weren't beyond her; she could talk about anything if she were interested. She just was bored to tears from suffering through a pompous, narcissistic soliloquy.

"I was asking if you would care for dessert? Perhaps we could share some tiramisu." His charming smile did help soften the self-absorbed monologue.

Payson smiled graciously, "Oh no, I couldn't. Thank you for dinner, this was excellent. I have a bit of a drive back home, so I'd like to call it a night."

"Of course," he responded. Was that condescension in his eyes? Huh. Figures.

As handsome as he was, of course he was conceited, and maybe a little sexist. He insisted on paying for dinner; Payson was a firm believer in splitting the check, but as she'd driven nearly an hour from home to meet him closer to *his* work, she didn't argue.

With perfect gentlemanly manners, he escorted her to her pristine blue 1965 mustang. 1964 and a half if she was to be more specific. As all men did, he passed the car at first, not convinced it was hers. "Thanks for a lovely evening," she said as she unlocked the door.

He ran a hand through his hair, stylishly messing up his perfect style, "I've not made this the best evening for you. I'm sorry, but I've been working 70-hour weeks and can't seem to relax. I was hoping my work would impress you enough to forgive me for talking so much, but I fear I've bored you to tears. Please, allow me to make it up to you?"

Fine. At least the guy knew how to apologize well. Maybe she shouldn't rule him out yet. "That would be nice," she accepted.

With a sigh of relief, he smiled, "You live in Seaview, right?"

She nodded.

"I went through there last Spring, ate at a lovely little Italian restaurant. Friday after next?" Without waiting for a response, he leaned in and kissed her gently, lingering but remaining chaste. Not bad.

"I'd like that," she said as she pulled away. She hopped into her car and gave a gentle wave. Turning the key, the engine purred like a tiger.

The car had been her father's baby, which he'd spent years teaching her to maintain, before finally teaching her to drive it. He and her mother died in the car accident a few months after she got her driver's license. She'd always loved the car, like he had, and had been grateful he'd shared his passion for antiques with her. Driving the car they'd worked on together for so many years made her feel like she always had a part of him with her.

Initially in Boston, and now in Seaview, she had always lived so close to school or work that she walked most everywhere, so she didn't get to drive it often. Every few weeks, she made a point of going for a joy ride along the coast. Shifting into high gear, she tore along the coastal roads, savoring the drive back home. The invigorating trek almost made up for the very dull date.

A god-awful buzzing sound woke Ronan from another vicious nightmare. Benadryl effectively knocked him out when he couldn't fall asleep, but it couldn't hold back the swath of nightmares that terrorized him. Every fucking night.

The buzzing started again. Dammit. Front door. Whoever it was, he or she clearly wasn't getting the message. He glanced at the glowing green clock. Yikes, one in the afternoon. He'd tossed and turned since three that morning, when he'd given up and popped the Benadryl.

Throwing back the crumpled sheets, Ronan dragged himself out of bed and tossed on his only sweatpants. Hobbling slowly, his joints aching like he was 79 rather than 29, he headed for the door.

"Okay, okay, I'm coming," he croaked. Was that him? He hadn't spoken aloud in two or three days and was so dehydrated he hardly recognized his own voice.

"Open the door little bro," hollered his twin sister from the other side of the door. Maddy, of course. Seven minutes older, and she still held it over him. No one else would be so damn persistent, not caring that he didn't want company.

Before opening the door, he quickly took down his makeshift fishing line alarm system. He knew he was safe; only a small handful at CIA knew that he was alive, and even fewer knew his real identity, but he just couldn't seem to break the habit. Unlocking the deadbolt, he opened the door to find his twin sister on the other side, shoving a steaming cup of black coffee in his face.

She shook her head as she looked him over, "Still haven't gotten around to a haircut or at least shaving off that ridiculous beard? You know, some guys can pull off the Grizzly Adams, but they actually maintain the bushy thing."

Knowing she wouldn't be deterred, he accepted the coffee and motioned her in. Making herself useful, she headed straight back into his bedroom. Blankets in a tangle, pillow several feet away from the bed, she started by grabbing the whole bunch in her arms and heading for the laundry.

Ronan leaned against the master bathroom doorway, watching his sister return from the laundry room and start ruthlessly cleaning his bedroom, complaining the entire time. "It stinks in here. Have you showered lately? You were so tidy and civilized and well-spoken since before you hit puberty, I'm just not sure what to make of this new Ronan." Without expecting an answer, she continued her cleaning rampage.

"Things change," he growled. He just didn't care anymore.

What good was being perfect when your head was full of secrets and lies, a body full of bullet holes. No future. Resume empty, as he couldn't be honest about anything that he had accomplished in the last 9 years. What might he say? *College dropout. Great at lying, breaking into places, listening in on conversations. Effective in taking down terrorist organizations...?* Sara had offered him a desk job, but he just couldn't stomach it.

Room acceptably tidy, Maddy finally stopped moving. About time; she was making him dizzy. "I love you. I missed you like crazy," she sighed, voice softer, "I know you can't talk about everything you went through. I know you feel like you gave up. I know that you're in pain."

Her expression was somber as she looked over the many scars covering his bare torso. "But... you survived. You're home now. I'd like to get to know you again. I don't expect you to know what to do and feel like you fit right in. That will take time. Can you start by letting your family in now and again?"

Shit. She always could get under his skin. "Yeah Maddy, I'll try."

She stared him down, trying to determine if he were telling the truth. Funny, as not even his twin sister would know if he were lying or not. He hadn't told many truths in the last few years. She was nearly cross-eyed staring him down, trying to read him.

A half smile crossed his lips, and he spread his arms openly in surrender. "As you can see, isolating myself isn't exactly helping to clear my head, so yes, I'll try to get out more."

With a grin, she grabbed back the now-empty coffee mug from his hands and gently pushed him into the bathroom. "Great. You can start by showering. I brought some of Chase's clothes that were bound for donation, as you appear to have little more than a pair of sweatpants in your entire backpack-sized wardrobe," she eyed him in his ragged sweats and bare chest. "I'm not sure how well they'll fit as he's broader, but they'll work until you get around to shopping. Now, I'm setting out clothes for you for tonight. You're on your own to finish washing your sheets and making the bed."

She dashed out to her car and re-appeared a few moments later with a small box of clothes and a few more covered on a hanger.

Still shocked at her efficiency, he hadn't budged from his perch against the bathroom doorway. "Tonight?"

"Sorry, I should have mentioned sooner. Mom and Dad are hoping to show you off at the gallery opening tonight; they already bought you a ticket. The gallery in town bought out and remodeled the old chapel on Beachside Street and are having a 'gala' tonight. I tried to talk her out of it, knowing that was too big of a step for you, but Mom has already told all of her friends that you'll be there."

Maddy's look was pained, and he somehow didn't mind her sympathy. Must be a twin thing, as he hated it from everyone else. Maybe it was because she knew him so well, even still. He appreciated that his twin sister knew he wasn't ready to brave a big crowd. She'd never liked crowds either.

"That's ok. I'll go, but I doubt I'll stay long. I'll meet you there so I can sneak out when I get overwhelmed."

She gave him the details. At least he had a few hours to prepare. He watched as she opened the garment bag and hung a tuxedo over the back of the bedroom door. Cringing, he scoffed, expression one of pure horror, "I am not wearing a tux. I don't do tuxedos."

Maddy laughed at him. "Sorry, pal. It's a formal event. Black tie. I tucked the ticket into the chest pocket. The tux should fit you pretty well - I had Aiden try it on first. Besides, you can pretend to be James Bond," she teased, a half-hearted attempt to get him to smile.

Ronan rolled his eyes and found himself smiling with her, while begrudgingly accepting his fate. "Fine. Now get out of here, I'm hopping in the shower. Thanks for the coffee. And the clothes."

His dad had bought himself a new truck last summer, but fortunately had fixed up his old pick-up that had a few miles left in it. He'd given it to Ronan as a little welcome home gift. Not his style, but he was glad to have his own wheels. Actually, he really wasn't sure what his style was anymore.

Now, he was being clothed in Chase's hand-me-downs. He'd have to get off his ass and start doing things for himself. Not that he didn't appreciate having the cushion to land on, but he hated feeling so helpless.

After a hot shower, Ronan felt a bit cleaner and almost revived. He pulled his wet hair into the neatest ponytail he could manage, but a few strays kept falling out. The beard was a no-win situation. Hated the thing, was damn itchy and always in the way, but it was easy to hide behind.

Checking the mirror, he eyed the nasty scars Maddy had painfully gawked at. Yeah, they were pretty gnarly. They'd heal with time and match his other assortment of wounds. His damn shoulder was stiff, his hip ached.

His phone sang out a cheerful jingle. Wasn't there an I-don't-give-a-shit ringtone? Not that he had even checked; it was still the default.

Sara had bought him the phone to help re-introduce him into civilian life; knowing her, she'd probably picked the most obnoxious ringtone she could find, just to make him laugh. Next to the fancy smartphone that she'd tucked in the backpack-of-basics she'd filled for him, she had given him a drop phone for emergencies. She didn't say it, but it was clearly for emergencies, in particular, in case Connor Young found him.

"Hey, Mom." His mom had programmed as many numbers as she could into the smartphone when she'd stopped by a few days ago. He didn't even know half the people he now had on speed dial.

"Hello, honey. I hope you don't mind, but… I'm sure you're getting restless, cooped up all the time. So, I found you a job. Nothing permanent or too taxing, just some good old-fashioned manual labor to get you out of the house." Uh-oh, pep-talk coming. His mother was the queen of those.

"Sure, Mom."

She nearly stammered at his easy response. "Well, that's great. Payson, a good friend of mine, needs help around her antique shop."

He grunted an affirmative. This sounded terrible already.

"She recently lost her assistant, so she needs someone to fill in for a while. Honestly, I think she mostly needs someone to take charge and fix up her storeroom. It's a disaster zone back there. I told her you were handy with a hammer and nails, and she's thrilled. Dear woman is so tidy and organized, that storeroom must drive her crazy. She'll also need some help with deliveries, and other odds and ends."

Great. Maybe he should have listened before he agreed. Spending his days organizing some old lady's musty antique shop. He'd be spending his retirement folding lace doilies. He grunted his final acceptance.

"I'm so excited for tonight. See you in a few hours." He could practically see her humming with joy. Helping a friend, keeping her son out of trouble, and showing off all three of her children to Seaview's elite. She'd made out like a bandit today.

"See you in a few hours." Hanging up the phone, he looked over at the pristine penguin suit hanging on the closet door. Shit. Made him feel like such a cliché. Not that anyone but him saw it that way.

5

FULL DARK SURE CAME early in the winter around here. The air was just below freezing, but at least the sky was clear. Payson grabbed a warm wool coat and scarf before heading out the door for the gallery opening. She was thrilled that the gallery was re-opening, confident that it would be a major tourist draw, bringing more art-lovers to Seaview.

However, now Natalie was either making art or selling it full time, abandoning Payson. She'd run Flotsam Antiques alone for only a short time before she'd hired Natalie on part-time for deliveries and extra help, and she wouldn't be easy to replace.

Laura had called her about an hour before the event tonight, proudly announcing that she'd found some temporary help for her. A big strong man who would be able to help her with deliveries and reorganize the back room, which she'd been putting off for... well, since she opened.

Her son, Ronan, had returned from Europe a week or two ago. Apparently, he was a busy computer programmer that travelled all over the world. After a recent train wreck in Germany and getting laid off from his job, he was forced to move home.

Laura wasn't specific, but it sounded like he was having a hard time adjusting. So, Laura was hoping that working for Payson would give him something to do other than wallow in self-pity. Poor guy, losing his livelihood like that had to be rough.

Payson was happy to have the help around the shop; her backroom really needed an upgrade. It was getting more than a little embarrassing. Some folks appreciated good presentation, and she was one of them. But... the backroom wasn't seen by anyone but her, so she'd let it go... for way too long now.

If Ronan was half as handy with tools as the rest of his family, he'd have the room spiffed up in no time. Besides, she'd do about anything for the McAllisters. The whole family had taken her in as one of their own since she'd moved to town. Aiden, Maddy, now Chase, were her closest friends. Since Laura's retirement from her seat as a county judge, she was fast becoming a good friend as well.

The McAllisters were like that; bringing in strays and making them feel included and loved. They had taken in Chase when he was an angsty youth. Then, when he returned last summer, Frank had hired Chase as his right-hand man at McAllister Fisheries. Almost immediately, he and Maddy had fallen head-over-heels in love. The kind of love that always made Payson sigh wistfully.

Checking her appearance one last time before covering the gorgeous dress with her heavy peacoat, Payson admired her latest find. For the occasion, she and Maddy and Laura had made a girl's trip into Portland to go dress shopping.

She'd picked out a long black satin dress with spaghetti straps and a deep cowl neck that showed a hint of cleavage. The back was way more risqué than she'd ever been daring enough to wear before, with a very low cowl showing off most of her back. Laura had insisted, telling her she looked like a model in the gown. It didn't take much arm twisting for her to cave and buy the stunning thing.

Initially, she'd freaked at the idea of not being able to wear a regular bra, but it was surprisingly comfortable. Growing up, she'd envied her mother and sisters with their curvy figures, but as a late bloomer, she finally developed a decent rack. Not much to brag about in the hips still, so she flaunted the assets she had.

For the occasion, she'd worn jet black eyeliner with smoky eye shadow and mascara to accent her green eyes. She had pulled her auburn hair into a messy bun with plenty of wispies to frame her face so she could show off her back. Having started teaching a local self-defense class, Maddy had decided she and Payson should be work-out buddies. She had been dragging her out running and had them on a weight-lifting program.

Grueling as it was, Payson appreciated the results and was pleased to show off some of her hard-earned muscle. And good cardiovascular health, of course. Satisfied, she headed out the door.

The fresh air felt great, and the icy breeze only added to the messy bun look. Grateful the new gallery location was only two blocks down from her own shop, she walked despite her delicate lace-up heels. A little chill and some great shoes wouldn't slow her down.

Wow, they sure had decked the place out. Greeters dressed in formalwear took her ticket and directed her to the bar. Servers dressed in black pants and white jackets carried appetizer trays around to the guests.

Great turnout. The place was huge, and it looked like half of the permanent residents of Seaview were here, plus a hundred more from out of town. The local shop-owners had all been invited as they'd be key to promoting each other, but otherwise the event was primarily a fundraiser for budding local artists, including programs for kids.

Scanning the crowd, she wasn't seeing any of her favorite people. She made polite conversation with those she knew as she perused: the mayor and his wife, some fellow shop owners, a few of the single guys in town that she'd dated. One might think it would be awkward, but she tried to always remain friends. Which had been part of the problem; she was quite proficient at making casual friendships. It was the meaningful relationships that were harder to come by.

Natalie was standing by a collection of high contrast black and white photographs of lighthouses that she had clearly taken, beaming as guests asked her about her work. Although she was incredibly shy, she was in her element tonight. Payson snuck up and pinched her friend lightly on the arm and gave her a thumbs up, before giving her space to show off.

Dang, where were Maddy and Chase? Where was Aiden? She was looking forward to meeting their mysterious brother, and her new employee, Ronan. Payson made for the bar, grabbing a glass of red wine to take on her self-guided tour of the gallery while she waited for her friends.

Much of the art was impressive; great selection and variety, predominantly coastal themed of course. It was amazing to think there were so many talented artists in the area. She stopped to admire a colorful mixed media sculpture, appreciating the creativity involved in designing the ocean scene using re-purposed bottles and cans.

From behind her, a deep, rumbling voice interrupted her solo contemplation. "A bit contrived."

She turned abruptly with a scowl. The art critic stood right behind her, and she ran right into the rock-solid chest as she turned to admonish him for his rudeness. He growled and grabbed his right side when she bumped him, his fierce scowl deepening.

Art critic was a total grizzly bear... but filled out the tux rather nicely... a bit like James Bond. Didn't look like 007, with a gnarly beard covering most of his face, his hair tied back with a few strands falling out, as it was not quite long enough to pull into a neat pony. His icy blue eyes looked familiar, but they looked distant and lifeless.

In a huff, she stepped back to gain some distance and foolishly knocked into the sculpture with her butt. With another harsh growl, and with surprising cobra-like reflexes, he reached around her and righted the piece before it went crashing to the ground. Her face was now pressed right up to his chest. As much as she hated to admit it, he smelled fantastic, like fresh mountain air.

Not that she spent a lot of time in the mountains. Or smelling men for that matter. What was going on with her?

The grizzly wrapped his arm around her waist and pulled her away from the teetering sculpture, as she'd been frozen in place, totally confused by her reaction to him. His hand splayed across her bare back; she burned at his touch. Surprised and irritated by his effect on her, she snapped at him, "Get your hands off of me."

"Hey lady, I'm just trying to save the gallery before you destroy all the art in it." What was his deal? He could at least stop glaring at her and insulting her.

Payson pushed at his chest to get some distance from the conundrum of a man; spilling her wine on his jacket. Dammit, she just couldn't catch a break around this guy. At least she'd missed the white shirt. "If you hadn't grabbed me so... boorishly, I wouldn't have spilled." Where had her manners gone? She was raised better than this.

Not having a napkin, she grabbed the handkerchief from his chest pocket and attempted to pat the area dry.

He grabbed her wrist, "I've got it." He pulled the handkerchief out of her hand and brushed the wine off himself, then stuffed it back in his pocket.

They scowled at each other, neither willing to be the first to look away.

From down the hall, Maddy's voice reached them. "Looks like you two have met, fantastic." Payson turned at the sound of her friend's voice. *You two*? Those familiar eyes... they were McAllister eyes. That meant... Ronan. Shit.

Shit. He'd just completely offended Maddy's best friend.

"Payson, you are so lucky Ronan will be helping out at the shop. He's got a good eye and will have that storeroom organized in no time." Maddy beamed at him as she introduced him to her best friend.

And, apparently, his new employer.

Still recovering from a serious lack of sleep when his mother had called, he'd easily been suckered into accepting the role of handyman, delivery driver, and shop-boy for what she had implied was a frail old lady. At least, he had assumed. In his mother's defense, he shouldn't say suckered, he knew he was on a downward spiral and needed to get his ass off the couch. Wasn't dead yet, so may as well find something to do.

He extended his hand for the introduction, but it was really more of an apology. He even attempted a smile, but he was downright rusty at it and was sure it came off as more of a grimace. Payson took his hand

and shook it politely, if only to avoid Maddy knowing she thought he was an asshole.

Yeah, he was that. Although, she was no prize herself. Sure, she was fucking gorgeous. Amazing body with just the right curves. Intense green eyes, straight out of a fairytale. He'd nearly gotten his first hard-on in months just standing so close to her, inhaling her delicious scent, his hand on her bare back.

Regrettably, she was too much of a snooty priss for his taste.

"Payson runs the finest antique shop on the eastern seaboard."

"Ronan, it's nice to finally meet you. Laura told me that you agreed to come help me out at the shop... now and again," her voice was gentle, but he couldn't miss the challenge in her tone. Her eyebrow raised defiantly, she bated him, begged him to back out of the deal.

At least he wouldn't be bored, working with this shrew in a smelly old antique shop. Maddy stood at his side, smiling and completely missing the disdain in either of their voices.

"Actually, I thought you were looking for someone to do some handyman work and serve as delivery driver and shop-boy until you find someone more permanent. I'll be by 8 o'clock Monday morning - that work for you, boss?" She rolled her eyes but agreed. Might be fun getting a rise out of her on a regular basis.

At last, Chase arrived, rescuing him from further making an ass of himself. Handing him a frothy beer, Chase winked at him. He gulped half of it down before he said something even more stupid.

Chase nudged him. "Glad you're here. This is really not my scene. I'm fairly certain Miss Hanson just patted me on the ass as I walked by. Have you caught her staring at you through her window yet?" Chase's former nosy neighbor, now Ronan's neighbor at the rental house, was a known busybody. But, her vigilance had helped save Maddy's life last summer when she'd caught intruders at Chase's house.

"Yeah, she's a real treasure. I'm surprised her nose isn't permanently turned up from pressing against her front window all day." Ronan found it easy to smile suddenly, more at ease with people that knew him.

Although he and Chase had never been close before, they had a lot in common. Both had run far and fast from Seaview as soon as they'd graduated from high school; both had spent their years away surviving on adrenaline. Chase had been making sure Ronan felt normal and welcome in his return. His exercise equipment still in the garage at the rental, Chase came over every day to exercise.

Each day, he'd opened the door to the house and blasted heavy metal, enticing Ronan out without any pressure to interact. He had quickly accepted the no-conversation-required invitation and was enjoying their routine. All while burning the edge off the temper he'd developed since getting shot.

Ronan started to relax. Chase continued, making friendly conversation to put him at ease. "Maddy's picked out half the gallery to go in the beach house; she finally settled on one of Natalie's lighthouse black-and-whites." They briefly chuckled, in a manly way of course, at Maddy's expense. Like a trooper, she took the teasing, knowing he needed a distraction.

Green eyes shining brightly, Payson pasted on a polite smile and tried to carry the easy conversation. "Settling back into town?"

Ronan managed a tight, ironic smile, "Not really trying."

Maddy tried to re-direct, but Payson continued, "Is Seaview not meeting your expectations?" The smile was there, and he could hear the tease in her voice, but he sensed she was baiting him.

"Seaview's fine."

Before Payson could fire back, Chase jumped in to diffuse what he must have noticed was already a ticking timebomb of a relationship,

"It's hard coming back. If it hadn't been for Maddy, it would have been a hell of a lot rougher."

Ronan understood. Chase must have had a rough return, the local bad boy and son of the town drunk, returning to take a lead position at the biggest business in town.

Maddy linked arms with Payson. "Let's get you a fresh drink, bet you could use it. How'd your date with Gregory go? Soothe your dry spell?"

Payson's blush was unmistakable, as was her elbow's direct hit to Maddy's ribs. Before he could hear the answer, they strolled off toward the bar together. He didn't care anyway. She could sleep with whoever the hell she wanted.

6

Lying flat on his back, fat snowflakes falling all around, Ronan drifted on an open Viking ship. Not alone. Above him, a goddess with silky auburn hair and fairy green eyes, rode him like an avenging warrior. He grasped her breasts as her back arched in glory and cried out in spectacular orgasmic bliss.

Beep, beep, beep. Ronan jerked awake.

What the hell? Sealing his eyes shut, he tried to ignore the obnoxious alarm, holding on to the dream. Stupid, he knew. But, for the first time in months, he hadn't awoken screaming in horror.

Not that he'd slept great, but this was a pleasant change. Hadn't slept last night for imagining peeling off that black satin dress she'd been wearing at the gallery. Over and over again, stuck in an indulgent erotic loop.

7:00. Shit. He couldn't stall any longer. Nor should he dwell in that little fantasy, at least, not now. His new boss wouldn't exactly appreciate it if she found out where his subconscious had lingered. Hopefully his imagination might stray in her direction again tonight...

Payson locked up her apartment and dashed downstairs at 7:45 Monday morning. Why was she so nervous? Something about Ronan unsettled her. Every time she closed her eyes since meeting him, even to just blink, he'd take over her imagination, in many, many forms. Searching those wounded eyes for the source of his pain... peeling that tux off of him...

Why? From the neck down, yeah, he thoroughly fulfilled the 007 fantasy. Pure muscle under that tux. But he was a scowling, classless, unkept mountain man from the neck up. And rude.

Ok, time to dump the judgments. He'd been through a lot; experiencing a train wreck couldn't be easy. She knew he'd need the money having lost his income as well. Shaking off the annoyance with Ronan, Payson turned her irritation inward. She hadn't exactly been friendly either, which was not at all like her.

She'd give him the benefit of the doubt. Unlocking the back door to the shop, Payson let herself into the storeroom and disengaged the alarm. Let's hope Ronan at least has a sense of order, as she apparently didn't. Not in any practical sense, anyway.

The sales area of Flotsam Antiques was meticulously laid out, both welcoming and drawing buyers in to explore every last treasure. The back room, however, was embarrassing. If an item didn't sell, she might store it in the back for a few months, then return it back to the sales floor with a different collection. Other times, she might hold an item before showcasing it up front when the time was right.

Hiking up her black and pink flowered maxi dress, she stepped over the flotsam and jetsam that blocked the hallway to the salesroom. She fired up the sales register up front, did some light dusting and organization while she waited. At 8 o'clock sharp, the expected knock at the front door interrupted her solitude.

Ok, she told herself. Be nice. Ronan McAllister stood outside the door, dressed in a faded, loose black t-shirt, threadbare jeans, and sturdy hiking boots. He must be handsome underneath everything; his family sure was attractive. It was just too hard to tell under the terrible-fitting, worn clothing, the fierce scowl and all that hair.

Pasting a polite smile on her face, Payson hoped she looked happy to see him. "Good morning. Sleep well last night?"

He snarled as he brushed past her, through the narrow opening as she held open the glass door. Pressing his body against hers, again. Damn, he smelled so good. Was he doing this on purpose? She tried to be irritated, but found herself noticing that he was quite a bit taller than she was, and she wasn't short.

"Yeah, fine. What do you need?" He didn't bother hiding the bad temper in his voice.

Payson glared at him, hands on her hips. "Can we try to get along? I need help, and you need a job. If you can't be civil, maybe we can just not speak to each other while we work. I'll post a daily checklist for you on the door, so we don't even have to look at each other."

Ronan shrugged, sarcasm dripping from his words, "Fine. I slept great. Did you have a nice weekend?"

Payson found herself growling like a deranged grizzly herself. This was already a disaster.

"This the back room?" Ronan headed back, not waiting for her response. Stopping fast, he narrowly missed tripping over the box blocking the narrow hall to reach the back room. "Shit, doesn't the fire department ever audit around here?"

Cussing the whole way, Ronan made it to the back miraculously unscathed. Hands on his hips, he surveyed the room. It wasn't huge, much smaller than the large retail space. A warped old 3x8 foot folding table sat in the middle and was covered with boxes. Several feet of walkway surrounded the table. An eclectic assortment of plastic shelving lined the walls, housing even more boxes and trinkets draped with old sheets.

Watching as Ronan scrutinized the space, Payson stayed silent. He didn't look impressed. She found herself biting the inside of her cheek, anticipating his insults. Surprisingly, he didn't outrightly insult the disorganized storeroom. Not that he needed to. They both knew it looked awful. "Do you have the new shelves yet?"

Well, he wasn't exactly complimentary, either. She shrugged, overwhelmed just looking at the daunting task. "No, not yet. I keep meaning to pick them up, but I don't even know where to start. You know when something spirals so far out of control, you don't even want to face it?"

Ronan nodded grimly. "Yeah, yeah I do." He walked around the room, pushing at shelves and boxes, testing stability. "Mind if I head to the hardware store to pick up some materials? I'm not much of a carpenter, but I can throw together some decent shelving units, maybe a sturdier table, with shelving for supplies. Do you have any tools?"

Again, she shrugged, adding a sheepish smile, "I have a hammer and a few screwdrivers, but I don't know where I left them. Maddy was going to fix it last summer but got a bit... busy, with falling in love. And the whole abduction business."

Ronan winced, "Yeah; she sure had a unique summer. She's probably a much better carpenter than I am, but I've got the time so you're stuck with me. Mind if I pick up some tools while I'm out? I can use my dad's table saw at his place to save on costs."

For all his crankiness, and the stories she'd heard about him - mostly that he was a loner in high school, he clearly cared about his sister and felt terrible about what she'd gone through. Which, almost, endeared him to her.

Nodding in agreement, Payson started to head for the front. "Let me grab you some cash. How much?"

A rusty laugh passed his lips. When did he last have a carefree, hearty laugh? He sounded out of practice. "I have no idea. I haven't been to a hardware store in quite some time."

Payson smiled. "Well, neither have I. I don't usually open for another hour, and it's looking to be a quiet morning. Why don't I go with you and bring the credit card?"

If she wasn't mistaken, Ronan visibly stiffened before responding. "Sure. My truck's out back."

Just what he needed. Miss Prim and Proper in a long, flowy dress following him through the hardware store. He wasn't even sure what all he needed but had planned to make it up as he went. He watched as she pulled a pink wool sweater over her head as they went out the back door. The wind was bitingly cold against his bare arms as they walked to his truck.

Pulling herself up into the truck easily, she buckled then sat silently. Her eyes wandered everywhere, except that she avoided looking directly at him. He was fine with that. He'd rather not chat anyway. On the drive to the hardware store, he quickly calculated what they would need. He'd always been able to think quickly on his feet.

Through the hardware store, she sashayed along behind in her little heeled boots. He almost said something... almost. Although, he had to admit, he liked the way the dress swayed with her hips. It had too been a damn long time since he'd even noticed a woman, work had been so busy tracking the fucking mercs that ruined his life. Now he was fantasizing about Payson and couldn't get her out of his brain.

At least it hadn't been a night riddled with nightmares every time he closed his eyes. That was a plus in the insomnia department.

He shook off the invasive thoughts; she still wasn't his type. Leave those thoughts at home. Pissing her off didn't seem to be buying him any space, but at least it was a good reminder for himself that touching her was a downright terrible idea.

7

IT TOOK DAYS TO organize the backroom so he could even get started on the new shelves. Each day he'd find a new reason to piss her off, and she'd find new, creative ways to snipe back at him. They'd picked up some storage bins so he could re-organize the stock on the shelves, while stacking the surplus stock against one wall while he cleared out the flimsy shelving she'd had before. It was a miracle she hadn't had a major collapse and destroyed what must be thousands of dollars in antiques, maybe more.

Which she hadn't been pleased to hear. "Payson, are you insured?" he asked as a box filled with glass fishing floats slid down the shelf toward him. Luckily, he caught the box just before it crashed to the ground. Delicately balancing the flimsy container, he set it neatly on the floor next to her so she could re-package it into a sturdier bin.

"Of course I'm insured," she glared fiercely in his direction, pulling the box closer toward her. Gently, she loaded the glass balls into one of the wooden crates they had picked up.

Shaking his head, he pulled down the rest of the boxes a bit more gingerly. If he didn't start from the top and work his way methodically down, ensuring the weight distribution was even, she'd lose half her stock in a collapse. "Where did you get these flimsy shelves?"

Payson looked up briefly to shoot daggers from her eyes in his direction. Exasperated, she snapped, "If you're going to be judgmental, you don't have to help. I got them second hand to save on start-up costs."

"I'm seeing the job clear through from start to finish, so don't think you'll get rid of me that easily," he fired back.

Furious, she tossed her silky auburn hair over her shoulder and wiped the early beads of sweat from her brow. She pulled the heavy knit sweater off and tossed it on the already overloaded table, then bent forward to pick up the next bin. Moronically, Ronan glanced over, ready to keep firing out insults, but got distracted when he caught an unexpected glimpse down her top.

Locked onto the prize, his eyes couldn't move from her incredible breasts, just barely held in by a white lace bra. She was right, it was hot in here. His heart and lungs completely quit functioning as he got lost in the vision, hoping the flimsy lace would bust... then she glanced up.

Luckily, she mistook his lustful gaze for a scowl and glared right back. He abruptly turned away and continued to clear the shelves, his scowl now becoming quite real. Angry at himself for losing his historically unwavering control.

Regardless of the state of her storeroom, she didn't seem to shy away from hard work. Quite the opposite. Despite the long dress she'd worn at the hardware store, she hadn't hesitated to jump in and grab heavy items. Had given him the evil eye when he had even implied that she might need his help. He couldn't help the smile that formed when he pictured the dirty looks that she'd given him over the last week since they first met. Had some serious fire behind it.

She operated a nice little shop too. As with its owner, he'd been pleasantly impressed by the shop. In contrast to the cluttered mess of a storeroom, the front of the shop was neatly organized, welcoming, and quite charming. She cleaned daily and had fresh flowers displayed throughout the shop, with fresh air wafting through regularly so the shop had a fresh smell rather than musty.

Ronan told himself he ought to lighten up around her. She worked hard and didn't deserve his bitterness. But, he just couldn't seem to pull himself out of this nasty disposition. Which just made things worse between them. He was rude to everyone these days, but he took it out on her the hardest.

He wouldn't deny it, his temper at her was mostly based in desperation. Needing to keep his distance, or it would be easy to give in to the desires of his subconscious, sex-deprived brain. When he put his mind to it, he could romance a woman more efficiently than his promiscuous brother; not that he would ever act so licentiously. He'd had to put on some mad flirting skills as an operative more than a few times.

Although, having a nice face had been a curse more often than an asset. Which was a small part of where the beard came from. For his sanity, much safer if he kept his distance.

After spending the next morning breaking down the flimsy shelving, Ronan loaded the last of it into the back of his truck. He'd drive by the dump this evening before they closed. First, he focused on measuring out and planning the shelves.

Maybe some different heights and depths, as she carried quite a variety of items. Would need to be sturdy enough to handle whatever she may try to overload it with. He taped an outline on the creaky wood flooring, ensuring the dimensions he'd imagined provided an easy flow.

Out of nowhere, the smell of rotting flesh came first. Coughing and gagging, he tried to purge his mind of the necrotic odor. Images flashed in his mind, dragging him into the flashback; eyes sunken or missing entirely, limbs bent in unnatural directions. Nearly 20 of them. Men, women, and children; no one had been spared.

There had been little intelligence to be gained from going into that building; the fucking mercs had been there first. Testing their latest biologic weaponry on those innocent people who had done nothing more than be in the wrong place at the wrong time; isolated, miles from anything.

Where would Young and his crew have gotten ahold of those weapons anyway? Young wasn't a weapons dealer. Didn't make a damn bit of sense.

It was the same horrific memory that plagued him every night, his subconscious remained stuck in an endless circle, demanding answers. Each night, he was Sisyphus, imprisoned in an unsurmountable predicament.

Sweat dripped down his brow, the salt stung his eyes. His ears were ringing in panic, the world around fading to black. Breathe in 2, 3, 4, 5, hold.... Release. Fuck. Fuck. Fuck. Every damn day. Other memories, good and bad from his years in the CIA surfaced periodically, but this one made an appearance every damn day.

Ronan stood from his squatted position and shoved open the steel door, its hinges squealing in protest at the impatient force. The ice-cold air blasted into the room like a welcoming flood of mana, cleansing him of the imagined scent. Propping the door open with a nearby chair, Ronan got back to work, trying to shake off the lingering panic. Calculating the dimensions, planning how many boards of how many inches.

The shrill jingle of Payson's phone broke his concentration. Her perky voice echoed from the front sales floor. "*Bonjour* Alain.... Yes, I would love to see your latest finds.... Alain, I can't just pick up everything and fly to France, can't you just send me pictures like usual?... That does sound amazing... No, I've never been... Ok, I'll think about it. Can I get back to you in a week or two?... *Merci*. Bye."

Her perkiness... and her atrocious French accent shattered the meditative bubble he'd built around himself. She called out his name as she approached. Dammit. He was still so shaken from the panic attack, his shirt soaked with sweat, his vision tunneled, he couldn't respond.

"Hey. It's freezing in here, if you're too hot, can't you just turn on a fan or crack a window?" She griped as she came into the back room.

On seeing his ashen pallor, his clammy skin, a look of sympathy washed over her. Not now. He really couldn't handle any kind words, any apologies. Not from her, not from anyone.

"It's fucking hot in here. I have to run to the dump anyway," Ronan stormed out, throwing down the tape measure he'd been holding. Knew he'd pissed her off even more. Hating himself for continuing to be a damn jerk every time she was around, he needed to get a grip.

Tearing the truck door nearly off its rusty old hinges, Ronan pulled himself into the truck and slammed the door shut behind him. Resting his forehead on the steering wheel, he calmed his breathing. Eyes closed, he took himself through the guided imagery techniques he'd learned from a PTSD app he'd downloaded.

Sitting on a wooden boat, eyes watching the steady horizon, the gentle rocking of the boat cutting through the choppy water, the hum of the engine.

Even the next morning, Ronan couldn't handle being around her. The sympathy was intolerable. Maybe worse, his nocturnal imaginings were becoming increasingly detailed, envisioning her perform many, many creative things with his body. Picturing her... very naked... was becoming a welcome diversion from the nightmares. But, the vivid fantasies made it so much harder to be around her.

Measurements finally done, satisfied with the plan, he headed to his parent's garage to use the table saw. Ronan made himself at home in his dad's enormous garage. Fortunately, his parents were spending the day running errands and left him to work in peace.

His dad had always enjoyed carpentry and had converted the 3-car garage into a 2-car garage with a well-equipped shop. Measuring each piece of material – twice, remembering the old adage to measure twice and cut once, he methodically cut the lumber down to size.

Details had always been his strong suit, which was why he'd been suited so well for his work with the CIA. Every little detail mattered. Sometimes it boiled down to one tiny nuance in a conversation that pointed toward the information he was seeking.

Headphones and safety goggles in place, he fired up the saw. Cutting the lumber was turning out to be downright cathartic. Who knew? Maybe he should have taken up woodworking a long time ago.

The smell of the sawdust was nostalgic, reminding him of when he helped his dad build their old pergola. Remembering how he had enjoyed the work. How his dad had tried to push him outside of his very narrow, hyper-focused academic and extracurricular activities.

Pushing the 2x4s through, precisely along the markings, he added the completed boards to the stack of other precisely cut lumber. Hours passed, but it could have been days or seconds for all Ronan knew, if it hadn't been for the cheerful cuckoo clock on the wall. That must've been his mom's touch.

"Hey son, you still out here working?" Frank shouted over the buzz of the saw as he sauntered into the garage, nodding approvingly at the neatly stacked 2x4s organized by length.

Ronan shut down the saw, pulled off the safety googles and headphones. Looking up, he realized every scrap of daylight had gone. "Guess I lost track of time."

"Nice work. Precise cuts. That's going to be a heck of a storage room. She know what you're planning?" Frank smiled, deep creases forming in his cheeks, eyes crinkled from years at sea. He leaned against the opposite side of the table saw facing Ronan.

Funny, Ronan was an inch or two taller, but he still thought of his dad as larger than life. Even though his dad worked strictly in the office now, just like when he'd been a little kid, Ronan could smell the salt air on his dad, coming home from a long day fishing, pulling in lobster. He would never have imagined how reassuring the scent could be.

"Sort of. She's uh... not my biggest fan. I'm trying to stay out of her hair until this project is done, and she hires a replacement." Ronan carried the cut plywood over to his stack of similarly sized pieces.

"Payson's about the friendliest person in town. We all know you've always preferred to keep to yourself, but you've always been more than likeable. Heck, you could win over just about anybody with a quick grin or a wink. What did you do to the girl?" Frank's voice projected humor and pride, but his crinkle-edged eyes harbored unmistakable worry.

Squatting down over the stack he'd just added the board to, Ronan double checked the cuts, keeping busy as he tried to think of how to answer. Which wasn't like him either.

His dad was right. Part of why he'd been hired on by the CIA was his ability to quickly win over others, his quick thinking on his feet. Where had that gone?

Lost in the pool of blood that had seeped into the floorboards of his London flat. "I'm not that guy anymore, Dad."

Frank sauntered toward his morose son, casually brushing off the sawdust that had clung to the elbow of his sweatshirt. With creaky knees, he squatted down in front of his son. Ronan had no choice but to look up and meet his father's knowing gaze.

"Ronan, I love you, son. Always have, always will. You've always been too brainy for your own good. Always followed such a straight and deliberate path, knowing exactly what you wanted. So much so, that the rest of us couldn't keep up with you. Left behind in your glorious dust. That path... well, that path is covered in leaves and dirt and muck of all sorts; completely obscured. Maybe even eroded away."

Pausing, the older man chortled, tugging on his son's ratty beard, "Hell, maybe it's lost under all that hair. Point is, maybe it's ok to get lost sometimes. Might be an adventure, forging a new path."

8

Payson paced up and down the storefront, afraid to walk back to the storeroom and disturb Ronan. He'd carted in loads of cut lumber and had been drilling and hammering all morning. How did she apologize for not recognizing he was unwell the last time she'd seen him?

She imagined he must have PTSD from the train crash. Or was there more? He'd looked so pale. So distant.

Resolved to make amends, Payson flipped the sign to *Closed*, grabbed her heavy coat and purse and headed out the front. She crossed the street to her favorite sandwich shop. Inside, Maddy sat with her partner, Ian, both dressed in their police uniforms.

"Well, fancy meeting you here," Maddy grinned at her friend as Payson headed to their table. Payson wasn't used to being the somber one. Whatever the occasion, she was always the one to find the bright side, to bring others up.

Standing at the side of the table, she nervously gripped her purse and tried to look calm. "I'm hungry. And, I should probably feed your brother, or I don't think he'll stop to eat."

She wasn't sure if she should sit for a moment or grab the sandwiches and run. Since meeting Maddy about two years back, they'd been best friends. Maddy was who she turned to when she needed help. Trouble was, this time her dilemma was directly regarding Maddy's own twin brother. But maybe that made her the person she should ask.

Ian, a few years younger, long and lean in build, joked back, "I can't imagine missing lunch. Or breakfast, or dinner... or snack for that matter." He took a huge bite of his gigantic sub.

Maddy kicked him under the table. "Uh-huh. You won't have that metabolism forever, pal." She looked up at Payson, "Is my brother behaving himself?"

Payson tried to say no, but she knew she was the one with the behavior problem. Overwhelmed with guilt for not having more patience, she admitted, "Mostly. I just feel so bad; I think that train wreck must have been really rough on him. I interrupted him in the middle of a panic attack the other day; he was so pale. Being me, I missed it and totally pissed him off. We've been avoiding each other ever since. So, I'm attempting to make amends with food."

Maddy nodded, a sad smile on her face, "Yeah, he's been through too much. I made him promise to socialize with his family at least once a week." In a lightbulb moment, Maddy pulled her phone out of her pocket to check her calendar. "Actually, he's passed due. Maybe we should drag him out tonight, distract him from his worries. How does Winter's after work sound?"

Payson smiled. "Perfect, maybe we can get him to loosen up a bit. You'll call Aiden and Chase?"

Typing madly away at her phone, Maddy was on it. "Group text officially... sent."

Swallowing a huge bite of sandwich, Ian piped in, "You know, it's dancing night. Maybe I'll see you there? I could show you a few moves." Ian was an incorrigible flirt. He sure didn't keep his crush on her secret but was never creepy about it.

Teasing him back, she rolled her eyes, "Nice try, hot shot. Aren't you dating Aliyah from the hardware store?"

With a playful eyebrow raise, he insisted, "Nah, she didn't hold a candle to you."

Payson's phone buzzed with the texted invitation from Maddy. For the rest of the group, she responded with a quick: *Wouldn't miss it!*

Ignoring Ian, knowing he could go on and on, she turned to Maddy. "Great idea for tonight. Maybe Ronan will relax a little. We'll liquor him up a bit. He may even have a laugh if we drag him out onto the dance floor."

Ian muttered to himself, "I see how it is. She likes them mysterious. I can be mysterious."

Maddy rolled her eyes. "Ian, no offense, but I'm not sure *mysterious* is your thing. Anyway, I'm not sure I've ever seen Ronan dance. Good luck with that one."

Feeling less guilty now, Payson headed up to the counter to order the sandwiches. She wasn't sure what he'd like, but something told her that he'd eat... or wouldn't... regardless of what kind of sandwich she chose for him.

Reminding herself she wasn't in the habit of terrorizing the wounded, she decided she would make it her personal mission to bring Ronan back to the land of the living. Berating herself, she couldn't believe she'd missed a classic wounded animal biting and snapping in defense. Reminded her a bit of herself after her parents had died.

"Sandwiches," Payson shouted across the empty shop as she walked in. For now, she left the sign on *Closed*. Not busy today anyway due the heavy snow in tonight's forecast. There had been light dustings of snow here and there, but nothing bordering on blizzard since she'd lived here, to her great disappointment. But, she'd heard the past few years had been unusually mild.

She found she looked forward to the snow like a school kid wishing for a snow day. Being snowed in for a few days sounded thrilling and relaxing all at once.

Finishing drilling the board he had been working on, Ronan didn't break his concentration. She knew he heard her for the grunt he'd given her, but so far, he hadn't looked up. He had incredible focus.

What would it be like if that focus were directed on her? Holding up the large board, his arms flexed, corded muscles tense as he drilled in the screw the rest of the way in. She could stand and watch all day. Was it getting hot in here?

Board in place, Ronan set down his tools and turned toward her. "Thanks." He accepted the offered paper-wrapped sandwich. Huh. Maybe he had a few manners. She'd been waiting for him to snipe at her for some reason.

Payson looked around for somewhere to set the drinks so they could eat together, but the table had disappeared. Reading her mind, he took the drinks from her and set them on the shelf he'd just finished.

"Grilled ham and cheese. I wasn't sure what you'd like, so I went with comfort food for a cold day. I was going to grab some tomato soup to go with it, but they only had chowder or beef stew today, which didn't sound as good." Was she babbling? Maybe. Wouldn't be the first time.

With a nod, he unwrapped the sandwich. Not the hungry bear devouring it that she had pictured, instead he ate politely as if they were at a formal dinner. Although, he certainly wasn't skilled at conversing politely. "Nice progress in here," she smiled serenely as she admired how the room was coming together, wishing he'd say something and spare her from further inane conversation attempts.

He finished the sandwich and wiped his hands and mouth with his napkin. After a sip of water, he finally replied, "Getting there. I've got quite a bit to assemble still, and the table will take me some extra time. I hope you don't mind going without for a while." He glanced her way, his glacial blue eyes locking with hers for the briefest of moments. It was enough to make her feel warm and tingly all over.

"Sure, of course. I'm so excited to see the whole thing put together. It was pathetic before. I'd just sort of moved in and spent as little money as possible back here where the customers wouldn't see, but I just hadn't gotten around to upgrading yet. Maybe I'll actually stay organized if I start fresh." Babbling again. What was going on with her?

She could hardly squeeze in a few bites of her sandwich; the butterflies in her stomach didn't leave much room for lunch. She wasn't even attracted to the grizzly. Not in any normal way; maybe in a pheromonal, primitive way. A deep warmth filled low in her belly, and lower, as she pictured him in very primitive ways.

Must be watching him working so hard, flexing those spectacular muscles, that sheen of sweat from the labor. The man exuded danger, competence... sensuality. Something in the way he walked like a tiger on the prowl, the deep rumble in his voice. The way his eyes looked into her, reading her.

Her hormones did a little dance every time he entered a room. Her ovaries stood and cheered every time he so much as looked at her. She needed to get a life.

9

Blustering wind nearly blew his truck off the road. Ronan gripped the wheel as he drove down Beachfront Street, heading for Winter's Tavern for his weekly socialization, as promised. This time, Maddy had insisted they go out with friends.

Last week he'd joined his family at his parent's for dinner, the week before he'd hung out with Aiden at his place. He was actually enjoying getting to know his family again. After all this time, he'd forgotten what an amiable, disarming unit they were.

Dark had fallen, the snow finally arriving, and he felt like he was flying through it at warp-speed. He'd spent last winter in Algeria, the one before in Iraq, and had forgotten what cold really felt like. He found it invigorating. Like a reminder that he was still alive. The numbness he'd shielded himself with couldn't withstand the freezing temperatures.

Winter's was relatively busy for such a stormy night. Although, this was nothing for the locals. Life went on, no matter the weather.

Not that he'd ever been inside; he'd left town well before he'd been old enough to go in and hadn't been back. The beloved local dive bar was the favorite watering hole for the fishermen and other laborers. He supposed that now included him. Not that his occupation was permanently as a handyman-slash-delivery-driver-slash-shop-boy. Once Payson found a new assistant, he had no idea what he was going to do with his time.

She wasn't such a terrible boss; sexy as hell and a bit snooty, but she was thoughtful. Always ensuring he was well fed and well paid. Not that he needed the money, but she didn't know that.

Nine years of not spending a dime of his own money made for healthy investments. Plus, the we're-sorry-you-almost-died money from the government didn't hurt. For larger deliveries, she'd come along with him and had shown some decent muscle, hadn't shied away from grunt work.

Yeah, maybe she wasn't so bad. Not that he'd tell her that; he didn't want to think what might happen if he let her get close. His demons wouldn't do her a damn bit of good. He'd stick to his bedtime fantasies; no need to ruin her life the way he'd ruined his own.

Backing into the parking spot, he saw Payson hopping out of Chase's truck. First time he'd seen her not wearing a long skirt or dress, but she was still purely feminine. She wore a leather miniskirt and black suede boots that just covered her knees, topped with a relaxed gray sweater. Ronan made for the group, trying not to stare at her mile-long legs.

Maddy and Chase held hands, laughing together about some inside joke, and headed into the tavern. Ronan stopped Payson before she went in, "I could have driven you." Why would he say that? She wasn't his responsibility. Maddy and Chase lived closer to her anyway.

A look of confusion passed over her as she looked up at him. With a shy smile, she added, "Thanks. I had planned to drive myself until I saw the snow. My old rear wheel drive doesn't perform very well in the snow." Still a few feet from the doorway, she stared up at him. Snowflakes nestled in her hair, her cheeks lively with pink blush from the biting wind.

Uncomfortable with the good-natured attention from her, the warm smile she was giving him, he cleared his throat and guided her inside. "We'd better head in. It's cold out here." When they weren't arguing, he sure had difficulty figuring out what to say to her. Damn cat had his formerly silver tongue and wasn't letting go.

The tavern was hopping. Winter, the seasoned owner and bartender, had pushed most of the tables into the corner for a makeshift dance floor, which he did a few days a month. Dancing hadn't started yet but was due to start soon.

The place was clean and inviting, but wasn't winning any beauty contests, with its scuffed-up floors, antiquated billiard tables, and a scattering of other well-worn classic tavern games. A delicious smell emanated from the kitchen, making Ronan wish he hadn't already eaten.

Chase and Maddy had already grabbed a corner booth for the five of them, ensuring enough room for Aiden when he arrived. Payson slid in first, scooting down next to Maddy. Ronan stood at the booth, not sure where to sit. "I, uh... I need the corner."

Might as well be honest. In his line of work, he'd always kept an eye on the door. Tough habit to break. In a pinch, a reflection from the window, or even a glass worked fine, but he wanted to be able to relax. Not chase shadows.

Payson looked at him like he was nuts, but Chase and Maddy promptly responded. Chase hopped right up, "Take my spot, I'll go grab us a pitcher." Maddy followed him, offering to grab the glasses. "Sit wherever you need. We'll slide in wherever."

Ronan nodded appreciatively. He slid around the circular booth, taking Maddy's seat next to Payson, his back to the corner so he could watch the room. She studied him as if he were an optical illusion and she was trying to make sense of the image. "I just can't figure you out," she finally said aloud.

"Sorry," he offered casually, his gaze scanning the room out of pure habit, but he kept his answer short; maybe also out of habit. Payson tugged her sweater off and tucked it into her oversized purse, revealing a snug white henley. Her spectacular breasts strained against the buttons, begging for release.

Cool your jets, he shook his head at his reckless thoughts. Perhaps letting his imagination run wild, building more detailed and creative fantasies about Payson each night was a stupid idea. It was rough before, but he couldn't seem to keep things in check quite so easily during the daytime now.

She tilted her head at him, a confused smile stuck in place. "Most of the time you're arguing with me, insulting me... generally being a pain in my ass. I'd toss you to the street if you weren't making my life significantly better by fixing my storeroom and helping with deliveries."

He managed to smile back at her, "Sorry about that, really. If it helps, I'm crabby with pretty much everyone lately," he trailed off, adding quietly, "even myself."

Payson reached her hand under the table and took his hand with her own, offering comfort. Instead of calming him, the connection set off an electric shock, singeing his nerves straight through his arm and into his chest, setting his heart into a rapid, irregular rhythm. Something flashed in her eyes; she was as astonished as he was.

Letting himself truly look at her, as he'd been avoiding quite intentionally before, he quickly recalled why he shouldn't. So fucking gorgeous, her enchanting green eyes looked him up and down, his own eyes wandering over her perfect breasts and subtle curves. Simultaneously, their gazes locked together.

She didn't say anything, she didn't have to. Both were drowning in foreign sensation. He was surprised the clouds didn't erupt with a crash of lightning right over their table.

Maddy and Chase returned with drinks a moment later, mercifully interrupting the moment. Payson pulled her hand away as they approached. Maddy set the frosty glasses on the table while Chase started filling from the pitcher before sitting down.

"It's so late, I assume everyone ate dinner already?" Maddy asked. "With Aiden's schedule, I tried to schedule as late as possible. He just texted; he's on his way."

Maddy and Chase finally slid into the booth, leaving Payson to squish up against Ronan. Didn't help his swirling emotions, which were only disrupted further when Maddy raised her glass in a toast, "To Ronan. I'm grateful to have my twin back in my life, safe and sound."

Ronan felt overwhelmed; even when he'd spent every waking hour studying or playing baseball, Maddy had made sure he'd surface to eat now and again, socialize sometimes. Always there for him, even when he wasn't there for her. When he should have been. Regretted that he hadn't been.

He thanked his sister with a smile and a friendly tap with his foot under the table and directed the toast to the right, as was an old McAllister family tradition. The familiarity of the action felt right. "To Payson, for keeping me busy so I don't spend so much time in my head."

Payson smiled back at him then raised her own glass, clearly at home to with the McAllisters and their habits. "Bringing it back around... To Chase, for coming back and making Maddy admit she needed love, just like we all do."

Ronan watched as she gulped down her beer. A hopeless romantic, she would never settle for an ass like him anyway.

Dang, she could chug, and this was a hoppy IPA. With her sleeve, she wiped the frothy moustache from her lip. Who was she? One minute she's in a delicate floral dress selling antiques in her quaint little shop, the next she's wearing a leather miniskirt and sexy-as-hell boots covering all but a ridiculously sexy scrap of bare legs, chugging an IPA in a fisherman's bar. She was rapidly throwing the uptight image right out the window. Not helpful.

As they set down their glasses, Aiden strolled in looking like he owned the place, as usual. Dressed to kill, he stripped out of his expensive-looking puffer jacket, strutting his stuff in his straight-fit black jeans with a pristine, snug-white t-shirt. For brothers not even two years apart, their lives had run on completely different trajectories. They looked a lot alike, sharing the McAllister blue eyes and chestnut hair, standing tall at an inch or two over six feet, with a lean but muscled build.

Personalities were a different story. Ronan had always been reserved, where Aiden was outgoing. Aiden was a pop-off and a troublemaker, but Ronan had been as straightlaced as they come growing up. Aiden was just starting out in his career, having recently opened his own legal practice in town, whereas Ronan was apparently now retired.

"Hey guys, thanks for saving me some," Aiden remarked sarcastically, noting the empty pitcher and half-finished glasses at the table.

Payson poked at him, as only a close friend would, "Maybe you should try showing up on time. Hang on, I'll go grab us another pitcher." She slid out of the booth. Rubbing his sternum, Ronan felt oddly hollowed out as she slid cheerfully away from him.

Aiden followed her up to the bar, visiting as they walked together, "That's alright, this one's on me. I won the case today."

Ronan couldn't help but watch the gentle sway of her hips as she walked away, her fingers running through her sleek auburn hair, still damp from the snow. He turned back to see Maddy observing his obvious ogle.

Quite rightfully, she didn't resist the obvious tease. "What's all this? Making eyes at my best friend?"

Done with living a life of lies, he didn't bother with hiding his feelings. "Eyes, yes. No more than that."

"Why not? You're perfect for each other."

Gaze locked downward; he ran his fingers along the frosty glass. "Funny. Regardless, I'm a fucking mess. I'm not dragging anyone else into my disaster of a life."

"I wasn't joking."

Pushing the accumulated frost into the shape of an arrow on the glass, he debated how to respond. Maybe they weren't as awful for each other as he imagined. Payson loved old, beautiful things. She was thoughtful, positive despite his recently adopted surly attitude. No doubt she'd be great for him, but he would drag her into his personal pit of despair. "I seem to crush her optimism with my very presence. I would be terrible for her."

Maddy stilled his fidgeting. "She's never let anyone get close enough to affect her imperturbably perky mood. The fact that you can rile her tells me you'll be equally able to raise her up further than anyone else."

Ronan snorted in disbelief.

Before Maddy could push further, the pair returned with a full pitcher of beer and a plate of nachos. Payson slid back in next to Ronan. Aiden tore into the nachos, talking through a huge mouthful of cheese and salsa, "I missed dinner. Too busy rocking the legal world of Seaview." Aiden flexed his muscles, ego inflated after what had clearly been a successful day in court.

Payson nudged him, "Uh-huh, way to go Mr. Hot-Stuff."

Grabbing herself a cheesy bite of chip, Maddy interrupted, "Speaking of hot-stuff, Payson, when's your next date with your new boyfriend, Mr. Fancy-Pants Neurologist? How are things going with him?" With a meaningful nod to Ronan, his sister seemed to imply he needed to move fast.

Aiden leaped in before Payson could respond, swallowing another huge bite, "Wait, boyfriend? Way to go Pace."

Maddy's question had the opposite effect. A boyfriend ought to help Ronan keep his mind off her. Well, it was at least a deterrent. He didn't poach.

Maybe. Not that he wanted anything to do with her romantically. She wasn't at all his type. Too damn stuffy.

Wasn't she? She had really been trying to be friendly the last day or two, which was slowly breaking down his well-constructed walls.

Payson rolled her eyes as she directed her attention to Maddy, "Thanks for asking. I'm supposed to see him next week. He's driving up here again. But, I think I'm going to cancel. He's so self-absorbed. I'm not putting up with one more asshole that doesn't see me for who I am."

Swallowing a mouthful of chips, Aiden teased, "Just take him golfing or something. If he doesn't appreciate you when you throw the club because you missed a good shot, then he's not a keeper."

Shocked at that one, Ronan actually found himself joining in, "Wait, throw the club? Weren't you just telling me how mild-mannered she is?" He raised his eyebrows playfully at Maddy and nudged Payson's knee under the table.

Laughing, Maddy scooped a huge pile of salsa onto her chip, "I said perky mood, not mild mannered. She's a bit... competitive."

Words defensive, but tone completely at ease, Payson nudged him back, "I enjoy healthy competition."

Aiden teased her again, "Is that what you call it? What happened to my tennis racket, again?"

Dodging Payson's under-the-table kick, Aiden leaped out of the booth in self-preservation. All attitude, and very maturely, she stuck her tongue out at him. Arms up, Aiden slid back into the booth.

Huh. Again, not what he was expecting. She was definitely not an elegant lady as he'd assumed.

"Children," Maddy interrupted, "Let's settle down. We're here to have a good time." She topped off glasses for those who weren't driving tonight.

Good thing he'd driven himself, didn't want to explain that he didn't drink to excess. Ever. Wasn't safe in his line of work. Or, what had been his line of work. Still, he couldn't risk a loose tongue.

Ronan threw a very drunk Payson over his shoulder. His shoulder still hurt like hell, but at least she wasn't wiggling too much. Just giggling. Maddy was too.

Aiden stumbled along behind, singing about Shaking You *All Night Long* in his horrendous ACDC impression, having decided to catch a lift home with Chase and imbibing along with Payson and Maddy. Chase didn't drink much either, having been raised by a raging alcoholic, so at least the two of them had stayed sober.

It had been funny, watching the three become increasingly silly as the night wore on. They'd attempted a few rounds at billiards, but that quickly became a bit dangerous when Payson and Maddy decided to try their hands at kendo.

Easily distracted, the tipsy trio had made for the dance floor as soon as Winter dimmed the lights and turned on the oh-so-classy disco ball. With no dancing clubs for miles, the turnout was great. Ronan was grateful, however, that it hadn't been karaoke night.

Despite the night of surprises where Payson was concerned, he was not surprised to discover that she enjoyed dancing. A lot. She, Maddy, and Aiden had rocked a few tunes solo while Ronan kicked Chase's ass at darts, until Maddy decided to drag Chase to the dance floor when the music turned romantic. Payson had initially made do with the equally inebriated Aiden as her dancing partner, but the pair looked downright awkward.

Quickly ditching her inadequate dance partner, she'd roped in Ronan. And danced with him very differently than with his brother, which his libido had accepted as a small victory, despite his better judgment. He rarely danced, but he had good rhythm. He'd actually learned to dance for a mission a few years back.

However, he wasn't trained for the kind of dancing Payson had in mind. The slow dance was sweet, her arms draped over his shoulders, her head leaned affectionately on his chest. Despite his better judgment, he let his arms wrap around her and let down his guard as they swayed together.

When the rhythm picked up, moving on to more contemporary, club-style music, she was all over him. Her hands were everywhere. Fuck, she had some incredible moves. He was certain she'd be mortified when she sobered up and realized she'd danced so... intimately with him. Like she wasn't disgusted by him.

If he wasn't convinced that sober-Payson found him to be a revolting dickwad, he would have thought she was looking for a booty call. He should have ended the dance as soon as she'd started grinding up against him, but... well... he hadn't. That ass pressed up against him, he'd been helpless against her wiles and pulled her tighter against him, letting his hands wrap around her hips.

Now, however, as he tossed her into the passenger seat of his truck, he hoped she didn't puke all over him. Ronan revved the old engine that coughed and sputtered, complaining in the freezing temperatures. He blasted the heat. They sure didn't make heaters like this anymore. Within a few minutes, the truck was toasty warm.

Before pulling out of the parking spot, he checked Payson's seatbelt. She looked over at him and reached across to tickle his beard. "I like this. Felt nice rubbing against me." She giggled again.

And, she talked the whole way back home. The woman could jump from topic to topic dang quickly and had yet to expect a response from him. Not that he was complaining. "And that's why I dumped Clive."

This time, she appeared to expect a response. "Who is Clive and why did you dump him?" he played along, finding himself curious as she described her many failed relationships.

"Clive, my ex-fiancé, haven't you been listening? Gosh. He just didn't do it for me. Nothing there. Yeah, the sex was decent, but nothing special. And he looked awful in a tux. Nothing like James Bond."

He smirked, keeping his eyes on the dark, snow-covered road. "You have a thing for James Bond, huh?" Although he quickly learned the life of a spy was so very, very different from the tales of James Bond, he wouldn't deny the secret agent had been part of the inspiration that had motivated his eleven-year old self's silently declared life plan.

Grinning from ear to ear, Payson responded, "Who doesn't? Sean Connery of course. Maybe Pierce Brosnan. All sexy... sexy," she slurred, gazing out the window with soft eyes. "That international man of mystery sexy spy business is hard to resist. Hard," she giggled.

Ronan bit his tongue. Well, that little tidbit certainly didn't help the little crush he'd developed. She was still not his type. Did he even have a type? Whatever it may be, it certainly wasn't his sister's friend, nor someone so eager to fall in love.

"Alright, we're here," Ronan said as they pulled in back of Flotsam Antiques.

With yet another giggle, Payson startled, "Oh, I guess this is my stop."

She swayed a bit as she hopped out, so Ronan decided he'd better walk her all the way in, else she may pass out on the steps and freeze to death. Ronan followed her up the steps, hands at the ready in case she slipped, but she did ok. At the door, she dug around in her purse, "I know I had keys when I left..."

She was a cute drunk. How could she possibly need to carry around that many things all the time to necessitate such a huge bag? While she stood fruitlessly searching her enormous purse for the keys, Ronan pulled out his own keys from his pocket. He discretely brought out his lockpicking tool - which, honestly, he didn't need anymore, but it came in so handy he routinely kept it on his keyring. You never knew when someone might lock themselves out of their house.

With a few quick flicks of his wrist, he had the door unlocked. He opened the door and motioned her inside. Honestly, he tried to not come in, but she dragged him in and slammed the door shut, shoving it closed behind him. Payson was a lot stronger than she looked. Her soft gaze drilled into him, her lush, pouty lips parted expectantly.

"Come on, to bed." He motioned her into the apartment, trying to get her to pass out before they did anything stupid.

She wasn't budging. Rubbing her hands across his chest, a sloppy smile growing, she purred, "Hmm, you know, you sure filled out a tux nicely."

If she only knew. Life as a spy was a hell of a lot more waiting around for something to happen, and his missions much less glamorous and without the nifty toys. He certainly never got to drive a fancy car or carry an explosive pen. He'd worn a lot more rags than tuxes, which is the official reason he'd grown the hair and beard in the first place, for a deep cover mission in Russia.

"Dance with me again. I like the way you move." Music playing in her head, she started to sway to the beat, still pressed up against him. Her hands wandered, exploring.

Imagining himself anywhere but here to distract himself, he turned her around to march her to bed. "Bed, let's go."

"Good idea." Managing to wiggle her way out of his grip rather than just cooperating, she turned and started to unzip the leather skirt. Eyes quickly looking up, at anything but her... Ronan had more willpower than most, but really didn't think even he could resist her wearing nothing but those boots, drunk or not.

He tried to leave, reaching for the door to make his escape... when she jumped him. Her sweet, warm lips locked onto his, her tongue not far behind. Holy shit, she wasn't messing around.

Digging her hands into his long hair, pulling it from its binding, she held him close with an iron grip. Nipping at his lip, she ran her tongue along the tender imprint she'd made with her teeth.

Losing the uphill battle, his control slipped away, and he pulled her up tightly against him, kissing her deeply. She didn't hold back, her tongue parried with his own, recklessly passionate.

Breathless, his brain finally kicked in, and he managed to pull himself away. Dammit, they didn't even like each other. At first, she looked disappointed at the rejection.

A quick second later, she laughed out loud with an indelicate snort. "Your beard tickles. What do you look like under all that hair?"

Ronan reached behind himself and put his hand on the doorknob, trying to sneak out before she jumped him again. Her kiss had pulled him under her spell so quickly, he feared letting her get too close. Neither of them would forgive him in the morning if he took advantage.

"I'm... sleepy." She yawned and closed her eyes. She collapsed towards him, fully trusting him to catch her. Of course, he didn't let her fall.

Still sore, but recovered enough from his injuries, he scooped her up for the second time tonight and carried her to the bedroom. Nice apartment, way bigger than he would have expected. The place went on and on, but he finally found what looked to be her bedroom. He gently set her on the bed, fearing she'd wake up and drag him down with her, but her soft snore told him she was totally out.

Standing and watching her for a moment, he didn't know what to do. What had that kiss been all about?

Her boyfriend. Shit; hope she doesn't remember this tomorrow. She wasn't the sort to fool around and would feel guilty.

He pulled his hair back into its binding. The least he could do was get her settled, then never mention tonight to her. Then, he'd go home and take an ice-cold shower.

10

Payson awoke with an unshakable grin the next morning. Must be her Irish genes to thank, as she'd never had a hangover in her life. She also hadn't been drunk like that since college. She woke up remembering an incredibly delicious dream—that she'd been lovingly kissed and tucked into bed by a sexy spy who loved her. Hard to let go of such a pleasant fantasy.

Looking down, she realized she was neatly tucked in the blankets, nude aside from her lacy bra and matching thong. Must have had more beer than she'd realized. She never slept in such delicate undies; damn uncomfortable. Nor did she remember getting to bed. Hopping in the shower, she wracked her brain trying to remember what had happened last night, but nothing came to her.

Letting her breezy mood guide her, Payson decided to follow through on her resolution. Hmm. In a spectacular lightbulb moment, Payson laughed at her brilliance and picked up the phone. "Good morning, friend."

The annoyed groan from the other end couldn't ruin her mood this morning. "Why are you so perky? Didn't you finish off as many beers as I did?" Maddy's voice croaked through the other end, surly and downright whiny.

"Oh, yeah... you've never seen me drunk. I don't get hungover. I think it's genetic; my sisters have an incredible tolerance too. Anyway, I want to thank your brother for all the hard work he's put into my storage room lately. I have a surprise planned for him. Would you mind watching the shop for the morning? I'll be back around lunchtime." Voice hopeful, Payson knew Maddy wouldn't refuse Payson if it meant bringing Ronan out of his shell a bit.

A loud, indelicate belch echoed over the line. "Fine. But you owe me."

With a squeal of delight, Payson thanked her friend. "I promise I'll make it up to you."

"Hey, I have your keys for some reason. Want to come by and pick them up on your way out?"

After a few frantic moments of figuring out where her purse had gone, she found the bag by the front door and searched its depths. Huh, not there. "That's weird. Why do you have my keys?"

"You were afraid you would lose them, so you made me put them in my pocket. Which, by the way, really hurt in my tight jeans. You owe me double."

"Since you already have the keys, I guess you can let yourself into the shop. Huh. I guess I have more than a few holes in my memory from last night." And that's why it was stupid of her to drink so much.

She really hoped she didn't do anything that she should be regretting. Beer, conversation, nachos... she also recalled miserably blowing it at billiards. Nope, nothing else.

Now to drag Ronan out of bed. Better not call first, or he would come up with any old reason to avoid her. Especially if she'd done something to seriously embarrass herself last night. Not wanting to risk his rejection, she headed straight over after a quick shower. For good measure, she grabbed breakfast sandwiches and coffee from the shop across the street to bribe him with food.

Looking at the state of the roads, she was not about to take her sporty rear-wheel drive straight up the snowy hill to Ronan's place. The morning was gorgeous anyway, so she indulged in a walk up the hill, marveling at the white blanket that had covered town.

The coffees had sadly gone cold by the time she arrived, but it was worth the rare quiet of the snowy morning walk. Not a soul in sight, the snow still untouched, she felt marvelously alone. Lingering flakes still fell from the sky, teasing at tapering off or picking up, but it wasn't telling which just yet.

She stomped the snow off her shoes and went to ring the doorbell. From the corner of her eye, she saw the blinds moving in a window next door. This must be the notorious Miss Hanson. She ducked out of sight when she realized she'd been caught... the ancient woman was awfully spry. Payson waved politely before ringing Ronan's doorbell.

Fucking doorbell. Not again. Did no one in this town respect anyone else's privacy? Between his voyeuristic elderly neighbor, his family, and even the dang high school glee club, his doorbell rang nearly every damn morning.

Resigned to this new complete lack of solitude, in stark contrast to his prior life, he rolled out of bed. Tossing on an easy pair of sweats and an old t-shirt, he headed for the door. If they had the balls to interrupt his morning, they were stuck seeing his delightful morning self, unkept mass of hair, and potentially a lingering bit of morning wood. Ok, maybe that was going too far, especially if it was the glee club again; they might not be so gleeful anymore.

After the snog with Payson last night, then moronically tucking her in and having to see her in that painfully delicate matching bra and panty set, he'd been hard all damn night. Before reaching the door, he stopped to think about baseball, calming matters a bit before scaring the intruder. After all, it could be his mother... well, that took care of the matter quite effectively.

Disabling the alarm, he swung open the door. A delectable sight filled the doorway. Looking bright as a spring tulip, Payson stood there with a bag of food and coffees for them both. Dressed in skinny jeans that hugged every curve, paired with fancy leather hiking boots and a sporty hooded sweatshirt under a heavy winter coat, she looked ready for anything. Her hopeful expression, waiting for him to invite her in, was more than he could handle.

He wasn't a complete asshole. With a gruff hello, he waved her inside. She breezed past him, a chipper smile pasted to her face.

"How are you so pleasant and wide awake so early this morning? You were so trashed last night." He griped as he hobbled his way behind her into the kitchen. *Make yourself at home*, he thought.

Grin even wider in response to his grumbling, she poured their coffees into mugs and zapped each in the microwave for a minute. "Sorry, the coffees got cold on the way over. I don't get hungover. Never have. Hope I never do," she was nearly humming with cheer. It was almost contagious... almost.

"Here," she held his coffee out in invitation. If he refused, maybe she'd go home and leave him alone. Her pouty lip was near quivering in anticipation of his refusal. Not intentionally, and she would be humiliated if he implied she was nervous, but clearly, she was worried he would reject her peace offering.

"Thanks," he accepted the re-heated coffee, attempting a smile. His mind flashed to last night. Her lips pressed against his, hands roaming across his body, those spectacular breasts pressed up against him so he could feel every subtle curve. "Payson, what do you remember from last night?"

She looked up, collecting her thoughts. "Everything... Right up until billiards." Tearing into her breakfast sandwich, she looked so damn sweet. "You're not going to ask why I'm here?"

Well, he had been thinking she was either here to apologize or... who knows, something to acknowledge last night. Either the *let's pretend it didn't happen* speech, or the *let's have sex* move. Honestly, he was accepting of either option at this point. Her complete lack of memory left him remembering the sensual embrace alone... it was disappointing.

"I figured you'd eventually get around to telling me what you're up to."

"Well, you're awfully surly. Which, I'm sure you are aware of. I don't want to pry, but I'm gathering that you haven't really felt like yourself since you've been back in Seaview. I just thought..." Wow, she really could babble when she was nervous. "I remember Maddy telling me you enjoyed baseball. I don't know much else that you enjoy since you never talk about yourself, so I thought maybe you'd like to come with me to the rec center. Not much going on there this time of year, but they have some fun indoor activities, like batting cages, an arcade, and laser tag. I thought you might enjoy hitting some balls?"

Like a well-placed kick in the balls, he nearly spit out his coffee at her suggestion. He hadn't played in years. Had made it to college on a damn baseball scholarship. Working for the fucking government had been more important, so he'd dropped baseball as quickly as he'd dropped everything else.

"Yeah, I'd like that," he said, accepting her as cheerfully as he could muster.

She grinned through a mouthful of breakfast sandwich as she annihilated the rest of her food in a few bites, somehow managing to remain neat as a pin.

"Can you wait for me to shower first?"

She nodded in ascent, delighted he'd said yes.

Payson felt an odd thrill at his easy acceptance. She'd seen a hint of something in his eyes. Nervousness? She watched him walk back to the master bedroom. His limp improved with each step as the soreness eased; was it the train accident that caused that limp? His shirt clung to his back, and she couldn't help but notice the way it hugged some seriously defined muscles.

Well, wasn't that interesting? She could imagine pressing her body up against his, feeling some ripped abs under that shirt. An intensely heated kiss. Her imagination was getting the better of her; she hadn't had sex in well over a year now. Yikes, that may be an optimistic estimate.

A few minutes later, he came out fresh and clean. Wearing yet another pair of antiquated jeans and what was likely the nicest t-shirt he owned, a baggy camo crew neck, with the same worn hiking boots he always wore. His wet hair was pulled back into a tight pony and a slightly less ragged massive beard that he had attempted to tame. Didn't seem to help, he still looked like a vagrant. Well, maybe more of a metal-head than a vagrant. A very appealing metal-head vagrant.

Where had that come from? From under all that hair, his penetrating glacial blue eyes watched her every movement. She'd thought they matched Maddy's eyes, but there was something... darker in them. Where Maddy's revealed a silent grace, his were piercing, like he was a hawk and she his prey.

Grabbing the re-heated breakfast sandwich he hadn't touched, she followed him out the front door. Ronan stopped and looked up and down the street, "Uh, Payson. Where's your car?"

She suddenly felt a bit embarrassed. "It, uh... It doesn't handle very well in the snow. I could try, but I don't drive in the snow very often so I'm not very good at it, and your house is pretty much straight up hill from mine, and the rec center up yet another hill. I like to walk anyway. I try to leave it covered in the carport most of the winter. I could drive the delivery van, but I would much rather walk than drive that ugly old thing all over town. Besides, it's only two miles on a beautiful day. But, yeah, that's why the food was cold." She was babbling again. What was wrong with her?

He shook his head after patiently waiting for her to finish her nervous speech and let out a warm laugh. "No worries. We can take my truck." Opening the garage, he ducked under when the door was up open far enough and unlocked the passenger door.

The garage was filled with Chase's exercise equipment. "I thought Chase brought all this equipment to he and Maddy's place?" She hoisted herself up into the truck. She had an odd sense of déjà vu as she sat down on the torn vinyl seat, she could almost feel blasting heat warming her bones.

As the engine roared to life, Ronan flipped on the radio and shifted the truck into reverse. "Nah, he comes here to work out most days; drags me out with him. Maddy refused to fill her garage with all this crap. She has access to gym equipment at the police station. He's trying to find some entrepreneur to open a gym around here. In the meantime, I don't mind him coming here."

"That sounds like Maddy. She was gracious enough to accept his fancy new bedroom furniture and gigantic tv when he moved in. She gets quite attached to her decor."

Ronan let out a rare, uninhibited laugh, smiling at his sister's quirks. "Yeah, that's Maddy. She doesn't put up with anyone's shit, even from those she loves. Want to hand me that sandwich?"

Unwrapping the breakfast sandwich to make a travel-friendly package, Payson handed it to Ronan. He managed to shift between bites, sipping his coffee now and again, too. She'd bet money he was a good juggler. "Do you have six arms or something?"

Smiling as he swallowed a bite, he joked, "Nah, I'm just talented."

Payson watched him as he pulled into the rec center parking lot. Through his beard, she could see subtle dimples that she hadn't noticed before. Frank's dimples; no one else in the family had them. They were adorable on Frank, and she suspected they added an irresistible charm when Ronan flashed his.

She felt oddly content; relaxed in a way she had never been with anyone else. Must be all the bickering that broke down some sort of wall between them?

"You coming?" He asked as he stepped out of the car. She realized she had been wool-gathering and shook away the heavy emotions that threatened, following him out of the truck. Pasting a smile on her face, she followed him into the rec center.

The place was pretty empty for a Saturday. There was a birthday party for a thirteen-year-old with about six adolescents running around screaming, and a small family with their young kids; otherwise no one was here.

The very wrinkled ticket-agent sat behind the front counter, eyeing them suspiciously as they entered. "Ten dollars each," was all he said. As it was her idea, Payson dug into her purse for the cash. Ronan pulled out his wallet and handed the guy a twenty before she could argue.

"I dragged you here, I'm paying," she insisted.

"And I'm thanking you for dragging me out of the house and making me smile. I've been a total asshole to you, and you're being awfully nice to me. Now shut up and put your money away this time." He flashed her a sly wink and led the way to the batting cages.

Payson slipped her hand into his and followed along at his side. Heart thundering, from her touch or from nerves, he couldn't have said. He hadn't been here in ages. This place had been his refuge in high school. He had usually come out here a few times a week, mostly when he'd been so enveloped by his studies that he needed to blow off steam.

Grabbing a wooden bat, he took a few practice swings and stretched a bit before loading the pitching machine. "You play?" he asked Payson, hoping she'd be the damsel so he could stand behind her, pressed against her behind as he taught her the proper stance.

Not Payson. She cocked out a hip and contrived a pensive look, "A bit. You're up first, cowboy." There were several cages, but it would be more fun to take turns and either rile or cheer each other on.

Gripping the wooden bat, he swung a few practice swings to loosen up his stiff muscles. Centering himself, he allowed in the rush and the calm before the first ball flew. Steady, he turned his gaze toward the machine.

Watching the rotation, he was ready when the ball launched. Muscle memory driving him, he pulled through with his swing and nailed it. Nothing like it, that moment when the bat connected with the ball.

Cheerleading from behind, Payson let out a "Woohoo. Let's see another just like it."

Ego nicely stroked, he readied for the next ball. Nailed it, too. Ball after ball, he knocked them out of the park. His shoulder was more than a little sore, but worth every swing.

He'd have to do something special to thank her. This was truly cathartic. So far, it was proving to be the best activity to make him feel like himself again. Well, one of the best ways. Getting lost in Payson last night for that brief moment had been damn effective.

Machine empty, he waved Payson in for her turn. She took her time picking out just the right bat, studying each one like a connoisseur. Finally, once she'd found the right one, she extended the bat like Babe Ruth calling his shot. "Load her up," she commanded. Her expression all seriousness, he could just make out the humor under the surface.

Crouching into ready position, he watched her wiggle that very fine ass, grateful she'd worn those tight jeans. Crack. She nailed the first ball like a pro. Damn, there go the batting lessons. "So, you play, huh?" he asked again, once the machine had emptied.

Puffing out her chest, quite the peacock, she gave him a condescending smile. "A bit."

He laughed uproariously, delighted with her attitude. She was cockier than he was. And in that moment, he loved her for it. It reminded him of how he used to act, used to feel. How he'd had the damn balls to earn his way into CIA and make his dreams come true.

They each hit a few more rounds, getting downright silly with calling their shots. She was a gifted athlete. He tried to contain his surprise, but she was always dressed so delicately, acted so proper... he was beyond pleasantly surprised.

The birthday party finally finished with laser tag, heading for the party room to devour the pizza that had been delivered. With a nod of his head, he gestured toward the laser tag arena. "Are you as adept at laser tag as you are baseball?"

She sighed innocently, "We'll have to find out. You?"

Stepping close, bodies inches away, he bit his lower lip in challenge. "Darlin', I'm only good at three things. Baseball and kicking ass are numbers two and three."

Leaning close so her lips were only a breath away, close enough he could smell her coconut-scented shampoo, she cocked out that hip again. "Why Mr. McAllister, I do believe you think you're quite the comedian. I presume number one is comedy." She turned on her heel and strutted toward laser tag.

Yeah, he'd walked right into that one... very intentionally. He had wanted to see her reaction, and she didn't disappoint. Couldn't help himself. It felt great to be normal again. To flirt completely carefree, bad jokes included.

Exhausted, sweaty, invigorated, Payson followed Ronan out of laser tag. First time she'd ever lost at laser tag. Ever. He'd dodged a serious attack when she threw the gun at him after it had stalled. Rather than being shocked or horrified at her angry outburst, he laughed gleefully and chased her across the course, tackling her and going in for the kill when he caught her.

"Stupid gun is broken. There was a delay. Poor craftsmanship, that's what it is. I'm demanding a refund."

Ronan took her hand, brought it to his lips and raised his eyebrow at her. "Face it, you got your ass kicked. Royally."

She wanted to be angry at that damn ego. But, she was too happy to see it. To see him smiling, giving as good as he got. This was that little light she'd seen flickers of before.

Walking hand in hand, they left the rec center and headed out to his truck. A few more inches of snow had stuck to the ground since they'd been inside. Forecast said six inches of accumulation in total, and she loved every last flake.

Her car, however, didn't. Nor did her delivery van. Maybe he'd let her borrow his truck if they needed to do any deliveries over snowy roads.

"Can I take advantage of you?"

His uncomfortable swallow was unmistakable. "Uh…"

Eyes dancing with humor, she took pity on him and expounded, "I mean your truck. I need to pick up a present for my nephew. He's turning seven and I need to go to the store."

Nodding appreciatively, Ronan forced a smile, "You almost had me there. Toy store off Beachside?"

"Please. And, any ideas that you have would be greatly appreciated, as I have never been a seven-year-old boy."

Cranking the engine, the old truck came to life with a deep rumble. Not caring if he noticed, Payson took advantage of the quiet on the drive and watched him from across the bench seat. His expression darkened, dimples lost. A little bit of her heart ached, missing his good humor.

Although she had only known him for a few short weeks, she already felt absurdly comfortable with him. Initially, he'd seemed insulting and rude, but she was beginning to see that it was an act. Pushing others away seemed easy for him, or maybe it was a defense mechanism. Yet every day, he seemed to open up a little more, he was calmer, kinder, even goofier. Recovering from his trauma. Accepting himself and his surroundings.

He'd been so... alive in there. She was hoping it would last a little longer, but something was eating away at him still. He'd managed to suppress it for a few hours, but it surfaced again. Was surfacing less since she'd met him, but not gone yet. The few hours they'd spent together this morning were promising.

With most everyone in her life, she maintained a sense of formality, of distance. Maybe it was a result of seeing him at his worst, but she felt she could say anything, and he wouldn't judge her unfairly. Not many got to see crazy-competitive Payson.

Even fewer laughed and encouraged her like he had. Jen immediately admonished any such inappropriate behavior. Clive had been embarrassed by it and consequently ignored it, or, more often, avoided situations that could potentially bring it out in her. Thus, she didn't let many people see that side of her.

Her parents were upstanding people. Well, her mother was downright uptight, but her father had always had an incredible sense of adventure. Jen, being the oldest, was the spitting image of her mother and just as overbearing. Maybe more so to compensate for the loss of her.

Whereas Payson battled the contradictory influences. She enjoyed lovely things, much like her mother. But when she let loose, she was purely her father's daughter. As she'd been at the rec center.

Lost in thought, she almost didn't notice they had arrived. Parallel parking the truck as if it were a mini, Ronan slipped into the spot in front of the local toy store. A few blocks away from Flotsam, Payson could have walked, but she'd been looking for an excuse to spend more time with Ronan. Fortunately, he hadn't called her on it.

"For the record, you can take advantage of me anytime." Ronan hopped out of the truck and dropped some coins in the meter. When Payson caught up to him, he still had a flirty smirk pasted on his face. Her hand slid easily into his as they walked into the store. Whatever black cloud had come over him, he was fighting it tooth and nail.

Brightly colored toys of every sort lined the walls. Where did she even begin? The two stood and gaped at the overwhelming selection. From outside, the shop looked no bigger than hers. Inside was a different story. The place was a gigantic toy madhouse.

Speaking hesitantly, eyes wide as he scanned the chaos, Ronan asked, "He's seven, huh? What does he like?"

"I don't see him as often as I'd like. But, I know he loves Legos." Eyes equally wide, she shrugged helplessly.

"Legos it is." He dragged her towards the massive Lego section. Dropping her hand, he briefly forgot he was a grown-up. "This is awesome," he grabbed a huge box with a Millennium Falcon kit inside. "I always wanted one of these. Never could afford it." He eyed the price. "Maybe I'll ask my parents for it for Christmas," he sniggered.

"If you're a good boy, maybe you'll get a bonus once you finish my storeroom," she nudged him playfully. Putting down the box, he shook his head.

"Once I discovered girls, Legos took a backseat. What does your nephew like? Superheroes? Minecraft? Star Wars?"

Brow scrunched in confusion, Payson couldn't cover her surprise at the admission. "Your brother seems to think you didn't date much."

Perusing the selection, he replied simply, "Not as much as he did anyway. And, not much in high school I guess, I was too busy trying to be the perfect student and athlete. When I did date, I didn't bring her around Aiden; guy's a menace."

Nodding, Payson agreed. "He is at that. What about after college?"

Subtly, briefly, Ronan's gaze cast downward in self-doubt. Payson wouldn't have noticed if she weren't caught up in his every move. "Didn't have much time to date. Nothing serious anyway." He grabbed a Minecraft set and studied the back of the box, "How does he feel about Minecraft? I know almost nothing about it, but I've heard kids like it. It looks fun. You can re-configure it in five different ways."

Rolling with the subject change, she held the offered set. "He loves Minecraft and can talk for hours on the subject. If he hasn't moved on by now. Want to grab some lunch before I go back to work? I could fix you something at my place."

Suddenly, he looked a bit... wary. Huh. After paying for the set and making their way back out, they climbed into the truck. For a moment, he paused, clearly deep in thought, as if about to say something but didn't know how to say it. Finally, he fired up the noisy engine. "I have a lot of errands to run so I'll just drop you back at the shop."

Trying to not feel disappointed at the rejection, she nodded. They'd made good progress; she was surprised he'd come out at all today. She just wasn't ready to part ways when they pulled up to the alley behind

Flotsam. Ronan hopped out and dashed around to open her door. Sliding out of the truck, she stood next to him, inches away as he remained in the doorway. Blocking her path.

"Thanks for a fun morning," she smiled shyly, looking up into those intense glacier-blue eyes.

Rather than thanking her in return, his look turned dark, dangerous. Eyes locked with hers, he sighed, fighting something. Biting her lower lip nervously, she couldn't break the eye contact with him. Waiting for him to make a move. Hoping he would. Fearing he wouldn't.

She wasn't disappointed. His hand gently brushed her hair out of her face, sweeping down to caress her chin and pull her toward him. Slowly, testing, he touched his lips to hers. His breath warm in contrast to the chill air, she melted into him.

Tenderly, he ran his tongue along her slightly parted lips, ending with a soft kiss on her plump lower lip. Her heart thundered in her chest, desire rising from deep within. Painfully familiar, as if she belonged here. With growing confidence, she kissed him back, yearning, begging him to continue.

Too soon, he pulled away. Suddenly unsure of himself, doubt flashing across his face. Payson wasn't finished, but the moment was. With a squeak and a groan, the storeroom door swung open.

Before anyone stepped into view, Ronan was already miles away, climbing back into the driver's seat. Resigned that she wouldn't know what that was all about for at least the rest of the weekend, Payson closed the truck door and turned to see Maddy taking out the trash.

With a quick wave to her friend and a "be right back," she dashed upstairs to change into work clothes. Completely off-balance and more than a little smitten.

11

Pulling his truck into the garage, Ronan visually marked his position against the tool bench as a marker. Tight fit, but worth it to avoid brushing snow off the windshield in the mornings. Sore from pushing his body past where it was used to, swinging the bat unlike he had in years despite his sore shoulder, adding a few duck-and-rolls to nail Payson at laser tag that bruised his healing hip wound, he ached as he hobbled into the house.

He grinned at the image of her diving around the course to avoid his shots. She didn't hold back. What else was she so... enthusiastic at? His mind went straight for the gutter.

He was starting to make a habit of letting loose. Enjoying himself. Laughing without reserve. Letting others see him for who he was, well, Payson at least. Felt fucking amazing. He wasn't sure he'd ever been able to let loose like he had the last few days.

He'd like to say it was lack of worry, but that wasn't true. It was Payson. Maybe her honesty. Maybe it was her passion for life. How had he ever thought her pretentious?

Whatever it was, he felt an overwhelming craving to be near her. Not going to lie to himself, it scared the shit out of him. But, like jumping out of a helicopter into a boiling sea without a parachute, it was as thrilling as it was terrifying.

He tossed his jacket on the back of the couch and walked back to his bedroom to shower. He'd worked up a good sweat this morning. Payson was no softy; he'd had to really bring-it. The laughter, the challenge, sharing the adrenaline rush with her, had felt like nothing he'd ever experienced.

Pausing on his way to the shower, he suddenly lost his smile, distracted by the drop phone he'd plugged in to the charger. He was out of the action, shouldn't even keep the damn phone anymore.

But, he couldn't help himself. Couldn't let it go. Not yet. Dialing, he pushed speed dial to call Sara.

Not addressing him by name, as always, she answered, "My favorite recruit. How are you enjoying retired life?"

Ronan shook his head with a half-smile, "Actually, I'm settling in. Relaxing a bit. No idea what to do with myself in the long run, but I'm ok with that for now."

Her voice soft on the other side, she said, "I'm happy for you. You know, you don't actually have to work. Ever again. You will be well compensated for your efforts."

"Money's not an issue. Thanks though, I appreciate you going to bat for me. I'm just going to take my time and figure out what I actually enjoy."

"I'm glad to hear it," she replied gently.

Finally, he got to the point. "I know I don't get closure on every mission, and not every mission ends well, but I just can't seem to let go of this one. Where are those damn biologics, and where the fuck did

Young get them to begin with?" Sara had played along with his casual conversation, but she had to assume he'd called for a reason.

Sighing, she agreed, "I know. It's getting at me too. I don't want you to worry about it anymore. I'm not letting it go. We're going to get Connor Young, those awful weapons, and find the source of all of this." She sounded as furious as he felt.

"Thanks, really. I'm retired; done with the whole thing. Except for those damn weapons. I can't shake the images of those families. If there's anything I can do to help, please don't hesitate to pull me in for one last op."

"I know. I hope it doesn't come down to that... but it might. Every lead we've gotten is just another dead end. Please, be careful."

He disconnected the call, her words bouncing around in his head like a pinball.

At least he wasn't alone. It was good to hear the whole fucked up situation disturbed someone else too. Stripping off his grubby clothes, he stepped into the brick-tile shower. He let the steaming water pour over him, trying in vain to wash away his worry.

Replaying the last year or two of his life, pulling out the important pieces, he tried to make sense of it all. Peter Young, with or without his brother and their team of mercenaries, was known to have contacted a group of terrorists, offering a deal on a cache of biological weaponry that he had acquired. Not trusting the notorious mercs to deliver the genuine article, the terrorists had demanded a demonstration, which had left behind the scene of mutilated remains that was permanently etched into his brain.

Apparently, the exchange never took place, as the last feed he received from the terrorists on the issue was a demand for the promised weapons. Around the same time, Young had gone to ground. Radio silence. Terrorists pissed. Mercs in hiding.

Ronan captures Peter Young. Connor Young somehow knows how to find Ronan and shoots him later that night. Ronan retires. Sharpe promises to locate the weapons. Sara has no new information to offer, nothing coming to light, but is still investigating. Trail cold.

If he could just find the source of the weapons, and where they were now, he could fucking rest. Mission accomplished once and for all.

Payson spent the rest of the weekend working on filling online orders and communicating with some of her dealers about new pieces. It was pleasantly quiet around town, which allowed her to refresh the layout, again. One of her favorite activities. A few tourists had come and gone, but things had been sedate.

By the end of the weekend, things had started to feel too quiet without Ronan around. She'd begun to prefer the days that he was around. She felt a thrill from deep in her belly that Monday morning had finally arrived, and he would be here any moment.

All damn weekend she'd been distracted thinking about that soft, testing kiss. Hoping he'd try it again. Daring herself to make a move.

Coffee brewing, stuffing in the last few bites of her oatmeal, she tossed on a stylish blue sweater and gray wool miniskirt, adding some tights and knee-high boots. She caught herself grinning like an eager debutante that was caught up in a fantasy about her favored crush.

Ronan was not at all what she would picture for herself, but she couldn't get him out of her mind. That first night, she had thought him a rude, hairy grizzly bear, but he was quickly morphing into a charming... something else. Something appealing.

Floating out the door, mood much sunnier than the cloudy sky, she carried two cups of coffee down the stairs at 8 o'clock sharp. Ronan would be punctual in meeting her at the backdoor, ready to work. She spotted him stepping out of his truck as she strolled down the icy steps. "Good morning. Did you have a pleasant day yesterday?"

He grunted as he grabbed both of their coffee cups so she could unlock the door and let them in, as part of the routine they had quickly adopted. As usual, he followed her in the back door and handed her back her coffee once she'd disengaged the alarm. "Well you're a sourpuss this morning," she commented.

"How are you so perky in the mornings?" He blew gently into is coffee cup, sipping the soothingly bitter liquid.

Was it her imagination, or was he less cranky than usual? He was still grumbling and sniping, but his teasing was more friendly than accusatory today. Maybe it was her trying to convince herself she was impacting him as positively as he was her.

She looked around at her half-built storeroom, pleased with the progress. Impressed with his carpentry. "I guess I just like where I'm going in the morning," she decided. Ronan nodded in agreement, assessing the progress, the work ahead of him. Enjoying the few extra moments with him, she continued, "Do anything over the weekend after we parted?"

Ronan shrugged. "Sure. Spent a few hours at my parent's house on Sunday morning. Went for a drive up the coast afterwards. The area sure has grown since I moved away."

Payson smiled, leaning against the nearly completed shelf closest to her. "It's nice to get out and just drive sometimes. Make any stops?"

Continuing to sip his coffee while he set out the tools he'd need to get started, he replied almost cheerfully, "Nah. I just wanted the view, the air. You make that drive much?"

Her heart did a little flutter as he actively engaged in casual conversation with her and asked after her interests. The open, fun Ronan was shining through more and more. "Whenever I can. Especially in summer; I like to put the top down and just feel the wind washing over me, feel the car hugging the curves."

Ronan nodded as he laid out the plans he'd sketched.

Payson's mind kept tripping up on something. Watching Ronan's lips, she could almost feel the heat against her, feel the scratch of his beard. More intensely than the brief tease he'd given her Saturday. She could almost feel his body pressed up against her backside, moving with her to the rhythm, hands gripping her hips. The memories were so vivid, she was overwhelmed by sensation.

Before she could make too much of a fool of herself, before she started drooling, Payson abruptly changed the subject, "Well, I won't keep distracting you. I'll just, uh, go open up the shop for the day." Turning on one foot, she skedaddled toward the front of the shop.

Listening to Ronan hammering away, Payson apologized to her one customer of the day for the noise. "I'd love to see what you make with the bottles; email me a picture so I can post it to the website." The customer happily left with a collection of pirate-era glass rum bottles.

Since Saturday, Payson had been floating and smiling when no one was looking. Ronan was still a grouch, but less and less so every day. No further action, unfortunately. She desperately wanted to taste him again, feel his breath mix with hers.

Despite the improvement in his demeanor, he'd been painfully standoffish. Like he was avoiding letting her in any further. His mother had brought them lunch, but he'd eaten quickly then found an excuse to run errands. Actually, every time she tried to spend any time with him the last few days, he'd found an excuse to not be around her.

Flipping on her computer, she sat on her stool at the register to update the shop website to distract herself. Getting sucked in, playing with different arrangements of the latest photos and reviews from customers, she didn't notice a visitor approaching her store. The jingling bells on the door managed to interrupt her deep concentration. Turning from her computer screen to greet her customer, she was startled to see her older sister standing in front of her. Eyes red and puffy.

"Jen, are you ok? What are you doing all the way up here in Seaview?" She walked around the counter to greet her sister.

Jen sniffled briefly, holding back her tears. "I should have called first, I'm sorry. It's just... I didn't know where else to go."

Fearing the worst, Payson wrapped her arms around her sister. "What's going on? The kids are ok? Cara is ok?"

"The kids are fine. Cara is fine, at least I assume she is as I haven't heard from her in a few weeks." She started blubbering again. "Tony and I got into a big fight. His work wants to transfer him to Colorado, and he expects me and the kids to pack up and move our lives." Jen pulled away, pacing back and forth.

Payson cringed as her sister flung her arms wildly in the air as Jen's sadness turned to fury, fearing she'd knock over one of the more fragile displays. She'd seen her sister this upset more than a few times. Having learned her lesson early on, it was best to let it run its course, else she direct it at Payson. Apparently, throwing things while angry was a family trait.

Jen continued in her rant as Payson looked for her opportunity to move the conversation to a safer location. "What about my job? I love working at the museum. What about the kids? It's the middle of the school year; we're not just packing up and moving across the country."

Payson hated to see her sister so upset. More, she hated the idea of her family moving even further away. It was hard enough to see them in Boston more than a few times a year. "Have you told him how you feel?"

Snapping back, her sister continued her tirade, just missing a 19th century crystal vase. "Of course I've told him. His job pays better, the schools are better, won't it be great for the kids to learn to ski and hike and all that nature crap."

Not wanting to stir the pot, but knowing her sister needed to talk it through, Payson risked interrupting to propose a change in venue. "Jen, can you hang on just a moment; I'm going to see if I can have Ronan run the shop for a while so we can go upstairs and chat. I'll make some tea, and we can have some privacy."

Confused, her sister looked at her, "Who's Ronan? What happened to Natalie?"

Well, Payson wasn't quite sure how to explain Ronan. "Natalie's working full time at the art gallery now. Ronan is... a friend. He's helping out for a bit."

Hoping her sister wouldn't knock anything over in another tirade, or scare away any customers, Payson dragged her along to the back room. Ronan was bent over the table top he'd just finished and was using it as a desk to sketch out the drawers and shelves he'd promised. "Ronan, can I interrupt you for a minute?"

Looking up from his drawings, he offered a sweet smile before he remembered he was supposed to be acting aloof, "What's up?"

"This is my sister, Jen. Jen, this is Ronan."

Jen faked a smile, but her heart wasn't in it. "Hi." She managed between sniffles.

"Would you mind watching the front for a bit? I need to talk to my sister." Her eyes glanced meaningfully in the direction of her sister, hoping he'd catch the urgent family drama situation, so she wouldn't have to explain her melodramatic sister just yet.

She didn't know what to expect, having never asked him to watch the shop before. He'd helped with a lot of the heavy lifting but had never had to deal with customers or the register before. He responded with a concerned, "Of course. Do you have a minute to show me the basics?"

Grateful, Payson asked her sister to hang on a minute. "Yeah, come on up."

Ronan followed behind her into the front of the shop. When they reached the register, he asked after her sister, whispering so she wouldn't overhear, "Everything ok?"

Nodding, Payson answered, "Yeah, she and her husband are having a disagreement. She just flails when angry, and I'm afraid she'll break something."

"Hereditary?" he teased. Quickly reverting back to his adopted scowl, he stood at the register and assessed his surroundings. She showed him the basics on how to ring up sales, how to take cash versus card. It only took a minute or two; he caught on quickly. "Head on up, I've got it. If you're not back down by five, I'll start to close up."

"Perfect. Thanks, you're a lifesaver." She nearly laid a quick thank-you peck on that tempting mouth but caught herself.

She couldn't deny how much she wanted to touch him, craved his closeness, but was thrown by how standoffish he'd been all week. For all the progress they'd made, he'd been so closed off. Had she done or said something? As much as she knew he probably wasn't looking for anything romantic, she at least wanted to be friends. Fearing rejection, she backed away and headed for the back room to meet her sister.

Glancing back, she admired the view. Despite the ill-fitting clothes, she could see he was built. However, he looked terribly out of place in her shop. She held back a laugh at the humorous appearance of the shaggy man in the classy shop.

She hopped over the few boxes in the hallway and made it back to her sister. Not as silently as she would have preferred, her sister teased, "Are you and he a thing?"

Payson rolled her eyes. There was no way she was having that conversation with her sister, when she didn't even know herself. A few days ago, she would have considered saying "maybe," but today... today she was afraid to even whisper the possibility.

In her sister's very poor attempt to speak softly, she pushed, "He's not at all your type. What happened to Gregory?" Fearing Ronan had heard, she shoved her sister out the door before she made things between them any more awkward.

Two hours of an enduring, exhausting, mostly one-sided conversation. Payson groaned to herself as she fought the vertigo from watching her sister pacing across the apartment. To save herself from decapitation, she'd had to walk on eggshells to avoid aggravating her sister. Watching her sister grumble and cry, she hoped they had it sorted out. Payson wasn't sure she actually helped, other than to be the ear her sister needed. Despite her sister's unmatched tirades, she was glad to be there when her sister needed her.

Jen finally decided to go home and talk with Tony, hear his concerns and his hopes. Ask him to hear hers. See if there was a middle ground or a trial period so they could fully explore their options. Be open to a new adventure, if that's what was best for their family.

Payson walked her sister down the frozen steps with the intent to escort her out. Not quite five o'clock, Ronan would still be manning the shop. She hoped to pin Ronan down for the moment and demand why he had been avoiding her.

Unfortunately, feeling much improved, her sister detoured and requested to stop in the storeroom to admire the new shelving that she'd been too upset to notice before. Begrudgingly, Payson agreed. She was glad her sister was at least noticing something Payson was proud of.

"This looks fantastic, did your friend build this?"

Payson rolled her eyes. Of course. Her sister hadn't bothered to even remember Ronan's name. Her sister was a bit of a snob; Payson hoped she got enough of the down to earth personality from their father to keep her balanced and approachable.

"Yes, Ronan built it. Isn't it gorgeous? I can't wait to see it finished and get everything organized."

Helping herself to a cup of coffee for the road from the tiny kitchenette Ronan had installed, Jen was clearly more relaxed. So much so, that she took a quick moment to grill Payson on her love life. Typical.

Didn't she wonder why Payson hadn't hesitated at the opportunity to move several hours away? As much as she wanted to be near her niece and nephew, she fared better with a little distance from her overbearing sister.

Leaning against one of the sturdy shelves, Jen asked, none-too-quietly, "Are you still dating Gregory? The handsome neurologist?"

Payson regretted telling Jen about Gregory. She'd been desperate to pause her sister's constant pestering, so she'd thrown her a bone and told her she was dating someone. Payson was dating for her own happiness, not her sister's. "We had a date planned for tomorrow, but I'm going to cancel. He's not the one."

Jen shook her head, "You haven't given him enough time to really know. He's gorgeous. And rich. And successful."

"He's just not what I'm looking for. He's handsome, but there's just no magic there. I don't think he understands me."

Jen tsk'd and sadly shook her head. "Of course he does. What's not to understand? You're gorgeous and outgoing and kind and have an eye for art and antiques."

Payson shrugged, pacing cautiously back and forth in the debris-filled room. "But I'm also bossy and competitive and compulsive and enjoy a night at the tavern... maybe even more than a night at the theatre. I like pretty clothes and antiques, but more because of the way they make *me* feel."

Payson enjoyed nice things. She loved dressing femininely, making her shop look inviting and sophisticated. Her apartment was the same.

However, guys didn't tend to see past that. They liked the appealing façade. Most didn't realize, the pretty picture was a very small part of who she truly was.

She doubted Jen saw that either. Her friends in Seaview did, or they wouldn't be her friends. Did Cara see it?

Jen shook her head in disagreement, unmoving from her spot she'd claimed against the shelf. "I doubt that. Think about what Mom would say. She would have been so proud to see you married and at the top of the social ladder. Not that there is much of a social life in Seaview, but maybe if you met the right man you'd move back to Boston, or at least Portland."

"I like it here." Steam started to puff out of Payson's ears. She rather missed Jen's angry ignorance all of a sudden.

Ignoring Payson's argument, Jen steamed on. "Clive was a complete bore and not the brightest bulb in the bunch; I understand why that didn't work out."

Jen sighed and rested her hand condescendingly on Payson's. "Since Mom and Dad died, you've been a bit obsessive about finding Mr. Perfect. You're nearly thirty and haven't even caught a glimpse of him. Maybe it's time to wake up and realize that perfect doesn't exist. Tony wasn't what I had dreamed of. Love involves a lot of compromise, sometimes including your own dreams. Don't cancel the date. I'll look forward to hearing how it goes."

Frustrated, she was done arguing with her sister. Jen could be damn stubborn. "Fine. You'd better head out, so you get home before the kids worry. And work on that compromise piece of your relationship."

Maybe she didn't need to conclude with the last part, but she couldn't help it. She wasn't looking for perfect. Perfect led to a boring relationship. She'd rather stay single forever than settle again, but Jen would never understand that concept.

Ronan heard the entire conversation from up front. He'd been keeping his distance from Payson all week, and it had been killing him. He was a damn mess, and she was so incredible. She deserved someone successful, confident. Despite her sister's craziness, she had a point. No one was perfect, Ronan least of all.

Jen was a piece of work, though. No wonder Payson had moved away from Boston. Not that Ronan was any prize, but she hadn't even bothered to remember his name. Hadn't given him more than a passing glance. Not like Payson; she saw past his gruff exterior. She was far too amazing to settle for a guy like him.

As Payson walked her sister out the back door, Ronan locked up the front and met her in the storeroom. Practically slamming the door behind her when she came back in, Payson leaned against the door as soon as it closed and groaned. "I'm so glad she's finally gone. I love her but holy crap she's self-absorbed. And pushy."

Ronan couldn't help but smile at her exhausted expression as she pout-laughed. "I'm sure she means well."

Rocking her head against the door, Payson whimpered. "Really, I ought to fake some wedding pictures and tell her I eloped, so she'll get off my back. I have no interest in going out with Gregory again, or anyone like him. If I'd said I was cancelling the date, she would have stayed all night and tortured me."

If things continued on the current path, he and Payson were going to end up in bed sooner than later, which, knowing both of them, would lead to more. Neither was the friends-with-benefits sort. Certainly not the one-nighter sort.

His life was a damn mess. Unsettled. What if Young found him? Even if he could guarantee her safety, what if he couldn't ever accept his past? If he couldn't accept himself, how could he expect Payson to accept him?

As much as it physically hurt to even say it, he needed to stop things before they went too far. "Maybe she's right. You already have the date set up for tomorrow, why don't you give him one last chance?"

The hurt look that flashed across her face was heartbreaking. Standing upright, she smoothed her dress. "I'm heading upstairs, mind locking up?" Without waiting for his response, she headed out the door. Never had he hated himself more than he did in that moment.

12

Friday frickin' night. Ronan had been working on the shelving for twelve hours, only taking a quick break for lunch when his mother had stopped by with another sandwich delivery. She'd insisted Payson come on back and the three had enjoyed the homemade messy sandwiches together.

His mother was making it a bit of a habit. For the last week, his mother appeared at noon with sandwiches for them all, insisting they stop and visit. Sometimes she hardly ate more than a bite or so herself, when she found some excuse to leave. At least she didn't keep crying anymore about how happy she was that he was home.

Payson had left on her date nearly two hours ago. She was welcome to date whoever she wanted. Her sister had certainly thought Payson should give Gregory a chance. Ronan had no claim. Tried to avoid making a claim.

He'd quickly remembered himself after their brief moment last weekend. Reminding himself that she had a boyfriend. He'd managed to keep his hands off her the rest of the week. Good thing too, after hearing her sister's rant about Payson's efforts to find Mr. Perfect, he reminded himself he was far from perfect. Not even close to what she was looking for.

He'd seen the fancy-pants neurologist come in to check out her store before escorting her out. He'd acted polite enough, telling Payson her shop was "lovely" and "quaint." He'd looked at Ronan like he was trash; all grimy and covered in sawdust with a ratty white shirt and jeans that had clearly been pulled out of Chase's giveaway pile.

Sort of how Jen had looked at him earlier in the week. His wild hair, his scraggly beard were nearly down to his collarbone. Not that Ronan had been much of a gentleman either, keeping his responses limited to feral snarls, playing up the lowly grunt worker façade.

Asshole had fawned all over Payson, hand on her back as they walked, complimenting her midnight blue velvet dress with its plunging neckline, her long pendant necklace drawing his eyes down to her spectacular cleavage. Pervert. Not that Ronan hadn't been admiring the view, but at least he was subtle about it.

She was probably out laughing and having a great time with Dr. Hot-Stuff in his spiffy black suit and tie. And the pink shirt, really? Clearly loved his own body, but his hands were pristinely un-calloused. Ronan looked down at his own rough hands, felt his own scruffy beard.

Payson and her Bond thing. Ronan considered himself more Bourne than Bond... not that it was any more accurate, but more raw anyway. That pansy she was out with was more Austin Powers than James Bond. Aiden was more her type; why wasn't she dating his brother? They seemed to be good friends.

Aiden might appreciate her quirkiness. All gorgeous on the outside; feminine and delicate. On the inside, she was a fireball. Competitive, bossy, daring.

Better than him. Better than the asshole she was out with. Hell, Aiden wasn't good enough for her either; player, pop-off.

He rather liked her crazy side. Furious with himself, realizing he'd put her on a damn pedestal, he almost called it a night. Almost.

At last, he heard the hum of the asshole's Mercedes SUV pulling up to the street. Not that he'd waited up for her. He legitimately had a lot of work to do.

He was nearly done with the shelves now, just some finishing touches. The table structure was finished, and the entire unit would be done as soon as he finished the shelves to go under the table. He'd see if she wanted them stained or left natural after he'd sanded.

Silently, he stood by the back door, which was conveniently located right at the base of the steps to Payson's apartment. Couldn't have chosen a better stakeout position if he'd tried. Not that he was spying; he was retired and that would be wrong. Their voices were muffled, but he could hear well enough.

Payson's tinkling voice echoed through the heavy metal door, "Thanks for a wonderful evening. Goodnight."

"My pleasure. What a great night." Ronan could picture the guy making his move, only momentarily deterred as Payson tried to head up the stairs, then trying again as she pulled away. "It's a long drive back home tonight." Creep; he could picture him trying to follow Payson up the stairs.

"Thanks for driving all this way; there's a great 24-hour coffee shop just at the south end of town." Way to go Payson. He started to relax, was about to start cleaning up to head home for the night.

"Payson, we've been out several times now, this is what, our fifth date? You know me well enough by now. Come on, invite me up for a nightcap." Was the asshole begging? Get a life.

"I know that Gregory, but I'd like to call it a night; I have to get up early tomorrow and it's late." She was too damn nice. Ronan would have punched him by now.

"Come on honey. I drove all the way here and treated you to a five-course meal. At least a goodnight kiss?" Asshole's voice dripped with rancid honey.

At the sound of shuffling, Ronan opened the door slowly, hoping to nail the bastard as he opened the steel door, but he was more afraid of hitting Payson, so he interrupted them cautiously. Charming Gregory had his hand gripped tightly around Payson's wrist.

Ronan startled, as if surprised to find anyone outside the door. "I'm real sorry to interrupt; I'm just finishing up for the night. Payson, do you have a moment to let me know your thoughts on finishes?"

"She's not interested in admiring your little woodworking project. Would you please give us some privacy?" Asshole still gripped her wrist, barely turning his body towards Ronan, making it clear he wasn't worth acknowledging. Payson stood casually, appearing indifferent to the situation.

"Oh, I think it's up to her who's wood she'd like to admire." Ronan raised his eyebrow in challenge, the corner of his mouth turned up arrogantly.

Payson rolled her eyes, "Oh for fuck's sake. Ronan, thanks, I'll check it out tomorrow. Gregory, goodnight." She tried to pull out of Gregory's grip to head up the stairs, but Gregory held firm. Pissed off now, Payson glared back.

She went to say something fiery, but Ronan just couldn't help himself. With a low growl, he stepped closer to Gregory, primed for a fight. "Let go of her, right now."

Gregory's voice was pumped full of superiority. "Go play with your tools, this is between Payson and me."

Ronan was hoping he'd say that. With a swift jab, his fist connected with asshole's cheekbone with a loud crack. Smile growing wider, Ronan taunted, "I'm sorry, it's just so icy out. I must have slipped."

Payson looked at him with confused wonder. The asshole, hand gripping his eye that would surely be purple tomorrow, fired back, "I'm pressing assault charges, you moron."

"I'll call the Seaview Police for you. My sister, Payson's best friend, is working tonight and would be happy to take your statement. Right alongside my report of your assault on Payson. The bruises you've left on her wrist should be plenty to incriminate you.

"Not to mention, I'm sure your patients and your certifying board would love to hear about how you treat women."

With a sneer of disgust, Gregory stormed away, loafers skating on the ice as he stalked back to his Mercedes.

Ronan's satisfied smile faded when he looked over to see Payson staring at him with a curious smile. "I'd love to see the shelves." Okay, guess they weren't talking about what had happened. Ronan held the door open as she walked in the back room of the shop. "I love it. Looks much safer too."

"I'll sand and stain it, make it look a bit classier."

"I'd like that. Maybe a rustic walnut? It looks good now, but a finished look will be really nice. I had no idea you were such a talented carpenter. I should have realized, as your mother volunteered you, and I know Frank has installed some beautiful built-ins at their house." She walked the length of the room, her hand running across the unfinished shelves.

"Thanks for the rescue," she finally acknowledged.

"Anytime. You were right, he's not the one." Crossing his arms, Ronan leaned against the shelves and watched her admire his handiwork. She'd been ready to clock that asshole herself. Ronan should have let her, might have been fun.

With an ironic laugh, she agreed. "I know what I want, and it's not another pompous ass."

Ronan had a hard time focusing on what she was saying. When she was around, just the two of them, he had trouble remembering why he couldn't pursue her. Remembering the taste of her lips, her body wriggling against his during their dance that night at the tavern, then again in her apartment. Then he noticed her pendant was lost between her breasts, her short velvet dress shimmying up a bit with every step.

Chest tight, anticipation building, Ronan teased, "Payson, what do you remember from that night at the tavern?"

His words ricocheted through her brain. What was he getting at? She turned to face him, hoping his expression would reveal his thoughts. "I remember having a fun evening, drinking a few beers with some friends. Drinking more than I should have, more than I have in a long time. Why?"

The corner of his mouth turned up in a devilishly handsome half smile - wait, when had she started to think of him as handsome? "Do you remember how you got home?"

Of course she did. Didn't she? "Chase didn't drive me home?"

He shook his head.

"Did you drive me home?"

He stood leaned against the shelves with his arms crossed, enjoying watching her struggle.

Her memories were totally muddled. Ok, she played some pool, but had to stop for some reason. Then the music... Oh god, she'd done some serious dirty dancing all over him.

Although, he had been an amazing partner. Her backside pressed up against him, his hips moving synchronously with her own, his hands splayed out on her abdomen as he held her close. He had driven her home, walked her upstairs.

Shit, what did she do? Maybe that wasn't a dream. A look of horror crossed her face. "Please say we didn't have sex."

"You don't have to look so disgusted by the idea. You seemed to enjoy yourself," he teased, holding her look for a minute as she looked panicked. "No, we didn't have sex."

"Phew. I'm not disgusted by the idea... I mean you're not unattractive... I mean, ack, I don't know what I mean." What was wrong with her? She was turning into a babbling mess, again.

Ronan's look was no longer teasing, smile gone. He slowly paced toward her, until his body was pressed against hers. *That* she remembered.

Her eyes locked onto his. The haunted look that kept plaguing him was gone, and in exchange was the arrogant, devilish charm she'd witnessed at the rec center.

With a slight angle of his head and a look that burned into her, he asked, "Do you remember yet?"

"You may have to refresh my memory."

Bringing his hands up, he softly ran his hands through her hair. His hand settled on the back of her neck, and he pulled her close. She had to stand on her tiptoes to reach him, but he met her halfway. Patiently, he waited with his lips a breath away from her own. "Anything yet?"

"Maybe..."

His other hand clutched her hip and pulled her against him. Hungrily, he kissed her. Desperately, passionately, nothing held back. Their tongues parried in a timeless duel, a soft moan escaping her lips that only deepened his kiss.

Ronan's hand shifted and subtly slid her dress upward until he pressed his palm against her bare ass. Glad she'd skipped the tights and worn that flimsy thong. His other hand joined in; gripping her tight, he hiked up her dress and set her on the sturdy table he'd just finished building. Thoughtfully, he'd set her on his sweatshirt so she didn't end up with sawdust in a sensitive area.

Hands encircling her waist, he positioned himself between her open thighs, holding her tightly pressed against him. His mouth strayed down her neck, giving her a gentle nip here and there, which he soothed with a soft lick of his tongue. "You smell so good."

Payson couldn't hold back; enthralled with sensations she'd never felt before, afire from the blaze he was igniting within her.

She slipped her dress down over her arms, revealing her breasts that were straining against the delicate black lace. He groaned appreciatively and ripped the flimsy fabric and tossed what was left of the bra, mouth on her before the lace hit the floor.

Gently caressing, kissing, nipping, he lavished each breast with attention. She arched her back and cried out in pleasure.

Abruptly, he pulled back, leaving her half naked and cold, the distance between them growing like they were on opposite sides of a vast canyon. A look of anger crossed his face, his hand running through his hair in frustration. "I'm sorry, I shouldn't have done that. We really can't."

With a huff of irritation, she pulled her straps up to cover herself, yet she still felt naked. "What do you mean we can't?"

He started pacing back and forth. "We can't do this. Every time I get close to you, I lose control. You don't even like me, at least, you shouldn't. I'm a grouch and a damn mess. We are not even each other's type. Gregory may not be the one, but neither am I. You're looking for James Bond. I'm broken, a damn timebomb; look at me. Trust me, you don't want to go there with me." He gestured to his wild hair and grubby clothes, arms out in demanding question.

Fired up, Payson hopped down from the table, not even caring if she ripped her dress on the way down. She started firing back at him before she'd even fixed the rest of her dress. "Yeah? I guess you have me all figured out. Did you see me making out with the successful stud in the nice suit, or was I in here with the irritable, scruffy, hired hand? I'll decide who and what I want. I know you're scared, but you don't scare me."

Fuming, she stormed out the door, leaving him alone to figure it out.

13

Ronan tossed off the last of the blankets at six the next morning, drenched in sweat from a long sleepless night. His soul flooded with self-loathing, growing worse after each nightmare grew increasingly horrific. Again. They hadn't haunted him the past few nights, but going to bed angry at himself had brought everything to the surface.

Maybe he should buy some whiskey and stand a chance at getting some sleep. Although, stuck in a drunken nightmare sounded so much worse. Benadryl wasn't doing shit anymore. His phone chirped with a text from Payson: *Don't worry about coming in today.*

What was that all about? She was pissed; he'd give her space, but he hadn't even finished the job. He texted back, *OK. I'll pick up the sanding material and stain tomorrow, then I'll be out of your hair soon.* Maybe he should have left off the last bit, but if she was going to be pissy, he would be too.

His phone chirped again. Really? Were they going to have a text fight?

Nope, not from Payson, but from his dad. *Can you call me as soon as you're up?*

Ronan calmed his rage a bit so he could call his dad without biting his head off. Forcing a smile, he responded, "Hey Dad, what's up?"

Frank's husky, yet gentle voice echoed back, "Sorry if I woke you."

"No worries. I was already up." Had been up most of the night. It was almost worse getting a few good nights of sleep. Somehow the bad nights felt more exhausting when he knew what good sleep felt like.

"Your mom has planned a little winter boat adventure. Thought we'd grab our children and cruise on up to New Sussex Island. Spend a nice day on the water, then spend the evening roaming around New Sussex. She's made reservations for a nice dinner together and booked a few rooms at a little B&B right near the docks. You kids can stay in the fancy rooms, and she and I will camp out in the boat."

"I'm not sure you can consider your boat camping." He thought of the good-sized Hinckley he'd seen pictures of, upgraded from the older model he'd spent his childhood cruising in. Hell, it was big enough that they could all camp out in sleeping bags on the boat like they did when they were kids. But, he'd rather his family not watch him toss and turn all night, periodically screaming with tears streaming down his face.

"Fair point. What do you say?" Frank wouldn't be pushy, as he wanted his son to join them because he wanted to come, not because he felt obligated. He sounded so hopeful; Ronan couldn't have said no for anything.

Running a hand through his wild hair, he sighed, "Sounds fun. What time do you want to meet at the boat?"

"Not until 11. Give everyone a little time to pack since it's such short notice. Same slip we've always had."

"See you soon." Ronan hung up and strode into the bathroom.

His reflection caught him off guard. Man, he was one hideous son-of-a-bitch. Why the hell had Payson kissed that ugly mug? Why did his mother or his sister not pin him down and shave it off?

Since his return, he'd looked disheveled and wild, a savage beast one feared provoking. His behavior hadn't helped either.

He grabbed the scissors and razor he'd had yet to even open from the drawer. Slowly, he cut away the hatred, the misplaced guilt, the self-loathing that been smothering him.

Seeing his completely unshaven face for the first time in years, he felt a growing motivation to like himself again. To let others like him. To give himself a chance with Payson, if he wasn't too late.

On a mission now, he picked up the phone to book an urgent appointment for a haircut. May as well grab some decent clothes while he was at it; quit wearing his sister's boyfriend's tattered cast-offs. He grabbed his empty backpack, threw in some basic toiletries, and headed out for some overdue errands.

At 10:30, Payson rushed to the door to let in the frantically knocking Maddy. Her friend tore into the apartment. "It's freezing out there, did you intend to leave me out there to turn into a Maddy-cicle?"

Laughing at her dramatic friend, Payson brushed the fresh snow off of Maddy's wild chestnut waves, "It was not intentional, I swear. I didn't hear you over my blaringly loud thoughts. Wait, didn't I give you a key?"

"You did, but I didn't want to actually use it without your permission. For all I knew you had a guy in here."

"Ha. As if. More importantly, what does one pack for an overnight boat adventure? It was so nice of your parents to include me, knowing I need a vacation, but don't they realize I've refused every time they've invited me because I'm too terrified? Will it be safe on the water in this weather?" Payson didn't mention that it wasn't just the wardrobe crisis or her fear of boating muddling her brain.

Last night's kiss had turned her world completely upside down. He wasn't at all her type. He was the type she filtered out of her online dating search. Yet, she was so drawn to him, couldn't stop thinking about him. Had never felt so... well, aroused quite frankly. But it was more than that.

Maddy patted her head. "They keep inviting you because they know you want to enjoy boating but are too afraid to give it a try. You know Mom, she's always trying to fix everyone."

Payson responded with a reluctant pout. "That sounds like Laura. If only I didn't like her so well..."

"You know she's right."

"Maybe. Dang it, I have always wanted to go boating. I'm sure I'll like it; it sounds like such a romantic hobby." Payson sighed, gesturing down to her outfit. "So... what do I wear? What do I pack?"

"How about you pack whatever you had been planning to wear tonight and tomorrow? It won't be cold on the boat; for winter we keep it sealed up tight and the heat on full blast. Mom has no cold tolerance, so we'll probably be roasting anyway. It's a perfect day for a cruise; snow is already starting to let up with clear skies predicted for this afternoon and tomorrow. The water is practically flat calm."

"You made it even more complicated. Do I pack for hot or cold or both? You should have been here sooner, before I reached a full-on freak out." Payson's voice moved from shrill to a pitch that only dogs can hear.

Maddy pulled her friend along back to the master bedroom. The bed was covered in discarded clothes of all sorts. If she was horrified, she didn't show it. She rolled up her sleeves and took charge.

"Ok, you'll need an outfit for the ride and shopping, maybe something for dinner tonight because they booked a fancy restaurant for us, pajamas if you wear them, a practical outfit for tomorrow for breakfast and the ride back."

Watching Payson's growing panic, Detective Maddy McAllister took over. "You grab your toiletries and I'll get you packed. I'll throw in a few alternates in case you want some options."

Payson obeyed and dashed into the bathroom, shouting, "Thanks, you're a lifesaver." She hoped her friend packed something cute, but it was better to trust her friend than continue fussing, or she'd be late. She was never late.

Nor had she ever been on a boat adventure before... or even been on a boat. The McAllisters had invited her out several times, but she kept resisting out of sheer terror. No more.

She was turning over a new leaf. Maybe Ronan wouldn't be so standoffish if he realized she didn't care about appearances. Honestly, she hadn't intended to appear caught up in appearances, and realized searching for *the one* by filtering out all the riffraff on her dating app was downright stupid.

She hollered to the next room as she madly tossed her make-up and toothbrush into her travel case, "Is Chase waiting outside?"

"He's playing on his phone, keeping the truck nice and warm for us. He knows us well enough by now; he'll know this won't be a quick stop."

Payson wasn't sure if that was reassuring or depressing that she was predictably indecisive. Her clothes were always planned out, often a few days in advance, then switched out at the last minute if it didn't feel just right for the occasion. She zipped back into the bedroom, clutching her toiletry bag. "Am I good in what I'm wearing?" She tried not to sound desperate, but Maddy would understand the dilemma.

Maddy grabbed the toiletry bag from Payson's paralyzed hands and stuffed it on top, zipping up the overnight bag. Payson felt foolish. After a lengthy internal debate, she'd worn her skinny jeans with knee high waterproof suede boots with a plain white t-shirt under a soft pink sweater with cozy cowl neck.

Maddy looked her up and down approvingly, "Yes, that's perfect. Do you have a hat and warm coat? The high is in the 20's today. I packed you a scarf and gloves that I found in your drawer."

Payson pulled on her coordinating wool cap and ski jacket - not that she had ever been skiing, but she'd found it on sale and fortuitously discovered it looked great on her - and locked up as they headed out. As soon as they were in the blessedly warm truck, Maddy turned around so she could see Payson in the backseat, and asked the dreaded question, raising her eyebrows suggestively, "How was the date with Gregory last night? Fifth date, right? Did you finally...?"

Looking horrified, Payson feigned offense, "Hey, just because it's the fifth date doesn't mean sex is on the menu."

Chase interjected, "Didn't he drive all the way to Seaview and drive you to a fancy dinner? Did he walk you to your door?"

"Yes," she admitted.

"Then he was expecting sex. Normally a third date milestone, so I'm sure he was impatiently presuming it was going to happen." Lucky he was keeping his eyes on the road, or he would have been turned to stone by the death glare shooting his direction.

Whacking him on the arm, Maddy tried to help, "You can have sex whenever you feel it's right. Did you at least send him away with a goodnight kiss to remember?"

A scorching, splotchy blush rose from her chest to her cheeks. Dammit. She'd certainly been on the receiving end of a goodnight kiss to remember. Not from dashing, successful Gregory. But from her irritable handyman, her best friend's brother. Yikes, she hadn't thought about that. Would Maddy understand better than Aiden had when Maddy and Chase hooked up? Aiden had flipped out at Chase, his best friend since childhood.

Chase glanced in the rearview. Seeing her blush, he granted her a reprieve. Nodding at Maddy, he advised, "You can quiz her later. We're here." He pulled the truck into a parking spot close to the docks.

Grateful, Payson mouthed, *Thank you* when Chase winked at her via the rearview. Grabbing her leather overnight bag, Payson dashed out of the truck as soon as Chase shut off the engine. Careful not to slip on the icy surface, Payson kept to the untouched snowy patches as she headed for the dock.

Maddy cautiously ran after her in her much more practical hiking boots. "Sorry. I shouldn't have pried." Payson linked elbows with her friend. She might be the one begging for forgiveness if things went further between she and Ronan.

"No worries. I'll fill you in later. It was a weird night, and I'm just not quite sure what to make of it myself. Can I vent when I'm ready? But, let's just say I won't be going out with Gregory again."

Frank approached from the docks, meeting them to unlock the security gate. "Did anyone want to help Chase with the bags?" He teased, gesturing to Chase, who was overloaded with supplies.

Payson glanced back to see Chase hauling his and Maddy's bags, as well as a heavy soft-sided cooler that must be full of snacks and drinks for the ride. Payson handed Maddy her own bag, "I got it."

She dashed back across the least icy spots to help with some of Chase's heavy load. Not that he needed the help. Guy was built; well over six feet tall with broad shoulders and bulky muscles from years of hard work as a deep-sea diver.

"Thanks for the ride," she said as she hoisted one of the bags over her shoulder.

Graciously, Chase accepted her help, "Anytime. Have you been out on the boat much?"

Payson shook her head. "I've never been out on *any* boat."

A look of shock crossed Chase's face. "What? How is that possible. You live in a boating town. How have the McAllisters not dragged you out before today?"

Payson bit her lip nervously. "I, uh, they've tried, but I've been avoiding it. I've been a total weanie. But, I'm turning over a new leaf and am determined to enjoy boating."

His jovial laugh didn't help her feel better about her confession. "Well, despite the cold, it should be nice and calm today."

Walking down the ramp to the dock, Payson's legs shook like jelly. The slope was at least nicely roughened-up so she didn't slip, but the dock was a solid sheet of ice. The others walked cautiously but confidently toward the boat.

Not Payson. She tiptoed as if avoiding potential land mines that may explode at any second, blasting her into the frigid ocean. She may have squealed now and again when her feet slipped, but she would never admit the mouse-like sound had come from her.

Frank took pity on her, taking the bags she carried and grabbing hold of her hand with his free hand. He led the way slow and steady, as if guiding a frightened filly.

Boarding the boat was another adventure in and of itself. Frank hopped down before her, standing and holding a hand out to guide her down. Payson looked down at the rolling gap between the dock and the boat. Gaping at the several-foot drop down to the floor of the boat, which she would have to survive *after* the deathly leap across the ice-cold water to the narrow ledge of the boat wall. How... why?

"You know what? Never mind. I just realized I really shouldn't close the shop today. Not on a weekend. That is just a reckless business decision. I'll just walk home. You guys have fun." She turned away and took a few steps back down the dock, willing to brave the slippery planks of doom, if it meant not having to cross the gigantic chasm between the dock and the boat.

Looking back toward the parking lot, she froze in her tracks, legs going numb, jaw dropping. Panic quickly subsiding, astonishment taking over. Sauntering toward her, swaggering really, was a genuine Adonis. Holy shit... Ronan?

Black t-shirt hugging chiseled abs and stretched across powerful shoulders, chestnut hair trimmed short in a sexy fade, face cleanly shaven... all topped off with his arrogant, devilish half smile as he caught her drooling reaction to his new look.

Huh. Maybe her hormones had been onto something. Made Gregory look like a chump.

Wicked smile somehow growing more arrogant as he approached, Ronan briefly glanced into the boat as he reached her, and tossed his bag and heavy coat to Chase waiting in the boat. Standing toe to toe, she looked up into his ice blue eyes that were warm with amusement. As they stared at each other, the onlookers quickly headed into the cabin, suddenly busy with official boat matters.

"'Don't bother coming in today?'" he accused with a teasing grin.

"I was irritated and wanted to piss you off. Did it work?" she asked hopefully, hip cocked out to the side tauntingly.

He shook his head, grin still in place as he feigned dismay, "Yes, yes it did."

"Sorry about that. Are we even now?" She'd been so angry at his rejection last night that she'd succumbed to the temptation to piss him off this morning. After all their fights, she had become adept at pushing his buttons.

"For now," he teased. He extended his hand in peace. She reached out to shake on it, but her hand trembled. Looking her up and down, he saw the panic setting back in, and his expression turned soft, sympathetic. "Give you a hand?" he offered.

With ease, he hooked his foot over the cleat on the boat and pulled the boat in closer to the dock. "I'm going to hop in the boat. You watch so you know how it's done. I'll be right here to catch you. I won't let you fall in."

With every fiber of her being, she believed in him; trusted him not to let her plummet to an icy death. Maintaining an iron grip on his hand, she stepped one foot onto the side of the boat, slowly lifted her dock foot up and swung it over the chasm, and somehow managed to drop into the boat.

Her landing was a bit wobbly, but as promised, Ronan was there to catch her. Hands pressed against his chest and gripping his new t-shirt, her breathing rapid, her heart finally started to slow as Ronan held her close and whispered soothing reassurances in her ear.

"Aren't you freezing?" she managed to ask, becoming increasingly overwhelmed by his new... well, his new confidence. Everything. He was ridiculously sexy. Aiden was hot, but Ronan, all fixed up and smiling and... holy shit. She wouldn't be so foolish as to say she wasn't outrageously turned on just looking at the most attractive man she'd ever laid eyes on, but there was something else that she'd seen bubbling just under the surface before.

She couldn't help but wonder what had spurred the change. Hoping that maybe he had figured out who he was, what he wanted. With all that he'd been through, of course he hadn't been sure what he wanted.

She certainly hadn't been silent about her not-so-simple goal of finding *the one*, nor had she given him much time to think about it, about them. Awfully pressuring for a guy that wasn't sure what he wanted for lunch, let alone the rest of his life.

Last night, precedence had died a tragic death. She wasn't the woman she had been a few weeks ago, looking shallowly for Mr. Perfect like Jen had insisted. Nor was he the broken man that had come home riddled with uncertainty and anger.

14

RONAN HELD HER TIGHTLY against him, knowing she'd feel more secure in the safety of his arms. Not that he had a choice; she still had an iron grip on his new shirt. "Yeah, I'm freezing, but I was hoping to get in the heated cabin quickly."

Blushing, she unclenched her frozen hands and released his shirt. "Sorry."

Laughing at her, he reassured her, "It's ok. I'm guessing it's your first time out on a boat?"

Payson nodded an affirmative, hands still clenched tight, but at least no longer stretching out his new shirt. He tried to ignore his family, as they were struggling to look like they weren't spying from the other side of the door.

"Come on, I'll give you a tour." He unlocked her rigid fists and took her cold hand in his. "The boat's made for year-round use, nice solid top to protect against the elements, but the thick canvas further blocks out the weather for rainy or winter ventures so we can go out year-round. Not much of a fishing vessel; Mom prefers a leisure boat.

There are plenty of seats so we can all visit while protected from the weather, but the cabin is nice and cozy if you get overwhelmed. This is a lot like the one we grew up with but upgraded."

Still holding his hand, she followed him in, checking out the cozy seating area outside, then down into the cabin. Frank hopped back out of the boat as Aiden and Laura approached with a few grocery bags in addition to their own overnight bags.

"Wow, it's really nice in here. I was expecting a bit more primitive of a living area." Payson's gaze passed over the kitchenette, corner bathroom, dining area with facing couch, and queen-sized bed at the front with all of their bags stowed on the floor around it. "I can't believe there's even a tv in here. The fabric and cabinetry are really tasteful. No wonder your parents would rather stay here than pay for a hotel." Payson still gripped his hand, unwilling to let go, but she explored a bit, feeling the textures around her as she took in her surroundings.

A sudden deep rumbling startled her. Ronan quickly reassured her, "It's ok, it's just the engine starting."

Defensively, she responded quietly, "Yeah, I figured that out. Just took me by surprise, that's all."

Ronan took her coat and added it to the stack of winter apparel already forming a mountain on the bed. The cabin door opened, and Laura headed down the small stairs, carrying one of the grocery bags. Dashing toward her, Ronan grabbed the bag from her and another from Aiden leaning over the threshold.

Aiden popped his head in, "Hey Pace, you seasick yet?"

Raising one eyebrow, she fired back, "Ha, ha. I've acclimated quite nicely to boater's life. I'm going to take a private moment in the head, then I'll move aft to join you all on deck. Save me a good seat, please."

And with that, she squeezed past Ronan and closed herself in the bathroom.

Laura whispered quietly to Ronan so Payson wouldn't hear, "She doing ok? I know she's terrified of boats. I suspect the only reason she finally agreed to come with us is because you're here."

Ronan scrunched his brow and gave his mother a *you're crazy* look. She chuckled at her son, patting his smooth cheek, "Don't give me that, I've seen the way you two look at each other. CIA operatives aren't the only ones who can read people."

"Mom, you're a hopeless romantic." He kissed her on the cheek.

She patted him on his nicely shaved cheek. "Welcome back."

A grimace of pain passed over his face briefly, but he quickly recovered. It felt good to be back, metaphorically speaking this time. All it had taken was a good kick in the ass from reality. Life was here to stay, and he may as well join in.

Reassuring his mom with a heartfelt smile, he headed up the steps. Chase had already nabbed the driver's seat with Maddy snuggled against his side. Frank sat across the aisle with a spot set aside for Laura. That left the couches that faced the aisle behind the front seats. Aiden was already crashed out on the driver's side couch, eyes closed. Ronan sat opposite. His brother had always had the ability to fall asleep, wherever he was. Not fair.

Ronan stretched his legs on the couch like his brother, reclining against the arm of the couch and facing the coastline behind them. Chase put the boat in gear and pulled out of the slip as Maddy dashed out to pull in the bumpers, then settled right back in at his side. The view wasn't great through the clear plastic that made up the rear door, but at least they were warm. The snowy landscape grew a bit smaller in the distance as Chase drove them northeast toward the island of New Sussex.

Hands firmly gripping the back of Frank and Laura's seat as the boat bounced across the ocean waves, Payson's gaze crossed back and forth between the brothers hogging the last of the seats on deck. "Ahem," she cleared her throat.

Ronan didn't lift his head but turned toward her. Eyes relaxed, his mouth turned up in a half smile, he spread his legs on the couch and patted the space between his thighs, "Have a seat; I'm happy to share." Rolling her eyes, Payson accepted the invitation and sat rigidly in the nest he'd made with his legs.

"Really?" she glared at him, eyebrow raised, arms folded.

Full grin now, Ronan apologized, "Oh, I'm so sorry." He spread his legs a bit and pulled her toward him. Catching the hint, she angled her body and pulled her legs up so she was leaning back against his chest, legs stretched out on the soft couch between his. She sat stiffly for a moment, resisting, but finally gave in and relaxed against him.

For a few moments, they cuddled in silence, neither verbally acknowledging what was happening. What had started for Ronan as an ornery challenge was now a rather painful reminder that he was human. Very much alive, and very much a man.

He inhaled the clean, subtly floral scent of her hair as he buried his face against her. How many different scented shampoos did she own? Her arms now wrapped around his bent legs. She finally settled in and wasn't going anywhere. He wrapped his arms around her middle and held her securely against him.

The first drunken kiss had been startling. The second the stoking of embers. The third had been an awakening. But, this... this intimacy, this was gut-wrenchingly, terrifyingly... miraculous.

Snuggling up against Ronan, Payson couldn't figure out how it had happened. One minute she was calling his bluff when he invited her to nestle up with him on the couch, the next she was in pure heaven. Heat emanating off his chest, the feel of his breath in her hair, the feel of his muscled thighs under her hands. The sensual feeling of his hands gently grazing her abdomen, initially frozen just to hold her in place, now tenderly caressing. Something shifted deep within her, something surprising and remarkable.

Who was Ronan anyway? He didn't seem to be a computer programmer sort; he didn't even look at his cellphone unless to text or call someone, and he'd had yet to even glance at her work computer. Actually, he didn't say anything about himself at all, save for a few comments about his family or his youth. Nothing about himself outside of Seaview. How could she trust him so thoroughly if she didn't even know who or what he was?

She couldn't deny she'd been inexplicably drawn to him before, even when he'd been disheveled and cranky and didn't seem to be at all the type she'd go for. Now that he looked and acted like a damn superhero, all confidence and strength and compassion, with a body of a warrior and a face that belonged on a magazine cover... now she was completely at a loss. As if her hormones were applauding, *See, I told you so.*

As she drowned in blissful sensation, she forgot to be afraid in the boat. The hum of the engine, the rocking as they crashed through the ocean waves; all soothing rather than frightening. She found she rather liked boating. Before she knew what had happened, her eyes were drifting closed as the snowy coastline disappeared on the horizon. Having tossed and turned all night, confused about Ronan, she needed some rest.

Quiet voices and shuffling bodies nearby disturbed her peaceful nap. Who would dare interrupt such a perfect moment? Payson had never felt so safe and cozy. Where had the blanket come from?

Eyes fluttering open, Payson saw the activity that had awakened her. Aiden was sitting a few feet away, digging into a bag of sour cream and onion potato chips. Maddy popped the top off a beer. Tummy rumbling, Payson accepted it was time to sit up and have a snack too. She hadn't eaten much this morning, fearing seasickness.

Shifting in her seat, she started to sit up. A strong hand pulled her back down and she thudded against the rock-hard chest beneath her. Turning in place against the brick wall that was Ronan's chest, she discovered he was smiling at her. Whispering, she demanded, "Ronan, I'm hungry."

Whispering back, he teased, "Me too," and waggled his eyebrows at her. Her sharp elbow went straight for the gut.

His face scrunched in pain and he held his hand over his low abdomen where her elbow had dug in. Oops, must have found one of his train-wreck injuries.

Quickly recovering, he whispered, "Don't move the blanket just yet. I, uh..." he gestured downward. Oh, of course. He had clearly enjoyed their nap as much as she had, his rigid erection digging into her.

Funny, she normally would have been disturbed by a surprise erection on her behalf, but this time she rather enjoyed it. Wiggling as she sat up just to egg him on, she sympathetically shifted the blanket to save his dignity a bit. Turning to face him, she grinned mischievously.

"Wench," he muttered with his devious smile she was already quite fond of.

Laura turned in her seat to look behind, "Well good morning sleepy heads. We're about another hour or two out. Thought we'd have lunch; it's almost two. I brought sandwiches, chips, and beer. Chocolate chip cookies for dessert. Hungry?"

Payson nearly drooled at the thought. "Yes, I'd love a little of everything. I was so afraid of getting seasick that I haven't eaten much today." She tried to stand but Laura waved her hand.

"I'll get it for you. On your second outing, I might let you help. This time, I want you to feel spoiled, so you'll want to come out with us more often. Sourdough, right?" Laura grinned down at her as she stood to head for the galley. Payson nodded and put in her order.

Ronan rubbed at his hip as he sat up, eventually swinging his leg around so they could eat. He nudged her with his good shoulder, "Did you order some for me too?"

"I'm sure your mother won't mind if you get up to help make lunch," Payson raised her eyebrow with a smile.

Laura appeared with two paper plates full of food and two unopened beers. "You both get a pass on helping today. Ronan's first time out in over a decade." She winked and headed back into the cabin to join her husband.

Ridiculously content, more than she could have anticipated, Payson tore into her sandwich ravenously. Ronan finished his by the time she was even halfway done, but he had still maintained those impeccable manners. She tried, but the chips were so salty and delicious. Something about the salty sea air.

Licking the seasoning off her fingers, Payson heard a groan from beside her. Glancing over at Ronan, she saw him watching every flick of her tongue. Laughing, she teased quietly, "Dang, Ronan, how long has it been?"

Eyes unblinking, still staring at her mouth, he managed to ask, confused, "What?"

"Never mind," she teased. Wiping clean with her napkin, she crumpled up her garbage and finally opened the beer.

Ronan grabbed her plate and took it into the cabin. She watched him walk away, then her eyes landed on Maddy and Chase. Chase still drove, and Maddy still snuggled up beside him. Not realizing they were being watched, she witnessed Chase turn his face to Maddy and steal a brief but incredibly sensual kiss. *Why couldn't it be that easy?*

From across the tiny aisle, Aiden interrupted her thoughts, "Can't it be?" *What?* Payson looked at him like he was nuts. "Pace, you talk out loud when you're tired."

Feeling foolish, she laughed at herself and took a swig of her beer. "Sure Mr. Commitment. How easy are you finding it?"

Rolling his eyes, Aiden scoffed, "Love? I couldn't give a flying fuck about love, so, yeah, I'm finding it incredibly easy to *not* fall in love." Leaning back in his seat, long legs stretched out nearly to hers across the aisle, he smirked back at her.

"Why didn't I see it before? Who was she and how did she shatter your heart so completely?" Payson knew he wouldn't say, but she couldn't help firing back after his sarcasm. Knowing she was right.

With a sneer, not at her, but at a memory, he retorted, "Does it have to be just one? There are many out there who proved to me that love is a bunch of bullshit. Not worth the effort."

Defensively, Payson set her beer in the nearby cupholder and leaned across the aisle and glared at her friend. "It's not bullshit. Look at your parents, at your sister and your best friend… that's a beautiful thing and we all should hope to be so lucky. I've been fascinated by love since before I understood the concept, and a disillusioned heartbreaker like you isn't going to ruin that for me."

Aiden fired back, their voices growing louder with each retort, "And what, my brother, drowning in PTSD, fixes himself up a bit and suddenly has your attention? Are you going to grab hold and then dump him when you realize he doesn't quite reach the perfect pedestal you've created? Like you did with Clive?"

"You don't have the slightest idea what's going on." Her fists clenched at her sides, her body stiff with fiery outrage. "I had hoped so desperately to love Clive, but it just wasn't there, so I ended it before we were both stuck in a loveless marriage. Your wounded, but very resilient brother, is stronger than you think. I started falling for him a long while before he cut his hair. If you looked a little closer, you'd see it's not just a shave and a haircut that's different about him today."

Shit, she hadn't meant to say any of that out loud, especially not here. Looking around, Payson saw Ronan standing in the cabin doorway, having witnessed the entire conversation. Maddy and Chase politely looked back at the water. And, thank goodness Frank and Laura were still in the cabin. They probably heard the whole thing, but at least they weren't there to witness her embarrassingly revealing, impassioned defense of their youngest son.

Stupid boats. She was never getting back on a stupid boat again. Where did one go after saying something so stupid? She debated leaving the heated part of the deck to sit all alone on the back bench in the windy, freezing weather, but didn't think frostbite would help her humiliation.

That wasn't exactly what Ronan had expected to hear when he came out of the cabin. He knew Aiden and Payson had been friends, but he'd never seen them fight. He'd actually never seen a woman fight for him before, stand up for him like that.

Not sure what to think, he froze in place. Did she really see him so clearly? Humbled the hell out of him that she saw beyond the superficial changes. She'd known him for a matter of weeks, and already placed him higher above any of the assholes she'd dated before.

Legs going a bit weak, heart racing, Ronan fought the panic attack brewing within. Not because she'd practically declared her love for him, that actually sounded... amazing. No one had ever loved him, other than his family of course. The pressure, the responsibility that came with it was more than he could carry right now. Yeah, he'd awoken feeling like his old self again today, but the self-assurance was waning.

Holding onto the back of Maddy's seat, Ronan inhaled slowly, held, released. Fuck, tunnel vision coming in. Payson saw the blood rushing from his face and immediately stood. Dammit, not now. Not when she'd been defending him.

She took his hand in hers and led him back to their couch. She opened the small window, directing the glacial air to blow right in his face, remembering how the cool air had soothed him before. The cold helped, but not as much as her hand in his. Pressing her cheek against his, she whispered reassuring nothings in his ear as his breathing slowed to a calmer rhythm.

Vision clearing, he glanced up to see that Aiden had disappeared, giving him the space he'd known his troubled brother had needed. Grateful, Ronan made a mental note to have a chat with his brother later, let him know what was going on with him. They hadn't been close since well before he'd moved away, but it was time for that to change.

Time to correct many of his past mistakes, particularly his relationship with his family. For now, he turned toward Payson and captured her mouth with his own. Icy air still blowing on him, the feel of her lips against his filled him with delicious sensation, an inferno brewing under the surface.

15

"Land ho!" Hollered a voice from up front. Aiden stood in the aisle, looking out the windshield, peering out at New Sussex approaching.

Laura laughed, as only a mother would at her son's lame joke. "Oh, my dear boy." She shook her head at her son. Maddy was driving now, Chase readying the lines and bumpers for docking. Frank was leaning back in his chair, finishing a beer and allowing the younger generation to take over.

"Thanks for laughing Mom. At least someone appreciates quality humor." Aiden shook his head, still smiling at his own joke, and headed into the cabin to pack up. The family made a good team, all well-trained and jumping into whatever role they needed to play.

Payson, feeling quite brave in the boat now, stood and held one hand on the back of Laura's seat, her other hand gripped across the aisle on the back of Chase's empty seat. The island-town was starting to come into view as they approached. Ronan moved in behind her, one hand gripping the seat next to them, and his other sliding around her waist to hold her close, his body pressed up against her own.

If she'd carried any hope of keeping things between them private, it was long gone after today. Frank glanced back and gave her a knowing wink. Better not screw this up. Ronan had been struggling until today. Yeah, his rather prominent ego now blossomed, but she feared it wouldn't take much for him to fall back to the lost soul he'd been the day she'd met him.

What if she let him down? That panic attack had been no joke; he'd looked like he was about to faint. Of course, she'd caused the panic. She'd been in the middle of saying she preferred Ronan to any man she'd ever even hoped to love... when he'd gone pale.

Dammit, she was already blowing it. Typical, she finally finds someone that stirs something inside her, and even the mention of her feelings drives him into a panic attack. Shutting up her own anxiety, she focused on their fun plans for the weekend.

"I've never been to New Sussex, is it as touristy as Seaview?" Payson was looking forward to seeing the town. She hadn't gotten out of Seaview much lately.

Laura turned sideways to visit. "I love New Sussex. If we weren't so settled in Seaview, I'd make the move. It's much smaller, and there's never as much happening as it's hard to get to. There's a twice daily ferry service, so anyone visiting has to really plan ahead before making the trek.

"There are a few small shops and restaurants, a few B&B's, a small hotel and some rental cabins. I'd say the population is under a thousand or so permanent residents, but the population increases dramatically during the summer months. It's a delightfully small town, village really, with a very restful pace. Runs on island time."

Payson smiled dreamily, "Sounds like a perfect destination for a cozy winter weekend."

"It really is; we come a few times every year. There's not much happening in winter, but the basics are open and it's mostly tourists just like us looking to watch the storms roll in while staying cozy inside." Laura snuggled up against Frank as they approached.

Payson noted Frank watching every adjustment Maddy made to the boat as they approached, ready to jump in if she needed help. Laura whispered something in his ear and he abruptly moved his gaze, remembering he didn't have to jump in and help anymore. Remembering he'd taught his family well.

Maddy looked back and motioned to Payson and the others, "Ok passengers; sit your butts down and out of my way until we've docked."

Payson abruptly moved back to her seat as directed. Aiden had been surfacing from the cabin but turned back to stay out of the way when he heard his sister's stern voice. Ronan pulled on the charcoal gray wool sweater he'd been using as a pillow and headed out of the cozy enclosed area to help Chase catch the dock.

Standing beside Chase, the two bantered pleasantly, gesturing as they remarked on the other boats in the marina. As they pulled in closer, Chase tossed out the bumpers while Maddy slid into the visitor slip like she was parking a sports car. Ronan hopped out and walked swiftly to the front of the boat, grabbing the bow line and tying up to the cleat. Chase did the same with the aft cleat. Nice system. You could tell the McAllisters, plus Chase, had always been a boating team.

Complimenting his daughter's excellent docking job, Frank couldn't handle sitting idle anymore and hopped up to help Aiden load everyone up with their bags and coats. Not wanting to be a total freeloader, Payson took her fair share.

Frank passed her Ronan's and her own bags and coats, "Head on up the dock, then Inn de la Mer is right next to the marina, that blue building," he pointed until she acknowledged.

"Got it. You and Laura heading up yet?" She slipped on her coat and swung Ronan's backpack over her shoulder.

"Nah, we'll tidy up a bit in here first. You young folks can get settled, and, if it suits your fancy, check out the shops and we'll join you in an hour or two. No cell service on the island, so we'll just poke around until we find you."

Laura piped in, "You each have your own room, except Maddy and Chase will share, of course. Already paid for, so just let them know your name and they'll show you to your rooms. We've stayed there before; they have a wonderful library looking out over the water you may want to relax in."

Payson smiled, "Sounds like exactly what I needed. See you around."

Thrilled, she headed to the back of the boat. She was about to climb out with confidence, as Ronan had showed her when they departed, only to find the dock wasn't quite what she'd imagined. There was an awkward wooden bar running down the side where the lines were tied on.

"Uh..." she stood open-mouthed, unsure how to proceed. Did she step over it or on it? It shouldn't be that complicated. Why was this minute detail of boating so oddly overwhelming? Last time she just stepped across then hopped into the boat, but this time she had to somehow step up and over?

Aiden stood behind her, "Come on already," he teased.

Payson stood to the side and watched as, arms full, Aiden hopped right over, despite the awkward wooden bar thing. Eyes wide, she tried to not panic. Ronan understood and took pity on her.

Speaking as if to a wild and terrified wolf about to lash out, he held a hand out and soothed, "You've got this. Hand me the bags and coats first."

Payson obeyed. He set their belongings on the dock next to him. With one foot on the dock extending over the bar and the gap, and the other foot on the edge of the boat, he took her hand. "Use the bench and step up onto the side of the boat, then put your other foot up on the dock on the other side of the bull rail. It's not as far as it looks. I've got you." Remembering how firmly he held her before, she trusted him and did as he asked. Not as scary this time, but still not her favorite pastime.

Clutching her hand in his own, Ronan balanced their bags over his opposite shoulder and refused her help. "You focus on walking; I'll carry the bags."

She shook her head at her own trepidation as she walked overly cautiously down the dock. "Thanks; I feel like such an idiot. I just can't shake the fear that I'm going to slide right into the Atlantic."

Ronan let her set the pace. "You're not being paranoid; I've seen people slip right in if they're not paying attention. The docks are a solid sheet of ice. It's good to be cautious." Smiling, she seemed to feel a bit less silly about her caution. He glanced back, noting Maddy and Chase were not far behind.

His parents had sealed up the boat and disappeared into the cabin. Which was rocking rather rhythmically. Smiling, he tried not to imagine what they were up to in there. There was little doubt their relationship was thriving, despite how rocky things had been 10 to 15 years ago. With a houseful of teenagers, both working long hours to save for college at the time, things had been tense more often than not. They'd even hinted at the big D a few times during that tough period.

Aiden always on the verge of committing a major felony with Chase right at his side. They'd taken Chase in as one of their own while his own father had been too busy drinking to notice his son was taking rebellion to dangerous heights.

Ronan was the opposite but hadn't been much easier on his parents. He kept his nose clean but must have worried them with how hyper-focused he'd been, totally self-centered and ignoring life around him. Maddy was doing great in school, knocking college credits out of the way to save on tuition down the road, but was dating a serious asshole.

He should have realized what was going on with his twin sister, as he'd been friends with her asshole boyfriend since childhood, but he figured she could handle herself. Which, she did when things had gotten unsafe, but maybe if he'd been paying more attention, he could have stopped things before anyone got hurt.

Shaking his head, he tried not to relive the past. Start fresh. No hard feelings between anyone. He'd returned to a happy, settled family. Not that Aiden was showing any signs of settling down, but he was at least established in his career.

Walking up the ramp, Ronan glanced over at Payson. She was already checking out town, an eager smile on her face. So gorgeous, her auburn hair was tangled from the wind, her green eyes wide and filled with wonder. She couldn't have ended up alone in Seaview without some serious drive, building her own antique shop from the ground up.

Although, she didn't make it look like she had to work for it. She ran that shop with ease, online sales processed quickly and with care, her brick-and-mortar shoppers leaving with huge smiles and arms loaded with bags, even after investing in some big-ticket items. He knew she did all of her own accounting and inventory. Had invested in the building using a chunk of the insurance money she had been saving after her parent's death as a down payment.

He'd seen the fire in her eyes that night when Gregory wasn't taking no for an answer; she clearly hadn't needed his help. Nor had she stood on her high horse when he'd stepped in. She was fucking perfect; beautiful but humble, kind, smart... competitive, a violently sore loser, a bit compulsive. But, more importantly at present, she didn't judge him for his many flaws.

"Want to hit some of the shops before getting settled?" he asked as they neared the B&B.

Nodding her head, she agreed, "Looks like there's an antique shop just across the street, I'd love to check it out."

"Always working, huh?" he teased. And received a jab in the ribs for his trouble, but it was meant well as she grinned back at him. "Let's drop our bags and check out the town. Dinner isn't for another few hours, maybe we can explore a bit before the sun goes down?"

Well, he hoped she wouldn't mind if he tagged along. Shopping was not his favorite activity, and he'd already spent his morning shopping for a new wardrobe. But he wanted the excuse to spend more time with Payson.

At each other's necks until recently with their quarreling, he rather enjoyed this turn of events. Silly, but he felt relieved that her feelings toward him had been developing when he still looked like a deranged mountain man. Like a reverse Cyrano de Bergerac.

"I'd like that," she responded, smiling shyly at him.

16

THE B&B WAS NICE; his parents hadn't skimped. Although his room didn't have the ocean view, he'd caught an incredible view from the library and dining rooms that he explored while waiting for Payson. Located right on the beach, it was like the B&B was floating over the water when he looked out the massive windows. Polished wood floors were covered with plush wool rugs. Classic coastal, thick white trim and warm green walls made for a homey ambience.

Ronan's room had a huge, beige area rug that covered most of the floor and a massive cloud-like bed took up most of the space. The bathroom was cleverly tiled in a decorative black and white pattern, with walls painted a deep blue.

Although, he had to admit, he was hoping to not spend much time in his own room. He'd had some incredibly vivid imaginings about seducing Payson, and after last night's kiss... he was beyond ready. She'd been ready last night, but he hadn't.

This morning, he gave himself a serious ass-kicking. *Get off your ass. You're alive, start living like it.* That look she'd given him when she saw him coming down the dock... He'd known then that he was ready for her.

Yeah, he was still a total mess. It didn't seem to matter, she liked him anyway. Just being around her made him feel so very human; she was hard to resist. Moth to the flame. Why keep fighting it when resisting just made them both miserable?

Having explored the place, Ronan finally dropped his bags in his room and went next door to grab Payson. Everyone else had decided to freshen up a bit before hitting town. Daylight was short this time of year, so there wouldn't be much shopping or exploring after dinner.

Knocking on Payson's door, he heard a frantic, "Just a moment," from the other side. Some more shuffling, and finally she swung open the door.

Her jeans discarded, she now wore a black wool miniskirt and cable-knit tights with her same boots and sweater from the boat ride. "I'm ready; let's go." Looking around, finding the hallway empty, she asked, "Where are the others?" She'd run into her room so fast to pee, she'd missed the conversation about everyone's plans.

Taking her hand in his, he led her down the narrow hallway toward the front door. "Maddy and Chase are going to take a short 'nap,' which I'm pretty sure is code for afternoon sex. Aiden already left, saying he wanted to check out town solo. Knowing Aiden, that means he's on the lookout for a local girl to hook up with for the night."

Throwing her head back in laughter, Payson teased, "Wow, your family is a bunch of sex fiends. Maddy and Chase, that doesn't surprise me. That rocking boat - your parents clearly still have a healthy relationship. Aiden was so isolated when he first moved back to town, but now the guy's a menace. I'm afraid to ask how much of Seaview's single - hopefully single - female population has surrendered to his charms."

Eyeing her suspiciously, Ronan frowned, "Wait, have you and he...?"

Payson took a moment to realize what he was asking. At his look of horror, she laughed out loud. "What? Me and Aiden? Oh god no. He's a handsome guy, but, no. Not a bit of romantic chemistry between us. He's a good friend. I would consider our relationship more of the brother-sister dynamic."

Relieved, Ronan pulled up their joined hands and kissed the back of her hand before opening the front door to leave the B&B. "Good. Not that it would stop me, but I'm really glad Casanova hasn't... uh... you know what I mean."

Playing innocent, eyes wide, Payson paused in the entryway and goaded him, "Hasn't what?"

Frustrated, Ronan jabbed back, "You know, I used to be good at this sort of thing. Talking, gathering information. Must be getting rusty. Let me try again: I feel reassured that you have not had sexual relations with my brother."

Not finished teasing him, Payson continued, her mouth quirked up in a sly smile, "Oh? And why is that?"

With a growl, Ronan pushed open the front door, the icy air shockingly cold. He let go of her hand long enough to pull on his brand-new heavy jacket. Grabbing her hand again, he led her purposefully a few steps along the sidewalk, then promptly spun her around and pinned her against the side of the building, framing her between his arms against the wall.

Faces inches apart, her gaze cast down to his lips in anticipation. Hovering a few millimeters away, he wasn't joking around anymore, "Payson, this shouldn't surprise you. I'm planning to peel that short skirt off you and make slow, scorchingly hot love with you all night.

We can wait until another night if you're not ready yet. But, if you are ready... I'm going to make you scream out my name in ecstasy."

Her twinkling green eyes unfazed, a seductive smile formed on her mouth. Without words, she agreed with a playful nip of his lower lip. From underneath him, she slowly teased at his mouth with her tongue, her hands reaching under his shirt, skimming her fingers along his skin, making him inhale sharply as she torturously caressed his abs.

Who was seducing who here? At the edge of control, he pressed his lips to hers, deepening the kiss. She kissed him back with equal fervor, a soft moan passing her soft lips.

Strolling by on the sidewalk, a voice broke the moment, "Come on guys, you have two perfectly good rooms inside," Aiden interrupted, protesting the public display of affection with a pitiful whine.

Ronan turned his head lazily, arms still locking Payson in place against the wall, and growled at his brother. "I thought you were out on the prowl."

Payson ducked under his arm and out of the cage with an eye-roll, winked at Aiden, and started across the street to the antique store. "I'll let you two boys compare dick sizes while I do some shopping." Ronan watched as her hips swayed with each step, her hair swaying in rhythm with her seductive strides.

Aiden caught his brother dreamily watching her walk away and cleared his throat, "Man, you got it bad."

Sighing deeply, Ronan had to agree, "Yeah, you might be right."

Aiden had a look of deep sympathy on his face when Ronan looked back at his brother. "You sure that's a good idea? You were in a pretty low place not 24 hours ago."

Introspective, Ronan ran his hand through his short hair, still surprised when there wasn't much hair to muss. He felt so much more comfortable with the new do, but it was a bit weird to feel so weightless. "I was. Still am, even if I'm dressing better. It's been letting up a bit the last few weeks. Getting easier."

The brothers stood side by side, looking across the street at the building Payson had since disappeared into. Ronan continued, wanting his brother to understand, "I've got some shitty memories, but some good ones too. The last nine years were actually pretty awesome. I did exactly what I wanted to do with my life. Saved a lot of lives, hell, saved the world. More than a few times. I'm trying to turn my focus to what went right during those years, rather than the shit that didn't."

"Saved the world huh? Any exciting stories?" Aiden was all ears, captivated.

Ronan looked around. No one in sight. Never could be too careful. "A few," he motioned his brother to follow him across the street. "Remember that 'false alarm' incoming missile threat to Hawaii a few years back? Or, better yet, want to know how they finally found Bin Laden?" Aiden shook his head, eyes suspicious. Ronan gave a wink and an innocent shrug, and disappeared into the antique shop, leaving his brother in the dust.

Payson had enjoyed shopping in the quaint village. Tourist-shop bounties were now safely stored in her room; she'd purchased a beautiful locally made woven basket and an artfully crafted coffee mug. Feeling inspired to help him fill up his new wardrobe, she picked up a knit watchman's cap for Ronan. She'd also made fast friends with the owner of the antique shop. They'd traded business cards and agreed to refer antique-loving tourists to each other's shops.

Finally, Laura and Maddy both surfaced, cheeks glowing from restful... or not-so-restful... afternoons with their significant others. Normally, Payson would have felt overwhelmed by a healthy dose of jealousy, but she had the promise of tonight to hold her over.

She normally waited until at least a sixth or even tenth date before considering sex. Not prudish, she just wanted to make sure they were compatible. She'd been with Clive nearly six months before they'd had sex for the first time.

Things were completely different with Ronan. They'd spent weeks working side by side, arguing constantly. The fire had been there from the moment they met at the art gallery, despite the bickering, and she'd grown to enjoy the challenge. As she got to know his quirks, she became more intrigued by him.

Then last night... well, more so the night at the tavern, she'd thrown out *Payson's Book of Dating to Find Your Soulmate* and jumped him. Yes, it had taken a large quantity of beer to initially lower her walls. But, she had yet to regret it.

Maddy walked arm in arm with her on the way to the restaurant. The boys had separated the last hour, checking out the fishing and boating-focused shop at the end of the main drag. The island ran a successful fishing tour, and, as Chase and Frank hoped to open one of their own in the spring, they'd scoped out the operation.

Maddy hadn't hesitated to drill her about Ronan. "So, you and Ronan, huh? That might explain why you're never going out with Gregory again." She teased. Laura had walked a few feet behind, pretending that she wasn't listening.

Payson blushed, unsure how to answer.

Maddy continued. "What changed things? At the gallery opening, you two looked like you were about to spear each other. Although, that night at Winter's... that was some naughty dancing. I wasn't sure if it was just drunk Payson or something more. With Ronan being Ronan, not at all the type to fool around, I should have suspected more."

With a sigh, Payson finally answered, "I couldn't even tell you what changed. I just... I like him. A lot. He's different from any man I've been out with, and you know how I've racked them up while looking for the right one."

"Different, huh? You've been going for the uptight narcissists, so, yeah, he is definitely not that. Not that he doesn't have an enormous ego, but he's both honest and self-effacing about it."

"Hey, I haven't picked that terrible of dates." Payson frowned.

Too impatient to wait behind and risk missing any of the good stuff, Laura dashed up and linked up to her other arm, "It was watching him work with his hands, wasn't it? Frank is at his sexiest when he's working with his hands, flexing those muscles." Laura grinned at the girls.

Shaking her head in wonder, Payson quizzed, "Laura, you sly thing. You set us up? Admit it."

Nodding, Laura fessed up, "Of course I did. I adore you and want you for my own daughter. I had initially thought of Aiden, but it's lucky you two just don't fit. He's a bit too much of a rogue. You needed someone a little more... enigmatic."

Maddy eyed her mother suspiciously, "Mom, you've got to cut back on the romance novels. You enjoy playing matchmaker a bit too much, don't you? Wait a sec, Dad's truck wasn't broken that day he told me to ask Chase to drive me to Portland - it was just fine, wasn't it?"

Laura rolled her eyes, "Oh honey, of course it was fine. It needed upgrading, and he'd been planning to buy a new one soon anyway, so we jumped on the opportunity to give you that extra push. You and

Chase had been obviously in love for years, you two just hadn't figured it out yet."

Payson laughed, "Aiden's a bit dense, though. Laura, did Maddy tell you his initial reaction?"

Maddy shook her head, "Mom doesn't want to hear about that."

Laura giggled and nudged Payson, "If Maddy won't tell me, you've got to. Aiden was a bit overly protective of his sister, and he can be a bit dense when it comes to girls."

Groaning, Maddy interjected, "Fine." Maddy went on to tell her mom about how Aiden had completely missed the heat that had been bubbling over between she and Chase, and that Aiden didn't notice until he'd found them in an awkward state of undress.

"Oh, that's our Aiden. I can't wait to tease him about that."

"Please, Mom, no." Maddy shook her head violently. "He's still a little squeamish about his little sister hooking up with his best friend."

"My eldest sure needs a good wake-up call when it comes to romance. He's going to be the last one standing."

Payson grinned, "Do you have someone picked out for him yet? I know you do."

Sheepishly, Laura smiled, "I sure do, but that's none of your business. I don't want anyone interfering with my process."

Entering the restaurant, the threesome laughed together as they unlinked arms and joined the guys, already seated. Ronan had saved her a seat, next to his - in the corner, of course. A glass of pinot gris sat waiting for her. "Thanks," she said as she slid into her chair next to his.

As she took her first sip, he whispered into her ear, "I'm trying to liquor you up a bit, seemed to work out in my favor last time."

Focusing on swallowing before reacting, Payson managed to not choke. "I'd like to remember jumping you this time," she whispered back. Not that she planned to jump him, exactly… well, maybe she did.

Grinning, he sipped his own drink and briefly glanced at the menu. She ordered a refreshing salad, not wanting anything too heavy as she had a work-out planned for later. Ronan ordered the fresh catch, apparently also going for a lighter fare. The restaurant had been quiet when they arrived, but the McAllisters had all been giddy and turned the sedate restaurant into a joyful, gregarious place with their lively conversation.

As they stuffed in the last bites of food, she felt the wine buzzing in her head, warm and bubbly in her brain. Dinner took an eternity. Longer than it should when she was desperate to get back to the B&B. It was delicious and she couldn't remember the last time she'd laughed so fully, but her mind kept wandering, planning her after-dinner festivities.

Her room had a massive king-sized bed overlooking the ocean, covered in plush white pillows and blankets. The bathroom held a walk-in slate tile shower with so many jets she imagined a full body water massage. There was a cozy sofa facing a wood-burning fireplace with logs and kindling already in place, waiting to be lit.

By the time dinner was done, most at the table had heavy lids, exhausted from a day at sea. As promised, Laura and Frank treated to dinner, as they had the entire trip. Payson would have to find a way to pay them back for the extravagance. Maybe she'd surprise them with some of the jewelry and pirate treasure they'd had their eyes on.

Laura rested her head against Frank as they led the way out. Maddy conned Chase into a piggy-back ride back to the B&B. Aiden was rubbing his eyes to stay awake as he followed shortly behind. Ronan held Payson's hand, holding her back to allow the others to filter out ahead of them.

17

Stepping outside, Payson inhaled the refreshingly chill sea air and admired the light dusting of fresh snow that had blown in while they'd dined. Isolated, small flakes still floated down from the sky. Hands linked together, she and Ronan walked slowly together down the two short blocks to the B&B. Payson's heart started pounding in her chest as they got closer to her room. Neither spoke, but she could feel as his breathing accelerated with her own.

Unlocking the room door, she motioned for him to follow behind, letting him know tonight was the night. Nervous but thrilled, she turned to lock the door behind them, taking an extra breath as she clicked the lock into place. Turning, she saw Ronan waiting a few feet away. His body tense, eyes full of fire.

Payson was overwhelmed with anticipation. Watching Ronan closely, she could see the tone change. Still frozen in place herself, he moved the last few feet towards her in a blink, hand diving into her slick auburn locks, pulling her in closely while his mouth devoured hers. Impatiently, hungrily, intensely, his mouth covered her own, his tongue mating with her own.

Breaking free for the briefest of moments, he pulled her sweater and undershirt over her head, lips quickly returning to hers. He slid her skirt down over her hips, her tights and panties following. She nudged off her clothes the rest of the way while his mouth slowly moved down and kissed along her jawline, down her neck, leaving a trail of fire.

As soon as she'd freed herself from her clothes, she snapped off the bra and tossed it aside, standing before Ronan completely naked, while he was unfairly still entirely clothed. Before she could complain, Ronan smoothly backed her against the door.

Taking charge, he raised her hands above her head, gripping her wrists with one hand, the other trailing down, gently testing, weighing, squeezing her breasts that were heavy with desire. His mouth followed closely behind, tongue grazing the curves.

Without warning, he covered a nipple and sucked her into his mouth, the surprise bringing out a cry of pleasure she'd never heard herself make. He continued stirring her deeply, erotic heat scorching her from the inside out. As she neared her climax, just out of reach, he moved back up and kissed her mouth, his desperation almost palpable.

His rough hand moved lower and cupped her; she bucked into his touch, gasping in reaction. Separating her soft, slick folds, he teased and caressed her sensitive nub, increasing the pressure and speed against her until she cried out his name, breath coming so fast she couldn't think.

With a sexy wink, Ronan quickly released her and unbuttoned his pants. Skillfully, he slipped on the condom before hungrily lifting and pressing her against the door. Payson held on tight, her legs wrapping around his waist as he thrust into her, both of them sighing with pure satisfaction at the sensation. Hips pumping against each other, the orgasm quickly ripped through her. Payson cried out as she flew, Ronan soaring right behind her.

Still inside her and holding her pressed against the door, Ronan rested his cheek against hers. Both gleaming in sweat and breath coming fast, Payson couldn't hold back a smile. Finally remembering where they were, Ronan lowered her down and saw her smile, his eyebrows raised in a questioning look.

Without answering, Payson gave Ronan a slow, savoring kiss before she pulled away. Looking him over, she laughed out loud, "Why am I naked and you're nearly completely dressed?"

His eyes wandering along her naked body, Payson didn't feel awkward like she would have expected, rather, she felt daring, glorious. Ronan finally grinned with her. "I guess I couldn't wait any longer." Giving her a quick pat on the ass, he headed for the bathroom to discard the condom.

Feeling suddenly quite wanton, for what may be the first time in her life, Payson headed for the bed and pulled down the luxurious comforter before she laid on the bed in a come-hither pose she'd seen on an Italian sculpture. Her breasts didn't quite stay as perky as the marble woman's had, but she didn't mind one bit. At the moment, she couldn't feel any sexier.

Still fully clothed, and buttoned back up, Ronan returned to the bedroom to find Payson waiting for him. Naked and looking so fucking hot. Erection stirring again, he knew he didn't have a choice this time.

She'd see his many scars; but he suddenly felt self-conscious. Hesitating, he stood at the side of the bed. Looking around, he scratched the back of his head nervously, not sure how to show her.

Payson watched him, finally speaking up, "Ronan, you have a nude, eager woman waiting. Get naked," she ordered impatiently.

With a quick laugh at her adorable impatience, he tried to find a way to warn her before he shocked her. He put his hands on his hips, trying to find the right words. "I, uh... I have a lot of scars. I just wanted to warn you first."

Rolling up on all fours, Payson crawled toward him across the bed and stood in front of him. "I know about the accident, the PTSD; and I sense there's something more going on with you that you are hesitant to talk about, but please, just trust me. Ok?"

He did trust her, completely. There weren't many he could say that about. She'd seen him at his worst, and still seemed to think the world of him. He nodded in agreement.

Payson stilled his nervous hands, slowly pulling his shirt over his head. She saw the puckered, healing wound on his shoulder and delicately kissed the gunshot wound. Her hands grazed his torso, migrating down to a healed knife wound on his left side. She followed the trail with her tongue, placing a soft kiss on an older wound before she lowered herself to her knees in front of him.

On a mission, she kept going. She unhooked his belt, slowly, tormenting him. Continuing the torture, she unhooked the button and slowly slid down his zipper. Rubbing her fingers with a feather-light touch across his tight abs, she stopped at the other recent gunshot wound low on his right abdomen, another, on his hip, she discovered as she lowered his jeans and kissed both softly.

Gently teasing at the waistline of his boxer briefs, she finally lowered his pants the rest of the way, his erection springing free. Glancing up for a reaction, she saw his eyes roll back in his head as she grasped his hard cock in her hand. Gripping her fist around the base, she traced her tongue along the long, thick shaft, with a teasing flick of her tongue at the tip before taking the length of him deeply in her mouth.

She continued, sucking, squeezing, until he pulled back with a gasp, "Payson you're killing me. Please..." With a quick motion, he scooped her up and tossed her on the bed effortlessly. Landing on the soft mattress, Payson didn't have to wait long before he was on her, sheathed, and in her with a swift thrust that took both of their breath away.

18

AFTER A DELICIOUSLY SLEEPLESS night, Payson awoke to a cloudy sky, gigantic flakes of snow rushing past the window in violent gusts. Her body still entwined with Ronan's, she didn't want to move, the moment so perfect. But all good things must come to an end.

Hopefully to resume in just a moment, but her bladder was full to near bursting. She tried to slide out, but Ronan's arm held possessively around her middle and pulled her back against him.

"Ronan... Ronan, I have to pee." She hissed.

With a grunt, eyes still closed, he released her. She ran to the bathroom to relieve herself, and returned to climb back in bed, but stopped when she saw the clock. Nine o'clock, dang, she never slept in this late. Remembering breakfast was between nine and ten, Payson started the shower and headed back to the bed to wake Ronan.

"Wake up, we don't want to miss breakfast."

Sitting up, the life quickly returned to his eyes. "I'm starving." He grabbed her and tossed her over his shoulder like a caveman and headed into the shower, setting her neatly on the floor so she wouldn't slip.

There were so many showerheads, they were able to shower together rather efficiently, both enjoying the view as they watched each other hungrily.

Turning the water off after a very pleasant shower, Payson tried not to stare, but couldn't help looking closely at his scars. "Ronan, what kind of train wreck was this? These look more like... bullet holes or something." She traced over the shoulder wound, curious.

Dodging the question, Ronan grabbed his towel and was suddenly in a hurry. "Shit, I forgot this isn't my room. All my stuff is across the hall. Meet you at breakfast?" He grabbed a quick kiss and dashed out of the bathroom, leaving her standing there, confused and frustrated. Holding the towel securely around his waist, he grabbed his room key from the nightstand and ran away before she could ask more questions.

Dashing into the hall, Ronan had known he was busted before he even opened the door. Not psychic or anything, just old habits. He didn't have to be caught, but facing his siblings was easier at the moment than trying to explain his scars to Payson. He didn't mind the ribbing from his siblings anyway; he was too fucking happy to care.

Maddy and Chase were just coming out of their room. Maddy adopted a serious lecturing face, "Little brother, what are you up to, coming out of my best friend's room in nothing but a towel?"

With a grin, he teased back, "You're only seven minutes older." Gripping his towel tightly, he unlocked his room.

Aiden came out of his room, joining the crowd, "Ah, come on man. Do you have to rub it in? Get some damn clothes on."

Ronan saluted and threw open his door, quickly dashing in to get dressed. Minutes later, he headed down to the dining room. His parents had just sat down at the long table; the owners normally only served guests of the B&B, but given the circumstances, they'd happily agreed to feed the whole family after Laura had booked all four of the rooms they had to offer in the off season.

He saved a seat for Payson next to him. She appeared in the doorway moments later, sexy as hell in tight skinny-jeans and her knee-high boots again, with a pale pink t-shirt that clung to those fantastic breasts. His poor brain quickly flashed back to last night, her gasps of pleasure, her hot mouth over his cock...

He had to get a grip. Biting his cheek, he tried to mask the smug grin and dreamy eyes that were a dead giveaway that he was falling fast and falling hard.

Glancing around, he noticed Aiden watching, the others were greeting Payson and making sure she had her coffee poured, alerting the hostess the last two were ready to eat.

Aiden shook his head, fortunately quietly, he whispered, "Another one bites the dust. I saw that same look on Chase last summer. Couldn't wipe off the smitten expression; hell, he still wears it most of the time." Glancing at his friend, he continued, "Like right now."

Ronan glanced up to see Chase staring out the window at the snow, looking just as sap-happy as he did.

He'd met Penny, their hostess, yesterday when she'd checked them in. She couldn't be much older than he was, but she still seemed young to be the proprietor of such an impressive establishment. Ronan had discerned that she and her husband, Dariel, had emigrated from a small town in Normandy a few years back to take over the small B&B that Dariel's grandparents built as an inn decades ago.

They'd done a lot with the place. Although small with only a few rooms, they didn't seem to be hurting for income. The place was pretty high-end. The upgrades made a difference; the place gave off a classy vibe, the sort of place you'd want to return to year after year. He hated to think what his parents had spent to rent out the whole place. Likely all part of the grand plan to get him out into the world of the living.

Penny arrived at the large dining table with a big smile and plates of delicious crepes covered in strawberries, with scrambled eggs and plump sausage on the side for he and Payson. The others had already started.

"Good morning," she greeted with her thick French accent. "I hope you slept well. Please don't hesitate to ask for anything." She was gone in a blink, leaving them to enjoy their breakfast.

Frank broke the silence that had come over the table as everyone devoured their breakfasts. He topped off his and Laura's coffee with the carafe before speaking. "Anyone notice the snow outside?"

Ronan looked out the window, the snow was really coming down now; mostly blowing sideways, the sky darker than it was even half an hour ago. Wind more screamed than whistled through the harbor.

Frank continued, "Nor'easter blowing in, already nearing white-out conditions. A full day ahead of when a moderate snow forecast to hit, stronger and faster than expected.

"I talked with our hosts. This shouldn't be as severe as some of the bigger storms in years past, but the winds will be pretty strong given how fast she moved in. We'll need to hole up here until things calm down. Tonight, and quite likely tomorrow night as well. As no one can get in either, I have been able to extend our reservation."

As soon as he paused, Chase jumped in, "How are things looking for the boat, and the power on the island?"

Frank continued, "The boat should be ok. The marina is in a fairly enclosed harbor on the lee side. The island has a diesel generator to run when the wind generators go offline, combined with buried power lines; we should be good for electricity."

Lips turned up in a playful half-smile, Ronan interjected, "Uh, this may be a bit obvious, but you can take my room... I'm assuming you're not staying on the boat tonight."

Laura laughed, "Thanks for the offer. We sort of guessed, but we didn't want to presume. We brought our bags and the coolers in and stashed them in Aiden's room."

Next to him, Ronan noted Payson blushing, looking suddenly fascinated by the whirling snow. Reaching down, Ronan pulled her hand into his and gave a gentle squeeze. A sweet smile crossed her face, but she kept her gaze on the storm.

Finally, she spoke, "Well, I guess my shop would be closed today anyway, so I don't feel so bad about playing hooky anymore."

Their host, Dariel, a stalky man with a massive head of black hair and neatly trimmed goatee, entered the dining area. "*Bon matin*. I have some updates for you. This storm looks to last at least another 18 hours, but they're not very sure of the estimated duration as this was such a surprise."

Laura smiled up at him. "Thanks, Dariel; we really appreciate your flexibility."

Smiling back, Dariel responded, "I'm pleased you folks are so understanding."

Chased laughed, "We're from Seaview, so it's likely no calmer at home."

"You arrived in the boat, that's right. No ferry service today, of course. The marina here is very protected, even in some of the more severe storms the boats have no problems," he reassured them.

"This certainly isn't the first time we've had guests sequestered due to a storm. Today, like with similar occasions in the past with total white outs, we serve three meals each day. We'll plan to have a simple lunch around noon and dinner at six, if that works for you?"

They all agreed and thanked them for the offer. Normally it was a bed and breakfast with a light snack in the afternoon, but with the blizzard conditions, nearby restaurants were likely closed as well. Ronan appreciated that their hosts were prepared, else he'd have to suffer another of his mother's homemade sandwiches from the cooler. Not that they were bad, but he was getting a bit sick of her sandwiches.

Laura piped in, "I have plenty of sandwich fixings I brought in from the boat that I would be happy to share." Damn, he spoke to soon.

Dariel smiled, "I appreciate that, Laura. We are looking forward to preparing some non-breakfast items; we both enjoy cooking and are glad to cook lunch and dinner now and again. I stocked up this morning when I saw the storm approaching. We have more than enough supplies, enough to last for a week or more in case this storm decides to hang around long-term," he said.

Phew, close one.

"That sounds excellent. I'll keep everything stored in the mini-fridge in our room for midnight snacks then," she winked at Frank.

Oh boy, not much better.

Getting up from the table, everyone cleared their plates and were quickly shooed out of the kitchen by the host and hostess. Ronan was definitely going to have to repay his parents for this extravagant trip.

After stopping briefly in the room to freshen up and grab her book, Payson went to join the others in the library. When was the last time she'd sat and done truly nothing? There were always online orders to process, new items to purchase, budgeting; there was always something that needed to be done.

On the rare instances she treated herself to time off, she spent it with her sisters in Boston, which was never relaxing. She'd brought a book, a hokey romance which she had been looking forward to digging into, all while snuggled up beside her own romantic interest. She headed for the library-slash-social room.

She heard them the moment she entered the hall. Shouting, cussing, accusations flying, gunfire, maniacal laughter. Rounding the corner, she stopped at the wide doorway and peaked in.

A massive flat panel tv took up a good chunk of the library wall, and on it was a first-person shooter game divided into four panels with an intense game underway. Ronan, Maddy, Chase, and Aiden sat on the expansive L-shaped couch, each focused on the screen and throwing taunts at the others.

A loud crack echoed through the screen. Aiden stood and tossed the controller onto the couch, arms flailing. "Ah, come on. Where did that come from?" One corner of the screen was covered in blood splatters, and the words *You have been killed by RONAN* flashed on the screen. "Where the hell are you?" Aiden glared at the screen searching for clues.

Ronan sat smugly in his end of the couch, body completely calm, his legs stretched out on the chaise in his far corner of the couch. His character ducked around a corner in a dark room or cave or something so no one could see where he'd hidden. Payson watched his screen.

A few minutes later, a similar outburst echoed from Chase. It was still tough to see where Ronan was by looking at his screen. His character stashed the sniper rifle and started to sprint across the map.

Maddy's character was frantically searching the screen for her remaining opponent. Watching Ronan's corner of the screen, Payson saw him draw a pistol, round a corner, and fire three shots right at the back of Maddy's character's skull. Gruesome, but effective.

Maddy's screen flashed as red as the other's had. "What was that? I was just in that room." She glared at her twin brother. He shrugged innocently. "Guess I should have considered who I was up against; cops got nothing on spooks, is that it?"

Maddy turned and discovered Payson standing in the doorway, quietly taking in the scene. The room went silent. What was that all about? She suspected there was more to Ronan than he let on, but she'd get it out of him later.

Clearing her throat, she entered the room with her book, "Guess this is not the best choice for a quiet place to read." She smiled as if she hadn't noticed the change in tone.

Sitting on the plush sofa next to Ronan, she slipped off her boots and curled into him. He passed her the controller, "Want to give it a try?"

Maddy and Aiden erupted in objections. Aiden spoke loudest, "No, no, no. Haven't you played any sports or competed against Payson in, well, in anything?"

Ronan glanced at her, clearly remembering their day at the rec center. Payson rolled her eyes.

"She's ridiculously competitive. Unless you want a head injury from having a controller thrown at you if she loses, or worse, a non-stop ribbing for the next week if she wins."

"Hey, I'm not that bad," she rolled her eyes and shrugged defensively.

Chase, previously sitting quietly in the opposite corner of the couch, spoke up, "We all love you, but you have a serious competitive streak. And you're a terrible loser."

Scrunching her eyebrows, she thought about the last time they'd tried playing video games together... and the football match last summer... and the 5k they'd run last Fall... and when Ronan beat her at laser tag. "Ok, so I may get a bit absorbed in the game."

Ronan nudged her gently. "Really, I'll take you on, anytime. I never lose, so as soon as you get used to that, I'm sure you'll figure out how to lose more gracefully."

"Oh my, that ego sure came back with full force bro," Maddy teased.

He continued, raising his eyebrows, "But, as I'd like to get some tonight..." He handed Payson his controller. Groans echoed through the room.

Smugly, Payson snuggled against Ronan on the chaise end of the sofa and designed her character. As she selected her weapons and armor, she offered, "I promise to not throw anything if I lose, and if I win, I promise only one day of gloating."

Aiden threw a suspicious look at her, "One hour, tops."

Payson nodded, "Agreed. Now get ready to get your ass handed to you."

Rolling his eyes, Aiden muttered, "Again."

The game was intense, with some close calls. Maddy found Payson and fired off a single shot before Payson dove out of the way and hid again while her health regenerated.

Aiden took out Chase, with an outburst of surprise from Chase, and ran for the hills, tracking down his sister next. Sneaking behind as Ronan had, he nearly took her out, but a shot rang out from a distance, and the kill went to Payson.

Payson managed to quiet her normal smack-talk, as promised. She'd been hiding on the cliffside and took off running, moving into position to take out Aiden.

Aiden kept his eyes glued to the screen, but conspicuously whispered to Ronan from across couch, "You distract her so I can win this one, and I'll buy the first round at Winter's when we get back."

Ronan shook his head, unblinkingly studying the positions of the remaining characters on the screen. "Nah. I can buy my own beer."

Again, Aiden made an offer, as his character searched the field for Payson. "Fine. I'll take your share of boat clean-up when we get back."

Still glued to the screen, Ronan countered, "You clean the boat, buy my drinks, and shovel the snow in my driveway when we get back."

Grumbling, Aiden agreed, "Fine. Now get on it before she kills me."

"Hey, no cahooting," Payson argued, her eyes darting across the screen as she searched for Aiden.

Chase laughed, "Cahooting?"

Maddy clarified for him, "As in, being in cahoots."

Focusing, almost to Aiden, Payson pulled out her sidearm. Just as she was about to take the shot, Ronan snuck his hand under her shirt and tried to make his way under the bra.

Shrieking, she wiggled away. "Stop it," she yelled, eyes still focused on the game. Lowering his hand, he tickled her abdomen mercilessly. Unable to hold back the laughter, she tried to wriggle out of his arms.

It was too late. *You have been killed by AIDEN* popped up on the screen as her character's blood splattered across her corner of the screen.

"Not fair," she hollered between laughs as she tried to throw the controller at Aiden. Ronan grabbed it from her hand in the nick of time and tossed it on the couch, throwing her over his shoulder yet again. "Hey, I'm not a ragdoll," she protested between giggle fits.

Aiden leaped off the couch and cheered, quite pleased that his plan had worked. Payson heard the laughter and cheers as Ronan carted her out of the room. She wiggled more, trying to break free. "Hold still, dammit," he chuckled, reaching up and tickling her again until she gave up on trying to break free.

Tossing her on the bed as soon as they reached their room, Ronan dove down and laid next to her on the bed. "I like your crazy."

Giggling, she squirmed against him. "Crazy?"

Tracing his hand along her side, he gently caressed her side. "I heard you talking to Jen. You're bossy in a nice way. Competitive in a fun way that makes everyone else enjoy the game even more. I like that you can rock it equally well at the tavern or at an art gala."

Touched, more than a little, Payson beamed and snuggled closer.

19

EXHAUSTED, YET EXHILARATED FROM the afternoon romp, Payson slipped on her favorite jersey skirt with her pink t-shirt from this morning. She curled up on the couch facing the fire with her book, finally. Ronan headed back out, leaving her to herself for a few hours.

Oddly, she missed him even for short time they weren't within touching distance. She was alone so often; she usually craved solitude after spending too much time with others. Especially if she spent too much time with her sisters. Somehow, Ronan didn't seem to fit into that 'not-solitude' category. Well, wasn't that something?

With a stretch and a yawn, she slipped on the sneakers Maddy had packed for her and headed to the dining room a few minutes before six. Laura was waiting alone, sipping a glass of wine and watching the dark, snowy sky. "Payson, I'm glad you're here early, too."

Walking over to the makeshift bar with the help-yourself wine and beer, Payson poured herself a glass of wine and sat beside Laura at the table. What did one say to the woman whose son she'd started sleeping with in the past 24 hours, that she was quickly becoming more than a little attached to? Wracking her brain, nothing was coming.

Thankfully, Laura rescued her. "I have a proposal for you. You know I enjoy visiting you in your shop. If you want some help so you can take some time off or just need an occasional day off, I'll be happy to pitch in where Natalie used to. Not permanently, just until you find a replacement for Natalie. I'll leave the deliveries to Ronan, or whoever I can rope into helping if you're not around."

Payson was taken aback, grateful for the offer. "That sounds fantastic, thank you. I would love to take you up on that offer. I was going to ask Ronan to watch the shop, but now I'm wondering if... I don't know."

She hesitated, finding the right way to ask. "I have a business associate in France, a friend really. Anyway, I buy pieces from him on a regular basis, from his own family winery or from his travels. He does some antique wholesaling, in a sense. He says he is selling some of the more valuable items from his family's collection and invited me to fly out and take first dibs.

"I wasn't picturing Ronan running the shop alone, so I'd hesitated." Payson trailed off and took a sip of her wine. She heard the end of another very heated video game match echoing down the hall.

Laura leaned back in her chair. "But, now you're considering asking Ronan to come with you?"

Payson nodded hopefully, but sensed the likely negative response.

Laura stopped as if to collect her thoughts, wondering how to proceed. "I'm not sure he'll agree. I'd like him to get out and do something fun like that, but... I'm not sure he'll be too eager to cross the pond again just yet. You should ask him, but I wouldn't get my hopes up if I were you."

Payson saw the worry on Laura's face. "I can imagine. He worked over there a long time; he must have a lot of memories. I'm certain he'll want to avoid the train, so if he agrees to go, I'll be sure we avoid trains." Laura nodded in vigorous agreement, then took a big gulp of her wine.

Rowdy voices echoed down the hall as the gamers approached. Payson had never seen Ronan smile so much. The goofy grin he wore lit up his face, bringing a whole new light to him. A happy, trouble-free version.

She was still getting used to the new look, too. The slick cut showed where he naturally had streaks of lighter brown mixed with the darker. Wearing clothes that fit so nicely didn't hurt, either; Payson must have blushed like a virgin bride as she pictured that very fine body, naked and pressed up against her. Ronan flashed her a smile, clearly reading her mind.

Rapid French could be heard bouncing back and forth in the kitchen; perhaps a quarrel between their hosts. They all sat for a moment and listened, hoping for even a brief lapse into English to discover what the conversation was even about. Their hosts had been so kind as to extend their stay to full services, so Payson hoped they hadn't done anything to wear out their welcome.

Ronan rose from his seat and walked silently to the kitchen, leaning casually against the open doorway. "*Ca va?*" He inquired from the doorway. More conversing in French, but less heated now, Payson wondered what was happening.

Penny and Dariel had moved closer and could be seen in the doorway separating the kitchen and dining area to speak with Ronan. Neither looked angry, but Penny had tears in her eyes. Dariel rested his arm on around her shoulders, pulling her against him.

Speaking in impressively fluent French, Ronan had a detailed discussion with the pair, his expression sympathetic. He patted Penny kindly on the shoulder and returned to the table as the pair returned to the kitchen. The entire table stared at him, waiting to hear the results of his conversation with bated breath.

Before sitting, he walked over to leisurely pour himself a glass of wine. He returned to his seat and took a slow, savoring sip. Finally, Aiden kicked him under the table none-too-gently, his eyebrows raised in question.

Ronan finally gave in. "Penny's mother is on her way for a visit, but due to the weather she's stranded on the mainland. She was to arrive tonight, but they're saying it may be another 2 or 3 days before ferry services are back up again. She's ok, she's just upset. She's newly pregnant and was looking forward to celebrating with her mother."

The table all expressed sympathy, comparing notes on how frustrated she must be feeling. Laura poked her head into the kitchen, offering to help wherever possible.

Payson poked Ronan on the shoulder. "You speak fluent French. I didn't know that."

Ronan smirked across his glass of wine. "Yep."

And that was it. *Argh*. He was like talking to a brick wall sometimes.

After dinner, everyone went to their rooms for a quiet evening. Payson was restless, thinking of all the work not getting done in her absence. She called Natalie from the landline in the library.

"Hey, Natalie, how's it going?" She tried to sound pleasant and nonchalant.

"Well, hello Payson. Going well, still a total whiteout here. How are you enjoying New Sussex? I've never been but I hear it's a beautiful island." Natalie's voice was friendly and welcoming. Relaxed. Life at the gallery must be good for her.

"I'm wondering if I can ask you a favor?" She bit her lower lip nervously; she hated asking for help.

"Of course. I would be happy to go and check on the shop as soon as the snow slows down a bit." She could hear Natalie's smile in her voice.

"Thanks for reading my mind. The internet out here was limited anyway, but it's now totally out because of the storm. I'm going crazy not being able to notify customers of potential delays. I know it's a lot to ask; I know you're busy." Payson babbled, afraid of pushing too hard.

Natalie laughed out loud, "Please ask me favors like this. You were so good to hire me on and be so flexible. I would make the time for you, but I don't even need to; the gallery will be just as slow. Why don't I just try to catch you up a bit once I can get out?"

Payson thanked her profusely and reassured her that she would be back as soon as the weather permitted their departure. She was about to head back to the room, when she caught a glimpse of a stack of magazines. Finding a very computer-nerd sort of magazine, she added that to stack of fun-looking magazines she'd found for herself to take back to the room. Maybe Ronan would tell her a bit about his work. Maybe even explain how a computer programmer ended up with gunshot wounds, and why he was so dodgy about it.

As she entered their room, she saw Ronan stretched out across the sofa, fire blazing in the fireplace. He didn't seem to notice her, so she tiptoed, hoping to scare him. Magazines gripped in one arm, walking as quietly as she could, when she was finally in arms reach, she leaned in and whispered, "Boo." Not very clever, but she was at least going for a laugh.

He didn't move, not even a twitch. Was he asleep? His chest rose and fell as if he were. Oops, startling him probably wasn't very considerate. Payson set the magazines on the ottoman, feeling guilty now and trying to not wake him.

She turned slightly away from him as she adjusted her skirt to sit down. Before she hit the couch, strong arms came around her. She indelicately squealed in alarm, and before she knew it, Ronan had her pinned beneath him on the couch, a huge grin on his face. "Boo," he whispered.

Frowning, Payson reached up and pinched Ronan. "It's not nice to scare people you know."

He raised an eyebrow, grin still pasted to his face. "Really Miss Roberts, I don't think you're one to talk." He leaned down and kissed her with soft but brief contact and released her.

Returning to his end of the sofa, he stretched back out again, this time putting his feet on the ottoman so there was room for her on the couch. He glanced at the pile of magazines, sparing only a brief glance at the computer magazine on the top before returning to his own book.

"Tom Clancy fan, huh?" She inquired. Naturally, she'd read a number of them herself. Jack Ryan was a particular favorite of hers, in the books or on screen.

Ronan nodded, eyes glued to the book. "It's pretty good. I'd never actually read any. Fun piece of fiction."

Leaning back and putting her feet on the ottoman snuggled against Ronan's, Payson defended one of her favorite characters, "It's spectacular fiction. He's an analyst for the CIA, but always ends up in the field and saves the day. For all we know that's exactly what happens in the CIA. And Tom Clancy does great research on his books."

"I'm sure he does. Just some extra exciting scenes for the readers." Ronan continued to read, pretty far into the book considering he'd just started it today.

"And you don't think the true, unfluffed stories of a CIA analyst would make for a good story?" She crossed her arms, a bit defensive.

"No, I'm sure that they would be interesting, but much less exciting." He turned the page, eyes darting swiftly across the page as he read impressively fast.

Humph. Payson picked up the fashion magazine she'd brought with her and started to peruse. She'd flip a few pages, then huffed again. Finally, she gave up and tossed the magazine back on the stack.

Without looking up from his book, Ronan asked, "Yes, Payson? Something bothering you?"

Starting a thought, then giving up, then trying again, Payson tried to figure out how to ask without making him run away again. "I'd really like to know, where did you get your scars? Between the scars and the PTSD, I'm just thinking there is more to you than a computer programmer that was injured in a train wreck. And, you completely ignored the computer-nerd magazine I brought; what kind of computer programmer are you?"

Ronan bit his lip, "The kind that doesn't enjoy reading about it." And he stopped talking. Brick wall for sure.

"And... the gunshot wounds? Scars?"

Pausing for a moment, he finally answered, "I was shot. It hurt, a lot. Yes, I have PTSD. I really didn't like getting shot."

That she'd already guessed, so she hadn't learned anything new. "What about the bigger one?"

"Which one?"

"Which one? There are more?"

That sexy half-smile forming, he shook his head and cussed, finally marking his page and putting the book down. "Could you be more specific than 'the bigger one'?"

Payson scooted closer and pulled up his shirt to show him the scar she was talking about on his abdomen. "Oh, that one. Cut myself shaving."

Laughing out loud, she jabbed him gently at the wound, "You're so full of shit."

Feigning injury, he accused, "Last night you kissed them and made them better, now you're jabbing at my wounds. Heartless wench."

"So, where's the other 'big one'?" She demanded.

Ronan sighed and shook his head again. He turned away from her and pulled his shirt over his head to reveal a rough, furrowed wound taking up most of his right shoulder blade. Payson delicately ran her fingers over the angry burn scar, voice soft, she asked, "Where did you get this burn?"

How had she not noticed it last night? Well, it had been pretty dark last night, and then in the shower this morning they'd been facing each other. She hadn't actually seen his back. And what a nice back it was.

Turning toward her, he looked her straight in the eyes, "Africa."

Well, at least he might be telling the truth this time. Before she could ask more, he held her chin and pressed his lips to hers. "Please. I want to say more, but I really can't, not yet." Without leaving her any room to object, he pulled her onto his lap. Palms gliding up her thighs, he slid her skirt up, shifting her panties to the side.

"Ronan..." She tried to argue, but she quickly gave in to his obvious diversion as his thumb rubbed her sensitive clit, his fingers plunging in and caressing her from both sides. Tension building inside her, she tipped her head back and rocked against him.

20

AFTER ANOTHER AMAZING NIGHT and day of sex and video games and spectacular French food, the storm was over. Light filtered in through the soft clouds as the sun rose on Monday morning. The sky was quiet, no more snowfall, the wind no more than a gentle breeze, the ocean calm. Ronan laid awake in bed, Payson wrapped around him, sleeping soundly.

Back to reality. Reality sucked. He'd made a huge breakthrough over the weekend and had felt more like himself than he had in a very long time. Anxiously, he anticipated regressing a little when they returned to town. The hustle and bustle, strangers walking around who could be out to kill him, the noise of the day and the isolation of night.

He'd have to call Sara for an update. Did they have the asshole who shot him yet? They'd pronounced him dead, or at least, the him everyone but the select few knew. In all likelihood, no one was looking for him, but he just couldn't let it go. Something didn't smell right about the whole thing.

Young's brother had known exactly where and when to find him. Had been waiting. Couldn't have trailed him to the flat, as the shooter was in perfect position across the street seconds after he'd walked in the door. If he'd been one flat up or over, they wouldn't have been able to make such an accurate shot.

His covers had been blown thanks to the intel Young had gleaned, but that had been a newer identity. Where had Young's brother, Connor, obtained that information?

Payson stirred, breaking him from the painful mind games he'd tortured himself with since he'd first woken from the attempt on his life. "Can't we just stay here forever? This place is ridiculously relaxing." Her eyes still closed, her voice sleepy as she snuggled closer, which he hadn't realized was possible with how tightly she'd clung to him already.

Gently brushing her hair out of her face, he smiled softly, "I can't say I would object to that. Might get a bit pricey though. And I'm not sure either of us could do nothing forever."

"Good point." She un-clung and rolled off him, heading into the bathroom.

Watching her walk away, his heart did a little lurch. Fuck. Didn't matter what he did, he was going to screw this up. It wouldn't take her much longer to figure out his history and be furious with him for the lies. Not that he was trying very hard to keep it from her.

She wasn't likely to forgive him if he got pulled back out on a mission. He'd promised Sara he was willing to go in for one last op if it meant tracking down those damn weapons. Worse, he still didn't trust that the Young brothers wouldn't track him down eventually.

If they did, would he be able leave and never come back - if it came down to that? If it meant keeping her safe, he'd have to.

Even if they didn't, and he was just being paranoid, what the hell was he going to do with himself? He was enjoying working around Payson's shop, but he couldn't do that forever, could he?

Trailing after Payson, he stood outside the shower and watched her for a few minutes. Watched the shampoo suds slowly pouring down her body, accentuating her curves on the way down. Stripping down, he stepped in and grabbed the soap.

Gently, lovingly, he ran the soap over her body. He felt her eyes on him, studying his face. Certainly, she was reading his sadness, his regret that he let this get so far, when he'd surely fuck it up somehow.

Slippery, warm hands caressed every curve, lingering in her most sensitive places. With an easy smile, she giggled as Ronan spent extra time ensuring her breasts were squeaky clean. "I think you got that spot already," she teased.

Moving behind her, he set the soap back on the tray and let his hands continue the work. His mouth trailed along her wet shoulder, while his hands continued to stroke, slowly working their way down. Payson felt his solemn mood, regretting that their retreat was ending. Fearing life would go back to the way it was.

Gripping her backside tightly against him, the steam creating a hazy mist around her, he stroked her core until she cried out, riding the crest of the wave that overtook her. Turning her abruptly, he lifted and pressed her back against the warmed tile of the shower wall and drove into her, greedy, reckless, obsessed. His solemn, heated passion propelled them both to aching release.

Melded in a petrified embrace, the warm water poured over their joined, sated bodies. Payson couldn't move if she wanted to. Her heart slowly steadied, beating synchronously with Ronan's.

Tears welled in her eyes, but she refused to let him see. After all her talk of love and soulmates, she had no idea the pain it could cause, the deep-seated desperation. The knowing that she would never be the same. Fearing he would disappear.

She'd stumbled upon him in such a dark, distant place in his mind so many times. Was he ready to stay with her? If not, she hated to give up her life in Seaview, but she felt deep inside, her heart was now completely his and she would follow him anywhere.

Her mind flashed to her sister. No wonder she was so torn; she had everything she wanted or needed in Boston, but to keep her love, she'd have to give it all up. Payson knew in that moment, she'd give it all up for Ronan, but hated that she might have to.

Worse, she feared that he wouldn't ask her to.

Things were sedate at the breakfast table, everyone sad to leave such a tranquil setting. They ate in silence, sipping coffee slowly, watching the calm sea and receding clouds.

Frank broke the silence after they'd all finished their breakfasts, "I checked on the boat this morning. No damage, but we'll need to remove quite a bit of snow before we can move out. Chase, you mind helping me with the boat? Aiden, you're on shoveling snow, and the rest of you haul all of our gear down to the dock?"

Aiden frowned, "Why am I shoveling snow and Chase and Ronan get the easy jobs? Why does Ronan get to help with the bags?"

Frank shook his head, "Because you're the only one of the young guys here that hasn't been in physical therapy for a shoulder injury in the past year; not that Maddy or Payson couldn't shovel just fine, but I'm not picturing either of them letting either of you do the packing?"

Maddy fervently agreed, "I trust Chase wholeheartedly… but he's not touching my clothes."

Payson nodded, "I'm sure you're a great packer Aiden, but you're not touching my underwear."

21

Ronan sighed and put down the paintbrush, stepping back to admire his work. The last week had been intense, but incredible. Spending a few days sequestered with his family and Payson had been therapeutic.

He'd spent every night with Payson since they'd returned home. Mostly at her place, but the other night she'd come over to his place to break in the huge bathtub. That was one for the record books.

She knew his story didn't jibe; his fault, he could have worked harder to maintain his computer programmer cover. Part of him wanted her to know exactly who he was, but he couldn't say it yet. For her, for him, for the secrets he held, he wouldn't yet. She'd stopped pushing him on it. For now.

Shelving fully installed and sanded, he finished the last sweep of the stain coating the slick new shelves. He'd even added drawers, shelves, and work stools for use at the sturdy new table. Payson had picked out an elegant dark stain that made the back room much statelier than the flimsy plastic shelving with hazardous boxes scattered across the floors of the non-public areas.

Part of him didn't want the job to be done, didn't want to not see her every day. He'd still help Payson with deliveries and around the shop when she needed him, but she was still looking for a permanent shop assistant. He dragged out the work as best he could.

After finishing a barrage of back-to-back sales, Payson snuck back for a peek at his progress. "This looks spectacular. I can't believe you're almost finished. It's better than I could have imagined," she twirled around the room, her dress swishing with her exaggerated movements.

"Once the stain is completely set, we can fill the shelves; I've got some ideas on that." Feeling self-conscious with the attention, but basking in her glowing praise, he didn't know how to respond. He settled for standing in one place looking stupid, hand nervously rubbing the back of his neck.

She paced towards him and stole a quick kiss, avoiding letting any of the stain get onto her clothes. The bell jingled again, and she laughed. "Busy day. I better get back up there." He watched her dash back up to the front and greet the latest customer in her cheery way.

A smile spread across his face as he heard Payson finally finish up with the latest customers; a cluster of sisters that had been perusing the jewelry section. Sounds like they'd each purchased a few items, making up for the loss of sales during the storm. Snow still lingered around town, but folks from the northeast were getting out and exploring now that the roads were passable.

A few moments later, the door chimed again. He immediately recognized the grating voice of her sister, Jen. Listening in, he paused his work and moved so he could watch the scene unfold from a safe distance. "I'm sorry to drop in on you unannounced again."

He heard her polite tone as she greeted her sister. "Hey, Jen. Everything ok? Did you and Tony have a good talk?"

Flustered, Jen tossed her heavy purse and winter coat with a thud onto the counter, knocking over the stack of magazines Payson had been planning to use for brainstorming décor ideas when the shop was slower. "We did. I came to tell you in person that we're moving to Denver," she dramatically sighed, quite the martyr.

Ronan rolled his eyes. Thank goodness Payson took things in stride by comparison.

Payson's voice was a blend of congratulations and disappointment; whether she was being genuine or not, she was a talented actress. Handy if she ever decided to become a spy. "I'm so glad you two worked things out. Do you feel good about the decision? Did Tony hear your concerns?"

Bubbling excessively, Jen responded, "Yes, of course. There are plenty of museums I can apply at in Denver. And, with his raise, I won't even need to work right away."

He could almost picture Payson's sweet disposition, supportively nodding as her sister spoke.

Jen continued, "The real reason I'm here is that I want to apologize for the last time I was here. You shouldn't rush into anything. I think it's great you're not settling for anything less than your soulmate. Why don't you move out with us? See if you have any better luck in Denver. Cara's thinking of making the move when she graduates in a few years."

Payson refused as politely as possible, "That is so kind of you. I'll pass, I-"

Persisting, Jen couldn't be stopped. "There are a lot of single guys in Denver. I met a few of Tony's new colleagues. Several that would be perfect for you: successful, good incomes, steady jobs. I'm sure they would love... old stuff, like you do."

Wow, she was a real treasure. Did Jen know her sister at all?

Payson was trying to stay calm. Jen was looking at her sister with such condescension. She continued, not letting Payson speak for herself. "We'll have you happily matched with one of Tony's investor friends in no time I'm sure, married with beautiful children and settled in a nice house. I'm sure we can relocate your shop without difficulty."

"Jen, stop, please. I'm not going anywhere. I'm happy in Seaview. I like where I am." Payson maintained a friendly disposition, but was clearly strained, trying to maintain a sense of calm.

Before Jen could interrupt, Payson continued, "I don't want to marry an investor and settle in a perfect house in a perfect neighborhood. I want marriage and kids, but I'm not in any rush. Besides... I'm actually seeing someone here in Seaview."

Jen rolled her eyes, arms folded and head shaking like a mother scolding her young child, "Come on, Payson, in this tiny fishing town? Who is he - the barista from the coffee shop across the street?" She was laughing mockingly as she listed the local possibilities that she clearly thought to be quite paltry. "A bartender? A fisherman?" On a roll, she was shocking herself with her own creativity, she dug lower, "Your grubby handyman?"

Nearly in tears enjoying himself, Ronan couldn't take it anymore. Remembering a cover he'd used a few years back, he pulled off his t-shirt and tucked it into the waistband of his jeans. He splashed some water in his hair and rubbed it all over to appear sweaty and like he'd been exerting himself.

Strutting out from the back room, he interrupted Jen's ridicule of him. "Pace, I just finished those shelves you needed done. If you don't mind, the ladies' club needs me to come in a little early today. I have a new routine I've been working on if you want to help me fine tune it, maybe later tonight?"

Enjoying Jen's look of total astonishment, he went for the gold. He walked up to Payson and grabbed her by the ass, pulling her pelvis against his as he leaned in for a steamy, erotic kiss, his tongue halfway down her throat until her brain was completely wiped of everything but him. Leaving both women speechless, he turned and strutted right out the back door.

Finding her words, Jen finally managed to speak. "Payson, was that..."

Payson threw her head back in sparkling laughter. "Yes, that's Ronan. My grubby handyman who's name you couldn't even remember." Done placating her sister, Payson enjoyed Ronan's interruption more than she could say. "That's the man I'm seeing. No, he's not what you would have picked out for me. He's so much better."

Jen wasn't letting it go. Setting her arm on her sister's, she shook her head patronizingly. "Sis, I understand you need a rebound. I thought you were past the rebound point from Clive, but if you need more time, I get it."

"I will miss you so much. I love you, Jen. Thanks for always wanting the best for me. Trust me when I say, I've found it. Let's promise to make it out to see each other a few times a year. I'll still call the kids every week, ok? But, please. Let me choose my own dates. I want Ronan, in whatever form that comes."

Pulling her sister in for a hug, Payson said goodbye and sent her flabbergasted sister on her way.

Ronan made his way back into the shop an hour later, carrying bags of takeout for both he and Payson. "You closing up soon? I grabbed fish and chips from next door. Meet you upstairs in five?"

She closed up shop for the night and dashed up the stairs, not sure if she wanted to knock his block off or kiss him for shocking her un-flappable sister. Walking into her apartment, he took her breath away yet again. He'd decked the place out for a romantic living room picnic. He had their fish and chips cleverly plated, beers poured, candles lit on the coffee table, and fire blazing.

"So... stripper, huh? Guess they didn't need you to work tonight after all?" She teased as she sat down at the charming picnic. Tearing into the fresh fish, she dunked the delectably breaded cod in tartar and finished the first piece before he had time to answer.

"Sorry about that. I just couldn't resist." He grinned, quite pleased with his cleverness.

Shaking her head, Payson sipped her hoppy brew and watched Ronan's very poor apology. "You're not a bit sorry, and she totally deserved it."

Reaching across the plaid blanket to wipe a smear of tartar from the corner of her mouth, Ronan licked the tartar off his finger. "Yeah, she deserved it. Did you say anything?"

Enjoying the image of her sister's complete and utter shock, Payson shook her head. "Nope. If you decide you want to become a stripper, you go right ahead. You certainly had the look down."

Swallowing the handful of salty fries he'd skillfully eaten in one bite, Ronan raised his eyebrows suggestively, "I think I might enjoy that. Want to see my routine? I wasn't kidding about that."

Playfully, Payson egged him on as she gulped her beer. "Really? I would be truly impressed. What can't you do? You have a knack for carpentry, play some serious baseball, are adept at video games.

You kicked my ass at laser tag, which is no easy feat. You speak fluent French, fill out a tuxedo even better than James Bond... I think I've finally found Mr. Perfect."

Switching to Russian and then into Farsi, which he spoke as easily as French or English, he whispered his intentions for tonight in her ear, or at least, that's what she thought he was saying.

"I know you can't, or won't say, but you're so much more than you claim. I'll have to accept that you're a mystery, because I'm keeping you... whatever the story may be."

Ronan sighed, realizing the time was now. Finally. He was desperate to tell her everything. Why was he stalling at telling her the truth? He felt like a nervous teenager about to ask the hottest girl in school to the prom.

Focusing on his beer, he stared into the amber liquid, hoping to find his courage. With a sigh, he began, "You're right. I'm not a computer programmer. I am pretty decent with computers, have to be in my line of work. But that's not my area of expertise."

She raised her eyebrows, mouth open to speak, but stayed silent, waiting for him to continue. Finally, he answered the questions she'd asked him forever ago. "I got the burn rushing into a building to ascertain the location of an enemy base so we could send in a SEAL team; they had discovered we were on to them and set the place on fire.

"The knife wound was a gift from a young boy that I pulled out of a gunfight in Afghanistan, not out of the goodness of my heart, but he had critical information, and my mission was to get him out of the area unharmed and without his people knowing."

"And the gunshot wounds?" Sitting still, as if afraid the slightest interruption would halt his story, she whispered her question.

Reverting to his professional demeanor, he found the courage to tell her his story, more than the truncated version he'd told his parents. His voice cold as ice, calm, collected as he told his story. "Those were more recent; the reason I came home. Why I was pronounced retired. Disabled."

Her gaze travelled down, seeking to learn more about the scars hidden under his shirt. So far, she hadn't rejected him. Vulnerable, he loosened his obstinate grip on his composure; let her see his raw emotions. She deserved to see him, as he was. No more holding back, especially with Payson.

"Fucking ridiculous if you ask me. Others have sustained injuries far worse than mine." Pausing, deeply absorbed in his internal conflict, his gaze was lost in the fire.

"Who do you work for? What is it that you do?" Her words drew him back to the present.

"I worked as an operative, as a spy, for the CIA for nearly 10 years." He gaged her for a reaction.

Staring at him, expression a blend of disbelief and I-knew-it-all-along, she succumbed to a satisfied smile. She struggled to find the right words. Each time she tried, she'd shake her head again and let an adorable laugh slip.

Finally, she sighed, "How smug did you feel when I shared my little James Bond fantasy with you?"

His devilish grin returning, enjoying the return of her open smile and humor, he teased, "I'm surprised you remember. You were pretty drunk at the time. Let's just say when you threw yourself at me a few minutes later, I thought you'd figured it out."

Face turning serious now, he admitted, "I wanted to tell you sooner, truly. Hell, I fell in love with you as soon as I saw you pompously wiggling that ass, then slamming the baseball right out of the park."

Face distorted with inner struggle, she looked like she wanted to say something. Or, at least, he wished she'd say something. Tell him she loved him too. That she was never letting him go. Not today; she wasn't ready yet. He'd dropped a hell of a bombshell.

Even he knew she'd been desperately searching for love for years. Dating for quantity rather than quality until she found *the one*. With Clive, she'd been mistaken, having settled for Mr. Nearly-Perfect.

Hell, her sister was so damn pushy and judgmental about the whole ordeal, it was a miracle Payson had given him the time of day. He could be patient, knowing she'd tell him when she was ready. When she was sure of her feelings.

Instead, she asked, "So, how did you wind up working for the CIA?"

"I'd wanted to join since I hit puberty. Worked my ass off to be the perfect candidate. I was recruited right out of college... well, not exactly recruited, that's just the official story," he laughed, enjoying the moment. Telling her the whole story was so much more gratifying than he could have imagined.

"I was actually lucky I wasn't arrested on the spot. Not yet 20 and a sophomore in college, I made my way into Langley under the guise of a school research project. While I was there, I, uh," he smiled as he reflected on the memory. "I made it into a restricted area. Found the highest-ranking person I could find."

"Does anything ever get in your way? Of getting what you want?" Payson was smirking now, teasing. She inched closer until their bodies touched.

"I wish. I got lucky; I found Sara before the guards arrested me. She took one look at me and knew what I was up to. Without hesitation, she offered me a job right on the spot. I hadn't even needed the puffed-up resume I'd brought, highlighting my studies on international affairs, fluency in French, Italian, and Spanish, budding conversational Russian. Since, I've developed passable Farsi and Arabic. I was active in sports, as you know; physical training an hour or more every day.

"Anyway, I was more than prepared for anything the CIA may throw at me. I was good at it. Damn good." He sighed, looking into the flames again. "Until now."

"What changed?" she set down her beer next to the last of the fries she'd been nibbling at. She cracked a helpful half-smile, "Aside from getting shot, of course. You sound like you were changing your mind before you got shot."

"I'm done with the fucking politics. The lies."

"Well, I can't say I am sorry that you're back to being a member of the civilian world. But, are you ok with it?"

Gaze still lost in the fire, he watched the dancing yellow, orange, red, and blue flames licking the fireplace grate. Not consciously aware, but grateful, he appreciated that she stayed snuggled up against him. "Hell yeah I miss the action, the intrigue. But more than anything, I'm done being someone else's patsy."

Payson gently angled him by the chin and turned his face until they were nearly nose-to-nose. She kissed him softly, releasing him from his impending wallow. "I'll bet you have some great stories. Maybe you could give Tom Clancy a run for his money?"

Smiling, kissing her in return, he reveled in the confidence she placed in him. "Actually, that's a great idea. Long ago, well before I joined, I was a writer, photographer, baseball player... recreationally. Maybe I ought to re-visit some of those dreams."

Playfully, she pulled her dress over her head and tossed it aside. Becoming the aggressor, wantonly, she climbed atop him and had her way with him. He didn't mind one bit.

22

HOURS LATER, THE SUN began to rise, shining down on their snuggled bodies through the vast window overlooking Beachfront Avenue and the Atlantic. Hinting at a beautiful day, the sun wasn't holding back. Blinking to adjust to the sudden brightness, it took Payson a moment to remember where she was. Sometime during the night, Ronan had grabbed pillows and blankets, as they'd fallen asleep in front of the fire.

Pleasantly, deliciously, she reflected on last night. She couldn't help but feel grateful that he had told her the truth, but she was terrified that he was so much more than he'd initially let on. So much more to his past than she could have imagined.

She'd always had her little spy fantasy but had always known the real thing was not known to be reliable to those left behind. James Bond was one sexy image, but even in fiction it was clear he couldn't keep a woman to save his life. Jack Ryan somehow maintained a marriage, but it couldn't be easy on his wife and daughter.

When Ronan had let it slip that he loved her, she was ecstatic. An hour prior, she would have danced with joy and professed her own love to the rooftops. After hearing his history, she was terrified. Of losing him, of him moving on and leaving her in the dust.

Yeah, he was retired, but his life had been in the intelligence world for a decade, and it had been his dream for a decade before that. How could she compete with that?

Her phone chirped and interrupted their peaceful wakening. She almost ignored the ringing, enjoying his possessive grip on her. Foolishly, she dashed into the open kitchen to answer the damn phone. Their relationship was tenuous enough at the moment. Had she realized the consequences of the brief conversation, she wouldn't have answered.

Ronan begrudgingly released his grip as Payson ran to the kitchen to answer her cell phone. He thought she had been ready to know everything, but now he wasn't so sure.

She'd withdrawn into a bleak shell when he confessed his love for her. Subtly, as he'd been too chickenshit to tell her the complete truth. That he'd fallen completely, fantastically in love with her. That he needed her heart in return.

"*Bonjour*, Alain," her perky voice answered in that horrific French accent. His ears perked up. He wasn't jealous or anything, of course not, but he couldn't say he enjoyed hearing her so happy to talk to some French guy.

He listened in to her side of the conversation, but she was too far away for him to hear the other end. "You know, I think I could make that work. Uh-huh... uh-huh... If I fly out on the 10th, I could spend a few days exploring then make my way to the vineyard on the 15th? Is there an inn you can recommend while I'm in town?... Oh no, I couldn't possibly impose... well, if you are accustomed to taking guests...

"Thanks, really. I'll let you know more once I've booked my ticket. I'm not sure if it will be just me yet, or if Ronan will be able to make it. I'll let you know as soon as I do."

Hanging up, Payson waited in the kitchen for a few. Clearly restless, not sure how to ask him, she set to work making coffee. Ronan desperately wanted to say yes. He couldn't do it, not when he'd come so far in feeling normal again.

Finally, after what seemed like an eternity, Payson hung up and turned to him, face lit up in good humor. She smiled shyly at him from across the room, hesitant to speak. Finally, she bit the bullet, "Ronan, I know you're going to say no, and you can say no, but... I was wondering... I spoke with one of my main suppliers in Europe. Alain; I've worked with him for a few years now. More of a friend anymore, we work together so often. He has been trying to get me to fly out there for years, and I'm finally planning to fly over to go through some heirlooms he has set aside for me.

"I've never been to France and was thinking it would be a fun trip... Anyway, you don't have to come, but if you wanted to think about it?" She babbled nervously, avoiding eye contact with him as she fussed with the coffee pot.

He couldn't say how much he wanted to go with her. Wanted to do just about anything with and for her. This... this was more than he could handle. "I would do anything for you, but I just can't make the trip right now. I'm not... ready to go back over."

"Okay, I get it," she nodded, forced a smile, and became quite engrossed in fixing the newly temperamental coffee pot.

Shit, he'd totally blown it. Hated to see her so upset; she was so optimistic about life in general, she never let anything get her down. Seeing her disappointment was unbearable.

He stalked closer to her and brushed a stray lock of hair from her face. "I don't think you do. I'm ready for you, for us. If it were Canada, Mexico, or even, heaven forbid, visiting your sister in Denver, I would be there with you in a heartbeat."

She nodded again, her eyes understanding, her broken heart mirroring his own, "Really, I do get it. It's ok."

Overwhelmed, feeling the need to travel with Payson for fun, but more strongly, feeling phobic about her traveling so far without him, Ronan suddenly had an overwhelming urge to check in with Sara.

She needed to open the shop, and he needed to get the fuck out of there before he lost his shit. Before he changed his mind and then had an outright panic attack at the prospect of using a passport under his own identity, which he'd never done. That was maybe more terrifying than actually crossing the big blue ocean.

"I've got to head home. Do some laundry, dishes, that sort of thing."

Settling on her stool at the kitchen island, Payson nodded. "That's fine. I should get ready for the day anyway."

Feeling unsettled, Ronan stood behind her at the kitchen island. He lingered for a moment, both of them looking at anything but each other. Finally, he rested his chin on her head. He kissed the top of her head softly, pensively.

Leaving her sitting quietly, brooding on her stool, Ronan left and drove home... feeling more alone than he had in decades. Too worn out, despite the fact that the sun had yet to fully rise. He avoided parking the huge pick-up in the narrow space in the garage for the effort it took; he parked in the driveway and trudged in through the front door. He dragged his weary limbs into his rental and slammed the door with miserable finality.

As was his habit, he leaned down to check his odd, paranoid fishing line alarm. For the first time ever, the trap was loose, disturbed. Had he remembered to set it when he last was here? Of course he had; he *never* forgot.

Someone was in his house. Or had been in his house. No one but Chase had the key; that had been very intentional. His family wouldn't have entered without talking to him first anyway. Staying crouched down as he stopped to listen, he craned his ears, ready to detect even the slightest sound.

Nothing.

Making long, silent strides, Ronan checked each room, every potential hiding spot. Checking for any signs of activity. The rest of the house looked untouched. No one was here now; he was sure of it. Still, he swept the house.

Another hour passed, his stomach rumbling. His latest drop phone—not that he needed it in any official capacity—remained in its hiding spot under the bedside table. He continued sweeping for bugs, cameras... anything out of place.

Finally, he got lucky. Rather, unlucky, he supposed. A tiny bug, audio only, was hidden behind his bedroom headboard. High end, top of the line. The intruder was no amateur, that was for sure.

Studying the device, it looked like one he had used before, but more streamlined. He took some detailed photos of it and texted the images to Sara via his drop phone, with a brief message: *Someone was in my house.*

Securing the place as best he could, he stuffed in a quick lunch and a shower, then climbed in bed to get some necessary shuteye before making his next move. He'd be on the run in a few hours, once he had some usable intel from Sara.

Late that night, Ronan's phone rang in its chipper tune, waking him from restless sleep. Not his regular cell, but the drop phone he'd texted Sara from. About time. Hopefully she knew something about the device.

Feeling cold, body and voice stiff, he numbed his emotions as he morphed back into the professional agent, "I'm here."

Sara's voice resonated through the phone, skipping the small talk, "The timing of your text couldn't have been better; I was in a meeting."

"Where are you? It's well past midnight." Ronan rubbed his eyes, just making out the glowing green time on the clock.

"I'm at Langley; it was that bad of a meeting. The bug is ours. Brand new, just approved for use by our field agents. I'm impressed you found it; it's tiny and not detectable by any traditional locators."

Swinging his legs over the side of the bed, Ronan leaned forward and rested his elbows on his knees. He ran his hand through his hair, hating where the conversation was going. "I was trained by the best."

She let out a soft chuckle, "That's sweet, but I'm too tired for flattery." Her voice trailed off; he could hear the poorly masked weariness in Sara's voice on the other end. "The meeting was about you, in a way. Rose is dead. She wasn't even on an op when she was killed. Three shots to the head."

"Someone was making a bold statement. Why? What did she know?" Images of Rose flashed in his mind. He hadn't known her that well, despite working together a number of times over the past few years.

Still, her death was a huge blow to the agency. He hated to think of losing a good agent; someone he'd relied on. She was damn smart; she wouldn't have been easy to take down.

"I couldn't say for sure, but with the timing, I'm willing to guess it boils down to those weapons. She must have known something... or knew how to get to you."

Ronan rubbed his non-existent beard, momentarily forgetting he no longer had the massive thing. "Peter Young was already sentenced, and the weapons were never found. CIA had moved on, case cold, Connor Young unfindable. At least, that's what Sharpe had implied."

Sara sounded equally exasperated. "Sharpe was here tonight; he was completely flabbergasted about the latest developments. He's convinced we have a mole. That one of our own hid the biologics and killed Rose. Sharpe wants the weapons, and fears that Connor Young will be wanting his money."

Seething, Ronan responded, "Now there's a mole and a merc after me. Fun times. And here I thought retirement might be relaxing, boring even."

Sara went silent for a moment. "There's more. The mole... they think it's you. Peter Young finally accepted a deal when we threatened extradition to Syria. Said you hid the weapons and faked your own death to escape further investigation."

"Fuck. That story's pretty thin. Is anyone buying that shit?" Ronan rubbed his hip, his wounds suddenly aching just thinking about Connor Young.

"Sharpe is; swears by his interrogation. Others aren't so sure. They're blaming Connor for taking out Rose and bugging you with bugs he stole from her. That he's after you to get to the weapons. Sharpe is pushing that you must know where the weapons are, as he can't find them, and he has his best spooks on it."

"Bullshit-" Ronan stood and paced, working out the knot forming in his aching hip.

"I don't buy it either, and I'm not the only one. You have an impeccable record, better than Sharpe's or Rose's. This isn't over yet. The fact that anyone believes this bullshit tells me they're desperate... or it's more than just a mole."

"Conspiracy? That's a pretty big word."

"And this is a pretty big mess."

"How did they find me?" On full alert, Ronan was already packing his bag, ready to get out. Quickly.

"Honestly... I'm not sure. Your file was sealed, and we'd ensured few knew your real identity. But, as you're now being paid out of the disability banks... your name would have popped up on new payroll reports. Depending on how high up this goes... someone could have connected you to Max Kennedy. I want you out of there. Now."

Fuck. He hadn't wanted to retire in the first place. But here he was, starting to enjoy feeling normal for the first time in well over a decade, since before he even joined the CIA. Now he was on the run again.

Sara's voice went soft on the other end, "Keep your nose clean. You're at the top of a very short list as the likely mole. Hidden weapons, dead agent... they won't be lenient. I'll have a new ID, phone, and flight information waiting for you at JFK in 12 hours."

"Aren't you going to be in trouble for helping me?" He was already tying his shoes and making for the front door.

"When this is all sorted out, and the real mole is caught, I am sure you'll receive a nice fat apology. I'm not worried about me; I've been in this business long enough. I have my own retirement planned. Far from prying eyes and ears." She sounded almost to be smiling.

As always, Ronan was grateful for his mentor saving his ass, again. "You be careful."

"Talk to you soon." She disconnected.

He had nothing more to offer the intelligence world. He was now a nobody. Didn't make a lick of sense.

Someone was looking for a scapegoat - the real mole. He had a hunch who that may be. Sara was right, he needed to get out of here. Whoever bugged him clearly didn't want to kill him, or he'd be dead already.

If they were waiting on him to reveal the locations of the weapons, who hid them in the first place? The Youngs would have lost a boatload of money on the deal of their careers.

Would the mole have hidden the weapons? Why? Was he trying to make a quick buck, or did he have other plans? How high up did this go?

Finally feeling settled, a part of something genuine, he hated to go. If he stayed, he put all of that in jeopardy. If he left now, he could draw the danger away from his family, away from Payson. He wasn't coming home until he'd sorted it out, no matter how long it took.

Deep in his chest, a clutching, gripping ache radiated outwards. This is why he didn't form attachments. Why he'd maintained such distance from his family all these years. Leaving was so much more difficult now. Leaving his heart behind, he hopped in his truck and drove away.

23

At two minutes to eight on Monday morning, Payson locked up her front door and headed down the stairs. Huh. No Ronan.

Straining her ears for the sound of Ronan's truck rumbling down the road, she tried to reason it through. Of course he wasn't here when he usually was, the stain was still drying. Nothing for him to do.

They hadn't parted on the best of terms, but they were still good, weren't they? They hadn't spoken since he'd sprinted out of there. He would have called if he wasn't coming in.

Hands full, she set down the coffee she had brewed for him on the back step and unlocked the shop. The shelves looked truly amazing. Still tacky, she didn't risk touching the recently finished wood yet. Starkly contrasting the rich stain of her new table, a crisp white note with her name written across the front laid on the darkly stained surface.

Payson,

I'm sorry to leave without saying goodbye. There was
an emergency with my old job, which has pulled me
away unexpectedly. I cannot say when, or even if, I
will be able to return. You and my family are not safe
if I stay. Please know that I have every intention of
returning to you, I want that more than anything. I
was nothing before you brought me back to life.

—Ronan

What the hell was that? Why? Where? This note says nothing.

She picked up the phone and called Maddy. Hopefully he'd told his sister more. Nothing, no answer. Payson recalled Maddy had been on patrol last night and was likely just getting home.

Next, she called Laura, who answered, fortunately. "I'm assuming you heard. He left a note for us, too." Laura's gentle voice lulled like a mournful lullaby through the phone.

Breath coming fast, frantic, she jabbered away, "I don't understand. He was retired, what could possibly have pulled him away without warning? When I spoke to him last, he didn't mention anything." Payson tried to hide the freak-out tremor in her voice, but she just couldn't process, couldn't grasp what was happening.

Voice breaking, Laura couldn't hold back her sadness either. "I am truly surprised, but his work has always been... critical. He wouldn't have left without a really good reason. I'm sure he'll get word to us when he can." She sounded as heartbroken as Payson felt.

"You'll let me know if you hear from him?" Desperately, Payson clung to any hope of contact. In the years he was gone from Seaview, his family had been used to his mysteriousness. Of his lack of contact for months at a time. Of him staying far away.

"Of course. You do the same." The women agreed to keep each other in the loop. Payson hung up feeling even more hopeless.

Numb, she managed to head to the front of the store and open up shop for the day. The second he'd mentioned what he did for a living, she knew he was going to leave. Knew his work was too important to stick around this quiet town. A man like him wasn't going to sit and work in a shop for a living. Or write, coach baseball, or become a damn carpenter.

Going through the motions of the day, she flew on autopilot. If she stopped moving, let herself start thinking, she knew she would crumble. That's what she gets for falling in love. Reckless sport this love business was. No wonder Aiden was so against it.

By closing time, Maddy appeared at her door, dressed in her uniform and seemingly ready for another night at work. Without even saying hello, she flipped the sign to closed, locked the door and insisted, "Ronan's coming back."

Payson couldn't tell who her friend was trying to reassure. "Is he? He's not coming back to this tiny town, to work as my handyman and shop-boy." Payson barely managed to hold back the tears she'd been keeping at bay since morning.

"He's just finishing up one last project that he was working on before... before the accident. He'll be back soon." Payson appreciated her friend's attempt, but she didn't sound convinced.

"He told me everything. I know he was shot in his last mission and nearly died."

Maddy walked her to the back door and helped her lock up. She noted the mug of cold coffee still outside the door. Silently, knowingly, Maddy picked it up and dumped out the coffee. She gently set the mug in Payson's hands and watched as her friend walked up the stairs. At Payson's request, she didn't follow her up or stick around to talk about it.

She needed to be alone. Would be alone for the rest of her life, might as well get started. After Ronan...

She couldn't even finish her thought. Dragging her feet up the stairs, she unlocked the door and neatly set the mugs in the kitchen sink. Steady, she walked the last few paces to her bedroom before throwing herself on her bed.

After the face plant, she finally released the tears, the emotion she had been holding back all day. Gut wrenching sobs echoed through the room. She cried until there were no more tears, heart so broken she couldn't feel anything.

Even if he came back, how could she trust he wouldn't disappear again? Stupid, stupid, Payson. Why did she have to go and fall in love with an actual spy? She knew better than anyone what a foolish idea that was.

Hours, maybe days later, daylight streamed through Payson's windows. She glanced at her phone, foolishly hopeful. Nothing. Not a word from Ronan. She sent a group text to the McAllisters, but none of his family had heard from him either.

Another day went by, and then another. She continued to make herself go through the motions of living but couldn't find the joy she normally did. Couldn't find the optimism in the face of adversity that she prided herself on.

Rolling out of bed on day ten of no-Ronan, she was startled by the loud buzzing. Her doorbell rang once, twice. The invader put a key in the lock and started rustling in the kitchen. Humming too.

Tossing on her bathrobe, she shuffled across the apartment to the kitchen. A white bag from the coffee shop across the street sat on her kitchen island, a tall coffee cup at the side. Cara, her younger sister, stood in the kitchen, still humming as she tidied up the mess Payson had made when she decided to binge eat last night. Her appetite was touch and go lately.

Cara acknowledged her finally. "Good morning, sleepyhead. Maddy assured me you might perk up a bit if I brought you muffins and a mocha from next door."

Payson eyed her sister suspiciously. "How did you know?" She struggled to open the bag, suddenly starving, but her hands were shaking too badly to open the bag without tearing it. Instead, she sat at the bar stool and put her hands in her lap to hide her emotion.

"I'd love to say I was coming to see you anyway, or that it was a sister's intuition, but we'd both know that's a bunch of bull." Clanking and scrubbing dishes from the binge dinner the night before, Cara sighed. "Maddy called me. Said she was worried about you. Broken heart."

Biting her lower lip to fight the tears that threatened yet again, Payson looked at her younger sister. "I'm sorry I didn't call you myself. I guess I'm just used you being the one that needs me, of the lost little girl that needs protection from anything serious."

Scrubbing the already clean saucepan, Cara continued her cleaning binge. Payson almost laughed at how alike they were. Cara didn't have her auburn hair, but she had her cope-by-cleaning habit - made a bit crazy looking by the intense green eyes.

"I know, and I understand. Whenever you get scared, you pull away. You love it in Seaview, I get that, but I know you also love having your own space." She paused, the warm water tinkling against the empty glass bowl she just washed. Inhaling deeply, she dove into the dirty pan that needed a good cleaning, coating it with too much soap. "I never made it easy on you."

"You were barely eight when our parents died, and I was practically an adult. I should have pulled it together for you."

Realizing the pan was starting to lose its finish from her over-scrubbing, Cara set it into the drying rack and dried her hands. Leaning against the counter, she swallowed the lump in her throat. "You did. It took you a while, but you did. But, unlike Jen, you gave me space when I needed it, but also kicked my ass when I needed it. Emotionally of course; you could never physically kick my ass." The corner of her mouth turned up in her weak attempt at humor before continuing. "Once you got it together, you filled in Dad's role where Jen filled in Mom's."

Chuckling at her sister's competitive spirit, she let herself enjoy that she had something in common with at least one of her sisters. Although, Cara at least had a sense of humor about it. "When did you get so... sensible?" Relaxing, she broke a piece off her muffin and enjoyed the warm, buttery carbs.

"No idea, but I'm hoping to take care of you for once. What happened? Maddy only told me her brother broke your heart. According to Jen, you're having a fling with some gorgeous stud that might be a stripper?"

Payson nearly choked on her muffin. Almost forgetting she was mad at Ronan, remembering how he'd come to her rescue quite creatively. "That was Ronan messing with her. He's quite normal, but Jen was being her usual overbearing self, insisting I should be compromising and settling down with someone rich and willing to procreate immediately."

"That sounds like Jen. She was thrilled when I broke up with Andrew. A professional snowboarder was not quite what she had in mind for me. Tell me about Ronan."

Payson swallowed a bite of her muffin and fought the threatening tears again. "He's everything I never knew I wanted. Has an ego bigger than mine, a devilish smile that makes me weak in the knees, and an incredible work ethic."

Pausing, she debated how much she could tell her sister. "Which is the problem. He worked overseas until recently, and something came up and he got called back to work suddenly. Even he isn't sure when or if he will be able to return, depends on how this project goes, I guess."

Cara stole her last, lonely bite of muffin from the paper wrapping. "This is really good; I should have gotten myself one."

Payson scowled at her. The distraction helped.

Eyebrows crunched as she swallowed the bite, she shook her head sadly. "I'm so sorry about Ronan... I'm staying here, but you're not."

Confused, Payson frowned at her sister. "And where am I going?"

"You've been talking about taking Alain up on his offer to visit him in France for forever now. Give him a call, get out of town. Natalie is on her way over to open up the shop so she can show me the ropes, and I'm going to stay here and run the shop while you're away."

"You can't be away from school."

"I'm actually done collecting data and need a quiet space to work on my dissertation. I have nearly two weeks until I need to get back and I brought my laptop. Besides, I'll get a lot more done here than if I stayed home with my chatty roommate."

Payson shook her head, fighting the threatening tears, "Thanks, but I think it's better if I stay here. What if he-"

Cara walked around the kitchen island and pulled her in for a hug. "What's better..." she applied her bossy voice that rivaled Jen's, but the loving smile was much better, "is that you distract yourself so you don't wear down to nothing, wondering when or if he'll return. Remember when Mom and Dad died, you dove into adventure in Ireland and somehow came back stronger than before? Go get dressed, and I'll start searching for a flight for you. You may not have realized, but you and I are a lot alike. Trust me, you'll be glad you went."

She shoved the untouched coffee at Payson and turned her toward the bedroom. Relenting with a guarded nod of assent, she complied. Or she tried to. She took one gulp of the lukewarm mocha, letting the chocolatey bitterness coat her throat and fill her belly.

And her belly rebelled. Shouldn't have binged on the last of the contents of her refrigerator last night... she ran for the nearest toilet and upchucked her guts. *Ewe*. Pale, clammy, she flushed the toilet and splashed cold water on her face.

From the kitchen, she heard Cara's concerned voice, "Pace? You ok?"

She ducked out of the guest bathroom and gave her a small wave, "Yeah, I, uh... as you must have gathered by the state of my kitchen, I had a bit of a pity party with food last night."

"I noticed. Go get yourself freshened up while I hop on your tablet and search for flights." Without argument, Payson suddenly felt much more motivated to get dressed, brush her hair, maybe slap on a little make-up. Clean up. Stop mourning so heavily that she neglected herself.

She'd survived the death of her parents when she was still a teenager, learning to cope with the worst sort of grief. Despite what was likely some raging ADHD, she trudged her way through college and graduated with not-terrible grades. When she discovered she'd hit a brick wall in her lackluster life in Boston, she left what others would have considered a charmed life to start her amazing career with her thriving business in Seaview.

Amazingly, her little sister had turned out ok after all. Maybe she ought to be a better example. Maybe she should have paid more attention to the confident woman Cara had become. Head held high, she stepped into the shower and washed away her self-pity.

Pasting a pleasant smile on her face, dressed in her favorite black maxi dress and light sweater, she strode out to the living room. Cara sat curled up on her sofa with her tablet. She had several flights to Paris up on the screen.

Looking up from the screen as she reached her, Cara smiled, almost cheerfully. "Ok. Pace, there's a direct flight that leaves day after tomorrow. I'll run the shop and let Maddy drive you to the airport. You already have your passport, right?"

"Yes, I'm all set to go, just need to pack. It's actually right around when I told Alain that I would leave anyway." Maybe she was right. A few days relaxing in a French vineyard, perusing marvelous antiques, spending time with a friend that didn't know Ronan… this sounded like a much-needed change of scenery. She grabbed her credit card and passport from her purse and handed them to Cara to book her flight, trusting her sister to take care of her, as promised.

"Alright. You'd better start packing. You only have 48 hours until your flight leaves."

Feeling a touch of good humor, she rustled her baby sister's strawberry blond locks. "It shouldn't take me more than 24; I had already planned what I'm bringing."

Cara stood up from the couch and hugged her sister. "I've got to run to downstairs to meet Natalie. Come on down if you feel up to it, and I'll bring up my suitcase this evening after closing."

Payson called Alain to update him with her itinerary. He recommended trains she should take, rental car information, sights to see along the way to his vineyard in Provence. She booked everything she would need, made all of her travel arrangements and got herself completely packed. Cara was right, the preparations took her most of the day and were a perfect diversion from her desolate thoughts.

Once finished, she headed down to the shop to check in with her sister. Natalie had already returned to the gallery, and now Laura was sitting next to Cara on matching stools behind the register. She watched as Cara checked out the sweetest couple that were apparently shopping for an engagement ring.

Staying strong, she didn't let the happy couple remind her of what she was missing. Trying to convince herself that he would be back. That a few weeks on a mission wouldn't tempt him away from her, from his family.

Seeing Payson entering through the front door, Laura hopped off her stool and bee-lined straight for her. Laura dragged her in for a very needed hug. Pulling back but still holding her by the shoulders, Laura looked her over. With a shake of her head, she tsked, "Honey, you look pale. Let's get you some tea."

Payson managed to nod. "Thanks, I'd like that."

Payson followed her friend back to the storage room. Big mistake. She saw the beautifully finished shelves. Neatly organized now, perfectly stocked.

She'd had to finish without him. The tears start streaming again. Dammit, once you let them out, they just didn't stop. Quickly wiping her face before Laura saw, she forced a strengthening deep breath and pasted a smile on her face.

Laura had stationed herself at the tiny kitchenette Ronan had thoughtfully added in when he'd seen her running up and down the stairs for coffee, lunch, tea. Turning to Payson with a steaming cup of chamomile, Laura frowned. "He's coming back."

Again, not sure who she was reassuring, Payson pretended to agree. "Why hasn't he called? Texted? Emailed?"

Laura shook her head sadly. "He would if he could. He mentioned in his note he wouldn't be able to. He's never made a promise he didn't keep; he promised to try to return, so he will."

Try, that was the key word. He didn't promise to return, he promised to *try*.

Payson took over the shop for the rest of the afternoon after shooing Laura and Cara out the door, insisting she was fine. Sitting on her favorite stool at the register, she sipped her tea. The slow, measured movement helped center her. Ronan's absence was making her downright ill-tempered. She was turning into surly Ronan.

24

THE NEXT MORNING, MADDY walked into the shop, carrying piping hot mochas for the two of them and a bag of warm, gooey muffins from across the street. "It's not going to work," Payson teased with a shake of her head.

Maddy shrugged, "What? I'm just bringing over breakfast for my best friend."

Payson eyed her suspiciously as Maddy headed for the back room and set the food on the neat and tidy worktable. Pulling up a stool across the table, Payson tore off a bite of muffin. "You only use mochas and muffins when you're trying to bribe me for something, what is it this time?"

"I'm really not bribing you, just visiting. I thought we'd make our plans for tomorrow. I'll drive you to the airport; we'll have to get an early start." Staring at her friend meaningfully, Maddy insisted, "Drink your mocha."

Frowning, Payson was still suspicious. She picked up her mocha and took a big gulp. Was it rancid? Again? What kind of crap was she pulling? She tried to fight the wave of nausea, but it was too late. She ran to the small bathroom and puked.

"Ha, I knew it," Maddy cheered from her stool in the storeroom.

"Knew what? That apparently mochas don't agree with me anymore?" Payson washed away the clamminess and rinsed her mouth. She eventually managed to eat a few bites of muffin, but she couldn't even look at the mocha.

"Cara said you puked up the mocha she'd brought you. Gilly at the coffee shop said you ordered tea the last few times you've been in." Maddy had a smug grin pasted to her face. What was her deal?

"So? I like tea."

Shaking her head and mocking her friend, Maddy asked, "When was your last period?"

Payson stopped and calculated. Having no luck recalling, she pulled out her phone and checked her app. Shit. No period for well over a month. That might explain a thing or two.

Maddy reached into her purse and pulled out a home pregnancy test. Without a word, Payson grabbed the test from her waiting hand and raced for the bathroom. Her heart was beating out of her chest. Longest three minutes of her life, waiting for the stupid test to process.

They'd used condoms. She hadn't gotten around to regular birth control. She hadn't anticipated falling for him so fast; she was stupid for not following her normal wait-a-damn-long-time-for-sex rule. Her last prescription ran out about six months ago, and she just hadn't gotten around to renewing it.

Glancing down at the strip, a little blue plus sign appeared. "Shit. Shit, shit, shit. What kind of faulty condoms do they sell these days?"

Payson wracked her brain, Maddy watched her with bated breath.

Finally, like a bolt of lightning hitting her straight between the eyes, she realized her faux pas. "Uh oh. That time in the shower..."

The moment she knew she was head over heels in love with him. Before he was the elusive spy. Not that she loved him any less when she'd found out, she was just scared. Regardless, she'd apparently given him much more than her heart in that moment.

How could she have been so stupid? She regretted all the judgmental thoughts she'd had for girls who foolishly got knocked up when they'd been caught up in the moment.

Maddy squealed with delight and danced around the table, pulling a very stunned Payson off her stool and threw her arms around her. "I'm going to be an aunty. I was planning on convincing Chase we need to get started making babies, like in a year or two, but you beat me to it. I'll have to toss out my birth control so we can have babies together."

Breath coming in shallow, frantic pants, Payson sat back down before she passed out. Pregnant. By that filthy bastard that ditched her. He should be here going through this panic with her.

"I can't be pregnant. Your brother is gone. He's not coming back. I don't want to have a baby all alone... without him." Payson broke down in tears, totally unable to hold back the waterworks. "Not again," she complained, grabbing the last empty box of tissue and chucking it across the room. Heading into the bathroom, she pulled a length of toilet paper off the roll and blew her nose like a lonely trumpeter swan.

Furious, she stormed back into the front and started meticulously dusting and polishing before she broke down again.

Glowing sidewalks, lit brightly by the full moon, made for terrible cover. Not that he was having much luck anyway. He'd talked to dozens of his old contacts in the past few weeks. No one knew who the damn mole was.

Rumors of the missing weapons were rampant, but no one seemed to know anything. Sara had told him to keep his nose clean. But he wasn't about to be this far from Payson, from his life, without doing everything in his power to get back home.

Connor Young was totally off the grid. Ronan had managed to find one of his team, well, former team, as they'd disbanded with all the attention and Peter's arrest. Said he knew about the weapons, knew the deal was shady, but the Young brothers had been secretive. Some risky trade deal they didn't want the full crew involved with.

Their old crew mate had been pissed to not be included in what was promised to be a huge payoff, but he hadn't trusted the cagy seller. When the deal had gone sour, the Young brothers took off. Couldn't verify anything, but he suspected the Young brothers backed out of the deal.

Ronan was running out of options. Going to ground, while quietly asking questions, had gotten him absolutely nowhere. Other than alone. Every time he closed his eyes to get some elusive sleep, images of Payson filled his mind.

He hated himself for what he did to her. Leaving her without warning. Had she come down with his hot coffee, waiting for him to hold their drinks while he grumbled about her perky morning attitude as she unlocked the door to let them in, only to realize he wasn't coming?

Did she hate him as much as he hated himself right now? Could she ever forgive him? What if he couldn't solve this fucked up situation and couldn't return?

Giving up for the night, he headed to the next cockroach-infested motel he'd selected for the night. Needing to rest but knowing there was no hope of that happening anytime soon. He'd run into dead end after dead end.

Seeing no other choice, he would have to leave a trail. Let them find him. Whoever was looking for him. He had some pretty strong suspicions, but not enough to take action. He needed solid evidence to prove his innocence and nail the bastards responsible.

Connor Young was likely involved, if not leading the charge. If he and his brother backed out of the deal, they may have hidden the weapons, or at least know where they went. Certainly, the mole would be out there looking for him; the mole was likely the one that placed the bug. Were they working together, Connor and the mole? CIA would be looking for him as well, thinking he had hidden the weapons, but Sara was hopefully covering his trail on that end. Not that even she knew where he was right now.

Crashing onto the rock-hard mattress, he tried to close his eyes. Letting images of Payson wash over him. The feel of her skin, soft and warm from sleep. Her long limbs wrapping around him. His guided imagery shattered with the chirp from his drop phone. Sara. "What's up?"

Sara's voice was panicked, "Your girl. She's on the move; traveling to France."

He smiled, thinking of Payson taking the trip alone. She must be holding up better than he was. "I know, she's been planning the trip for a while."

Sara's frantic voice shattered his hope that Payson was making the best of this nasty situation, living her life. "She's not safe. I've been keeping an eye on your family, like you asked me to do. When she disappeared suddenly, I worried. I swept her apartment and her shop right after she left. Personally. I'm not risking her safety by letting anyone else in on this. I found three of the bugs like the one you found in your house."

Awash with panic, drenched in sweat, Ronan was off the bed and gathering his gear in a flash. Stupid. He hadn't left a trail, but she had. They would think she planned to meet him, or at least make contact; that was the best-case scenario. At worst, they were planning to nab her and use her as bait to get to him.

Sara continued, "I checked her flight information, and there was one ticket sold after hers. Angus McEwan, Scottish passport. Fake; either that or this McEwan fellow doesn't ever travel or have any bank accounts. I'll send an image of his passport; I think he looks an awful lot like Peter Young. Must be Connor."

"I'm on my way. I know where she's going." He was already out the door. "What time does her flight land at Charles de Gaul?"

"Eight minutes ago."

Swearing, seething, he sprinted in the direction of the nearest train station. "I'll find her. Let me know if you hear anything else."

"Will do. Be careful."

25

PAYSON LEFT DIRECTLY FROM Charles de Gaul Airport for Provence. She'd planned to spend a few days in Paris, hopefully with Ronan, but now she wanted to go straight to Alain's. Paris sounded a lot less fun pregnant and alone.

Jet-lagged, she tried to close her eyes to catch a quick catnap on the train. Each time she tried, she was filled with dreams of Ronan. Of that wicked half smile he flashed her, knowing it would make her roll her eyes with amusement. That swagger when he'd walked down the dock that day, followed by the way he had been so gentle when he realized she was afraid. She'd trusted him so completely in that moment.

Against her will, she trusted him still. Trusted him to come back to her, to not make her a single parent. It was just hard to convince her insecure side that he hadn't ditched her to return to his dream job.

Drowning in confusing thoughts, she stood up to explore the train a bit, stretch her legs. She'd have to schedule a prenatal visit as soon as she got home. What the hell. She was planning to call for birth control, now she had the opposite problem. Stupid, stupid mistake. She'd been so caught up in him that she hadn't protected herself.

On her stroll, she passed a burly dark-haired man. She'd seen him on the flight over. If she were feeling more outgoing, she would consider stopping to visit, compare notes on their similar routes. Although, there was a dangerous vibe to him. Something deep within her was screaming *not safe*. Pretending not to notice him, she continued on her walk before returning to her seat.

Arriving at the station, she walked straight to the car rental desk. Surveying her surroundings, she was relieved to see the burly man meeting a gorgeous blond woman that was near her in age. The woman dove into his arms and kissed him in a rather dramatic PDA. Blushing, she looked away.

She hopped in her little Nissan rental car and plugged in the directions to Alain's. After a long, scenic drive, she found the well-marked drive. Covering the expansive hills, grapevines in perfect rows extended in all directions. Each row had neatly wintered vines covering acres of hills with just the tiniest green buds revealing the first signs of spring. Driving down the long gravel road, winding in and around the hills and rocky outcrops, with occasional olive groves and fields of lavender scattered across the terrain, she admired the breathtaking landscape.

A grand, yet somehow humble estate came into view as she approached. The cobbled driveway led to a large home constructed from ancient gray stone. Homey and welcoming, she felt immediately at ease. At the hum of her engine approaching, the front door swung open and Alain stepped out.

She'd only seen him in person once a few years back when they'd met at a trade fair shortly before she opened Flotsam. They'd hit it off immediately, both drawn to classic, meaningful antiques. He'd invited her to dinner where they'd talked shop for hours, and he had encouraged her to follow her dream to open her shop.

He must have seen her approach and met her out front. Although spring had only just begun, there was a smattering of colors around the large wooden front door. Alain was a handsome man in his late forties, his hair a distinguished salt and pepper, with hardly a wrinkle on his chiseled face. He was just a bit shorter than Ronan, leaner in build, but solid muscle. Despite his warm smile, there was an underlying edge to him; not frightening, but more that he was inherently capable, fearless.

"*Mon amie*, it has been far too long. I am so glad you are here." As she exited the car, he welcomed her whole-heartedly with a kiss on each cheek. His chocolate brown eyes twinkled as he smiled kindly. "You must be exhausted after your long journey. Please, let me help you with your bag and let's get you settled."

She nearly broke down in tears on hearing a friendly, familiar voice. "Thank you. It has been quite a trek, but well worth it. Your home is a work of art, so beautifully situated in this incredible vineyard. Truly magnificent."

"Thank you. It has been in my family for generations." He swung her backpack over his shoulder and led the way into the house. "Nicolas is finishing up some business for the vineyard but will join us shortly. I did not inherit the family desire to make wine, so I am fortunate in my husband."

"I look forward to meeting him." Payson felt herself smiling naturally; she was starting to feel her inherent optimism shining through her gloomy mental clouds. She'd felt so tearful and cranky since Ronan left. Cara was right, this was a great idea.

Alain led the way in through the large, heavy wooden door into a cozy foyer. Payson was already charmed by the place. The rustic tile floor and French country wooden entry table, circa late 1700's, next to an artfully re-purposed wine-bottle coat rack sealed the deal.

Directly in front of her, there was a wide doorway that clearly led to the rest of the main house, and on either side of the foyer were two narrow wooden stairwells. He led them up the creaky, worn-smooth stairs to the right and led her down a large white hallway.

A weathered blue rug, pastoral paintings and photographs of the region lined the walls of the sunny hallway. A classic old European home. They passed a sitting room, guest rooms, bathroom, and eventually the door on the end opened into a large guest suite.

"This will be your suite; as you are our only guest at the moment, you will have a fair amount of privacy. We are typically full to the brim during the summer and fall months; friends and business associates mostly, but we rent out rooms on a case by case basis." He walked Payson into the room and set her backpack down on an ornately carved high-backed bench just inside the doorway.

Enchanted, Payson immediately went to the terrace, opening the French doors to let in the fresh, cool spring air. "This is wonderful. Thank you, Alain."

"Nicolas and my living quarters are in the opposite wing. To reach the dining and common rooms, simply head back down the stairs and through that wide doorway you saw in the foyer. Please, make yourself at home. Will you be feeling up to dinner in an hour or so?"

Charmed, Payson was quickly finding her second wind. "That sounds wonderful. I'll wander down and find you."

After Alain left her, Payson took a moment to explore the grand room. Darkly weathered plank floors and contrasting white walls created an inviting, old-world effect, with an expansive green and beige wool area rug and more pastoral paintings warming up the space. A large, ornate wooden bed with lacy white sheets and bedding took up one wall. An oversized fireplace, nearly big enough to stand in, took up much of the opposite wall, with two cozy leather chairs on either side, and a small brass side table sat in between.

To the right was the bathroom, and to the left was a small table with wrought iron chairs for two that sat in front of the glass doors leading out to a small deck. Despite the cool air, she spent a few minutes gazing across the landscape. The small deck was adorable. Constructed of iron and wood, it had just enough room to sit and sip a glass of wine and watch the sun set over the vineyard. She suspected the table and chairs resided outside on the small deck in the warmer months.

Payson indulged in a quick shower before dinner. As inviting as the rest of the house, the bathroom had weathered clay tile floors, sky blue throw rugs, a double vanity sink made from a converted antique dresser. She helped herself to the lavender scented lotion to ease her sore muscles from long days of travel. She took some mental notes on how she could improve her own bathroom, loving the clawfoot tub and blue lace shower curtain that was delicate without being gaudy.

Slipping on a soft cotton dress and light sweater, she made her way down the creaking staircase for dinner. A stranger waited at the table, a massive figure with jet black hair and a neatly trimmed week's growth of beard. The man was solid muscle. She was nearly intimidated, but his mouth turned up in a welcoming smile as she entered the room.

"You must be Payson," he said as he stood from his chair. "I am Nicolas, Alain's husband. Will you please join me? Alain was held up in the kitchen; we have a regular cook as we have guests so frequently, but Alain enjoys adding his personal touches to the meal." He welcomed her with a kiss on each cheek as Alain had. He was so massive, she felt rather tiny standing next to him.

Payson relaxed at the easy conversation. She enjoyed hearing him tell her about the wine they make and the history of the house and vineyards. Alain entered a few moments later with hors d'oeuvres and a bottle of wine.

Eyeing the wine, she realized she couldn't keep her pregnancy a secret. Before he could pour her a glass, she grimaced, "I am very sad to turn down a glass of your wine, as I have really been looking forward to trying some. I quite recently discovered that I am pregnant."

What crappy luck, staying at a gorgeous French vineyard and unable drink the wine. Bad enough being all alone with an MIA baby-daddy, but she couldn't even enjoy her trip as she would have liked.

Bubbling with congratulations, Alain instead poured her a glass of sparkling water. "That is so very exciting. Your young man that you told me about, he was unable to come?"

"Yes. Ronan was pulled away for work quite suddenly, which is why I took the opportunity to come now or I'll go crazy waiting. I just found out about the pregnancy a few days ago; he doesn't even know yet."

"We are happy to keep you company while he is away and to celebrate with you." Alain toasted her water with his wine.

The trio enjoyed friendly banter through a spectacular dinner. The dining room was as marvelous as the rest of the house. Comfortable for ten or twelve guests, the table looked to be from an old friary perhaps, with ornate benches at each side. The setting sun cast a pleasant orange glow in the room.

For the first time in weeks, she was feeling at ease. Her worries weren't entirely at the forefront, for now. A shred of hope that she wouldn't cry and be lonely forever.

As a beautiful dessert of *Pears Belle Helene* was served, Alain asked, "Payson, you have not told us how you met your *petit-ami*. Was it romantic?"

At that, Payson laughed. As much as it had been hurting to even think about him, she found it reviving to talk about him now. "Not at all. When I met him, he was recovering from a train wreck he had barely survived in Germany. He was a downright irritable jerk when I met him. Surly, short-tempered, hair and beard wild."

She shook her head with an ironic smile as she described the p.c. version of their meeting. No one had ever asked that before, as they were still so fresh. Despite her anger at him, it helped to talk about him.

"His mother convinced him to help me in the shop; my stockroom was in terrible need of re-organization." Images flashed through her head as she recollected watching him come back to life; smiling more, teasing her, kissing her despite his own reluctance. "Eventually, he started to come back to life and, well, the rest is history." She took her first bite of the spectacular pear dish, letting the delectable concoction melt in her mouth.

"And what does he do for work that has called him away so suddenly?" Nicolas asked, sipping the last of his wine.

"Something with computers. I'm not entirely sure to be honest. He doesn't like to talk about his past." Not knowing quite how to explain Ronan, she turned the questions around, "How did you two meet?"

They two shared an ironic look, Nicolas reached across the table to join hands with Alain as he answered her question. "Until about five years ago, we both served in the *Commandement des Operations Speciales*; you would know it better as special forces. We had travelled all over the world, both in different battalions. Not long before Alain was injured, I was assigned to assist his elite unit on a top-secret mission; I speak many languages, you see, in addition to some other... particular skills." He paused, looking to Alain.

Payson interrupted with a friendly chuckle, "That was not exactly what I would have guessed, for an antiques dealer and a vintner. What happened on the mission, if you don't mind me asking?"

Alain continued for Nicolas, "The mission was a success, but I was wounded as we made our way to the extraction point. Nicolas wouldn't leave me. In the midst of gunfire all around us, he tossed me over his shoulder and ran for the helicopter. We made it back just in the nick of time. Entire place exploded as our helicopter pulled away."

Shocked, Payson could hardly imagine the circumstances. "That is... incredible. It sounds like something out of a movie. What happened after?"

"Nicolas refused to leave my side as I healed; he risked dishonorable discharge to stay with me. I told him about my home. By that time, my father was ready to retire. He and my mother live in Paris now, but they were not very active in the business anyway. My grandmother was happy for us to come live here with her. So, we put in our notices and left." They grinned at each other, sharing a sweet kiss.

Payson hid the pang of envy, watching the happy couple. They said their goodnights and she let the fatigue from the day, the sadness she had pushed to the back burner for hours, rise to the surface.

Exhausted from the long day and a whole lot of hormones, Payson sunk into the plush bed. She left the French doors open to let in the cool spring air. In the distance, she heard the soothing sound of frogs croaking, the smell of fresh rain starting to soak dry soil.

Letting the soothing smells and peaceful sounds calm her, she closed her eyes and allowed herself a secret moment to imagine what Ronan was doing. Was he as miserable as she was?

Drained and delirious from the jetlag, sleep finally took hold.

26

RONAN HAD BEEN RUNNING on pure adrenaline for the past twelve hours. He'd managed to find Alain's vineyard; it was both ancient and charming. From a distance, he watched as a light finally flickered on in the upper story of the east wing.

Like Romeo, he watched as Juliet came out the open French doors and took in the night air. She didn't linger on the terrace. Even from a distance, he could see she was weary and sad.

Knowing it was his fault, he berated himself for leaving in such a sudden, cruel way. She was such a bright light shining on his dark world; he wanted to do anything in his power to keep that magic. His chest burned at what she must be going through. Aching to hold her close.

Patiently, he waited longer, for just the right opportunity. Eventually, the main house lights turned off, the inside of the home becoming dark as night. To avoid detection, he waited until he was certain the household was asleep. None too soon either; fat raindrops were starting to fall from the cloud-covered sky.

Silently, covertly, he made his way through the dark field to the house. Assessing the area, he determined the best way to get into her room, avoiding being spotted by anyone inside the house or watching from the outside. Using a crack in the exterior wall, Ronan dug in his foot and lifted his body to the next crack and slowly climbed the stone wall.

Making his way up the stone house using the few-and-far-between cracks between blocks for leverage, he was finally near Payson's terrace. Checking his grips, testing his footing, he grounded himself into his footholds before leaping across the several foot gap to the base of the terrace.

Silencing a yelp at the near miss, he managed to grab hold of the support to the lower edge of the balcony with one arm. He laughed internally, thinking how awesome it would be if he could somehow create a YouTube video of espionage outtakes, showing the many times our heroes missed the handhold or bumped their heads. Certainly, he made sure that didn't happen when the outcome could be life-threatening, but in certain emergencies like this, making the leap was worth the risk of looking foolish or spraining one's ankle. Dangling for a moment, he used the momentum of his body weight to swing so his other arm could reach a bit higher.

With ease that came with experience and agility, he pulled himself up the rest of the way and climbed over the rail. Maybe he ought to take up rock-climbing? He was going to miss little adventures like this. Although, this time, the asset inside was more valuable than all the rest combined.

Gently pushing open her terrace doors, he found her fast asleep on a massive bed. Her auburn hair spread across the pillow in stark contrast to the crisp white sheets. Eyebrows scrunched together in a deep scowl, she appeared troubled even in sleep.

He'd missed her so much. Once he'd fallen for Payson, being away from her for so long was physically painful. Closing and locking the door behind him, shutting all the bedroom curtains, he allowed himself to pretend, just for a moment, that they weren't being chased by multiple parties out to arrest or likely torture him.

Stripping down to the skin, he slid into bed beside her. Aching to hold her close. Hoping she didn't wake and scream at the intrusion... or smack him for being such an ass. Hoping she would forgive him someday.

He nuzzled close, inhaling her soothing, lavender scent, and curled his body against hers. Sleep came quickly, for the first time in weeks.

The sky still dark, Payson listened to the raw, rumbling sounds of an approaching thunderstorm, feeling the deep booming resonate down to her bones. Stirring, she snuggled against Ronan, savoring the comfort of his warm skin pressed up against hers... *what*? Holding her closely, he slept soundly, peacefully.

She was torn between fury and bliss, thrilled he was here, regardless of how or why. Before she woke him to give him an earful, she twisted her body around in his arms to face him, brushing her lips gently across his in a soft, longing kiss. Whispering, she told him she loved him.

Running her hand along his jaw, darkened by the rough growth of beard that hadn't been shaved since she'd seen him last. When she knew he was sound asleep, drawing back her hand, she flicked him dead-center on his forehead.

"Ow," he awoke rubbing his injured forehead. Eyes slowly opening, he groaned, "What was that for?" His vision clearing, he saw her scowling at him, her face inches from his own.

"*What was that for?* You left me. With a short, stupid note. You couldn't have come to tell me before you left? Or even called to say, sorry honey, something's come up, but I have to leave?" Bubbling with emotion of every sort, Payson could hardly get her words out fast enough to keep up with her angrily babbling brain.

Expression remorseful, Ronan reached out, his hand running through her hair. "Oh, honey. I'm so sorry. I hated leaving you. More than anything. Please, I wouldn't have left if I didn't have any other choice." Testing, he placed a gentle kiss on her forehead. "Please forgive me, but it's not over yet."

"What's not over? I thought you were retired, but I knew you couldn't settle idly into small town life. I hate that I let you... that I gave you this... this... power over me. Dammit. I hate that I feel so... Just get to the point and tell me what's going on," she demanded as she sat up in bed, looking down at his naked form.

Eyes wandering over his many scars, she saw the dangerous side of him she hadn't realized was there before. She'd seen the edge the moment she had first met him, but hadn't realized how deep it ran. Looking into his ice-cold eyes, she saw why he was so good at what he did... saw the ruthlessness in them.

Despite all that, she also saw the warmth, the ache. Dark circles stained heavy under his eyes. No sign of the charming dimples or arrogant smile. He wasn't the broken man he was when they'd first met, nor was he the hard-hearted spy anymore. He was hurting as much as she was, maybe more.

Sitting up to get closer to her, he gently nudged her chin toward him, kissing her softly at first, apologizing with his touch. His lips trailed along her jaw, down her shoulder, sending electric shivers through her body.

Breathlessly, she struggled to refuse, but she missed him so damn much she didn't want to stop. "I'm still mad at you." Verbally, she tried to resist, but her damn traitorous body, and her heart, weren't listening. She knew he would stop if she really wanted him to. Rather than pushing him away as she knew she should, she pulled him closer.

Trailing kisses along her shoulder, her neck, her forehead, he needed her to know how he felt. With each kiss, he told her he loved her. Needed her. Wanted her.

He poured his soul into his kiss and his words, letting her know with each touch that she was the most important thing in his life. Returning to her lips, his kiss, his touch became more desperate, the raw need exploding between them.

With a feral growl, he pulled her closer against him and kissed her deeply. No more soothing, no more gentle seduction. He plundered.

And she responded unreservedly, granting him a temporary reprieve. She didn't have it in her to ignore her heart, as much as her mind was furious with him.

Fire igniting, each could no longer discern where one ended and the other began. Lowering her back down to the bed, Ronan followed close behind and tore off her flimsy nightclothes.

Greedily, he grasped her breast with one hand and devoured the other, licking and suckling until she cried out his name. He shifted and moved down her body, leaving a blazing trail with his tongue. Ravenously, he pressed his tongue against her core.

She gasped, breath coming faster and faster as she lost control. Riding the wave of her erotic response, he sweetly tortured her with circles, pressure, and vibration until she couldn't hold back the uninhibited cries of pure pleasure.

Still writhing in ecstasy, he flipped her over on top of him, putting her in control. Letting her know that he was at her mercy. Guiding the pace, she lowered slowly onto him. Tormenting them both, she rocked her hips back and forth until she found her rhythm. Taking what she wanted, what she needed.

Her back arched, head thrown back as she triumphantly climaxed. She cried out as the orgasm ricocheted through her. Enthralled, Ronan tried to hold back his own release to prolong hers.

As her movements slowed and the orgasm receded, he couldn't wait any longer and grasped her hips and renewed her rhythm. Gasping, she crested again, driving him even wilder as she refused to leave him behind this time. Body tensing, nearing his release, he increased the rhythm, carrying them both through a torrential wave of ecstasy.

Limbs tangled, breath calming, neither spoke for several minutes. Thunder rolled overhead, flashing lightning lit up the room in dramatic applause. The sharp clinking of raindrops on the roof evolved into a relentless roar.

Slowly, the magic of the moment faded. Reality came crashing back. He could feel her pulling away, emotionally as she did physically. Making it clear that he had blown it, big time.

Cautiously, he propped himself up on his elbow. After a quick check of the room, still undisturbed, he turned and rested his eyes on Payson. She looked so amazing, so beautiful. He hadn't come to ask for her forgiveness, nor to take advantage.

Needing her touch, he'd made love with her with nothing held back. If she had resisted, he would have stopped. They hadn't had a condom; he didn't exactly have time to stop to pick some up when he'd rushed across the Mediterranean to protect her from the danger that followed her.

Terrible as he felt that they hadn't made the decision together first, to risk it, he was thrilled at the prospect of making a family with Payson. Brought out some rather primitive, territorial feelings as well. He nearly laughed at himself and that odd testosterone-driven line of possessiveness.

His future was so clear now, that path his dad had described was no longer hidden. Payson, him, maybe living in the apartment above Flotsam together. He could pop downstairs with their little one anytime. Maybe he'd write during the day; he'd enjoyed writing way back when. Coach a little league team every summer, their little one bouncing on Payson's knee. Or, maybe she'd coach alongside him; those kids wouldn't get away with a thing with fun-loving, competitive Payson urging them on.

...*Shit.* That time in the shower in New Sussex. They had both been so caught up in the moment. What if...?

Shaking his head, he couldn't think like this right now. Getting lost in fantasy was downright dangerous when on an op. First, he had to get them both home. Safely.

"What time is it?" Still dark, Ronan couldn't tell how long he'd slept by her side, before the not-so-gentle flick on the forehead.

Her fury with him had returned in full force. She held her expression neutral, but he couldn't miss the fire sparking in those fairy green eyes. Blandly, she replied after glancing at her phone, "Six in the morning."

"I'm going to grab a quick shower. Is there any coffee or food around here? I'd like to explain, everything, but I need a shower first. I've been in four countries in the last three days. I stink." Warily, she nodded in assent. Every muscle in his body aching and tight, he hobbled across the room to the shower.

Payson climbed out of bed and tossed on a cotton dress that didn't quite come to her knees. Avoiding watching him slip into the steaming spray of the shower, she was out of the suite before he reached the bathroom.

A few minutes later, she returned with fresh croissants and coffees for them both. As Ronan pulled on his black low-slung cargo pants and a fitted black t-shirt, Payson set up their snack on the small table near the window. She went to open the curtains to watch the sun rising over the vineyards, but Ronan stilled her hand. "Not yet."

She sat and sipped her coffee, watching him, waiting, suspicious of his every movement. He sat in the other chair and devoured his croissant within seconds. Laughing at himself, his terrible manners, he apologized, "Sorry, I haven't eaten in a while. As soon as I found out you were on your way here, I didn't stop moving."

She continued to stare at him, arms folded. Still furious. He wasn't used to the silent treatment and didn't care for it. She wasn't giving him an inch.

Knowing she wasn't talking until he explained, he leaned back in the undersized metal chair and sighed, considering where to begin. "My last mission still haunts me. Every night, the disfigured images of the people I failed to save torment me. The mission stalled; I did as much as I could, as much as I was allowed, but then I was shot. Forced into retirement."

He leaned back in his chair, staring down into the dark liquid of his coffee cup as it chilled in his steady hands. She remained still, arms folded across her chest. "I recently learned there was... more to my sudden retirement. Forcing me on the disabled list was an easy way to get me out of the picture." He paused, reflecting on the words he'd finally said aloud.

It wasn't the toughest case he'd had to solve in his career, and it was proving to be the most personal. Tensing his jaw, a snarl escaped from his tightly drawn mouth. Fists balled up, he quieted for a moment, listening for unusual sounds, ever on guard. He managed to gulp the remaining coffee and set down the cup before he chucked it across the room; restless, angry, unsure.

He stalked to the window and peaked out through the gap in the curtains, watching for signs of activity. The sun was starting to rise, but the dark clouds and heavy rain kept visibility to a minimum. Perfect timing if someone wanted to make their move. What were they waiting for?

Payson finally spoke, no longer giving him the silent treatment. But she still followed him with distrustful eyes, her body stiff and unforgiving. "What happened that you had to leave Seaview?"

Feeling hopeful she might forgive him one day, Ronan was eager to fill her in on everything. Explain why he'd left and somehow make her see that he would do everything in his power to never leave her again. Hopefully, she would understand why he'd had to run.

27

A KNOCK AT THE door interrupted their conversation. Payson glanced to Ronan, shrugged as if to say he was on his own with explaining his sudden appearance to Alain. She walked to the door and opened it wide.

Alain waited politely a few feet from the door. "Are you alright? I came to see if you were joining us for breakfast, when I heard someone talking?"

Ronan leaped up to introduce himself. Not the best way to meet one's host, sneaking in during the night to climb in bed with their guest. He'd planned to have Payson out of there before dawn. Well, that had been the formal plan he'd told himself, but he knew better. He couldn't help but take advantage of the perfect opportunity get the answers he needed.

Payson introduced him as he reached the doorway. "Alain, this is Ronan. He arrived late last night."

Putting on his full agent charm, Ronan held out his hand and spoke fluently in his host's native tongue, "*Bon matin*. You must be Alain.

I am very sorry to intrude. My business brought me to the area, and I have missed Payson so much that I had to surprise her."

If he was taken aback, he didn't show it. Alain graciously welcomed Ronan to his home and invited them downstairs for breakfast. Alain exuded strength, intelligence. He was more than an antiques dealer, but he also wasn't the slimy smooth-talker Ronan had imagined. His body moved gracefully but fiercely, his gaze penetrating.

Walking down a creaky wooden stairwell, he followed their host into a small breakfast room connected to a large chef's kitchen. As directed, he sat at a small square breakfast table. Each of the four chairs were different, two wooden chairs that looked as old as the house itself, and two brightly colored metal chairs that had likely been there since the middle of the last century. A glass door and collection of large windows made him a bit nervous, fearing they were being watched. Staying on alert, he monitored for any signs of movement from outside.

A collection of pastries, breads, jams, cheese, and fresh fruit were set out in the middle of the table. Alain immediately poured them each a cup of espresso with a dollop of heavy cream. Within moments, a taller, dark-haired man with a panther-like edge entered the room.

If he was surprised to see Ronan, he didn't show it. The man took a seat at the head of the table and leaned back in his chair. Alain made the introductions, and the newcomer, Nicolas, was not quite as friendly as his spouse and greeted Ronan with a sharp, but dubious nod.

Where Alain was warm and welcoming, Nicolas was skeptical. He leaned back in his chair, sipping his espresso with a wicked poker face, watching Ronan like a hawk. Ronan tried to ignore the silent interrogation. The guy was intimidating as hell. Ronan could swear he saw Alain subtly kick him under the table more than once.

A few bites into breakfast, Alain broke the ice. Between Payson, who had not yet forgiven him, and Nicolas, who looked like he could wipe him off the face of the planet with the blink of an eye, he was grateful for Alain's friendly demeanor.

"We are so pleased you could join us. How did you come to be in town so fortuitously to join my good friend, Payson?" The clear show of support for Payson was not missed, nor was the suspicion, but the question, like Alain himself, was presented kindly.

After years of lies, Ronan nearly began with a story about the computer virus emergency, as Payson would have told them he was a computer programmer if they had asked. Regardless of the secrets he kept, he knew these were good people, and he knew they were more than the ordinary vintners they seemed to be. He couldn't put these good people at risk. Well, more than he already had by his very presence here.

Ronan tried to find the right words to explain his arrival... the honest words. "As I mentioned earlier, I was in the area for work." He inhaled deeply, forcing the truth from his lips. "I want to be completely honest with you, for your safety and for Payson's."

Nicolas slightly let up on the evil eye that rivaled Payson's spiciest death-glare. At the mention of honesty, he began to relax, the corner of his mouth turning up in a clever smirk. "Please, explain. We will welcome any friend of Payson's, but something doesn't add up for me. Thank you for bringing it up before I was forced to."

Ronan raised his mouth in a half smile to match his host's, finding his candor reassuring. Lifting an eyebrow to punctuate his curious smile, he inquired of his hosts, "What did Payson tell you about me?"

"Not much." Arms still crossed, but his expression almost playful now, Nicolas continued, "I know you didn't come in through the front door, or any other downstairs entrance, as we have excellent security. It's not easy to get to our second floor, except with some extraordinary acrobatics, so you're more capable than I would expect for someone who works in computers."

Curiosity peaked, Ronan nodded his head in agreement, "And you are a bit more astute than I would expect for a vintner."

Alain shook his head, getting to the point more quickly than his spouse. "My goodness, Nicolas, let up on the boy. Ronan, I am sorry for my husband's poor manners. He and I are retired *Commandement des Operations Speciales*, so you are correct, we are not what you would typically expect for our current lines of work. What is your story?"

That made more sense. And was a huge relief. These two would be perfectly capable of defending themselves... and protecting Payson. "Until a few months ago, I was CIA. Naturally, that isn't something I normally share, but this is an unusual situation."

Nicolas nodded, full smile now, "Not what I would have guessed, but I think I understand now. Please, what brings you so suddenly to our home? Your unexpected arrival is disconcerting."

Leaning forward and resting his elbows on the table, enjoying the quick, easy camaraderie, Ronan divulged the whole story. Payson sat back and watched quietly, absorbing everything. "As I am sure you can understand, this information cannot leave this room. A few weeks before I met Payson, I was shot within hours of capturing a mercenary that I had been tracking for some time. Due to the extent of my injuries, I was medically discharged. My final mission was not resolved, at least, not to my satisfaction, so my abrupt retirement was...unsettling."

Alain nodded and offered another round of coffee for the table. "I understand. I was similarly discharged, and if it had not been for Nicolas, I would never have recovered. Physically, yes, but not emotionally."

Ronan smiled, reflecting on his own return home. His family was so supportive that he would have been ok. With Payson there to ease his panic attacks and nightmares - before she knew she was helping with the nightmares. He bit his cheek and thought about telling her that little tidbit down the road, obviously, not today. Just by being her honest self, she brought back his sense of normal again... and, quite frankly, called him on his abhorrent behavior. Thanks to her, he became more than he had ever been. "Without Payson, I would probably still be drowning in nightmares."

He gave her a wink. Miraculously, she didn't glare at him this time. Rather than the scowl she'd been wearing all morning, she was easing into an almost neutral expression. "Is that why you left so suddenly? Or did something happen?"

Ronan went out on a limb and reached for her hand, desperate for her to understand. Amazingly, she didn't shake her hand out of his grip, but instead softened at his touch. "I discovered that I had been found, likely by the man that shot me, and that I was under investigation for serious criminal charges. In staying, I would have risked your safety and the safety of my family." Whether it was conscious or not, she gently squeezed his hand in reassurance.

He continued, "A year or so back, I'd caught of whiff of a very power-hungry terrorist group in the market for game-changing weapons. I couldn't dig up much more than chatter, but I had a bad feeling, so I put everything else on the back burner. From the chatter, I found that a mercenary named Peter Young had been in contact with the terrorists and had bartered a deal. Evidence was thin, and Young was not usually in the weapons business, but I went with my gut. I didn't let Young out of my sight... even when I was supposed to be on a vacation." He chuckled, lost in distant memories.

"Trusting my instincts paid off. Young had gotten ahold of some truly awful biological weapons. I saw the aftermath of their demonstration; the memories of that day drive most of my flashbacks. I uh... I won't burden you with the specifics."

His respirations increased as he battled the images threatening to take over his vision. Fighting the remembered smell that was just under the surface. Seeing his panic setting in, Payson put a hand on his cheek and gently traced her thumb across his jaw. Softly, she reassured him, "It's ok. Can you tell us the rest?"

Swallowing the lump forming in his throat, he managed to continue. "To this day I don't know why, but the deal went sour; terrorists didn't get their weapons. Worse, I don't know where the weapons came from to begin with or where they ended up. Young was just the middleman, but he went into hiding shortly after the demonstration. I managed to track him to London and arrested him.

"As soon as I returned to my flat that night I was shot. Sniper was waiting in the building across the street. Presumably Connor Young, Peter's brother. Three bullets, hours of surgery, and inpatient rehab. CIA faked my death and sent me home. Disabled. Retired. Call it what you like."

Nicolas' eyes drifted out the window, watching, waiting. Alain was in an equally dark place, reliving his own memories.

Mirthlessly, Ronan laughed. "It's crazy. I was so angry to be kicked out, but so grateful to leave. Coming home, spending time with my family... falling for Payson, was the best adventure I've had. I was so lonely, had isolated myself so severely, and I hadn't even realized how it was destroying me."

Slowly, long shadows contrasted the brightening fields as the sun rose in the sky and broke through the clouds. Scanning the rows of vineyards and outbuildings while he paused, Ronan wished he could have told Payson all of this sooner. He hated putting her through all of this.

When he had dropped the L-word again last night, she had cringed. Desperate to see some sign of her feelings, he glanced her way, only to find she was lost in thought herself, staring at the impressionist painting that took up most of the far wall of the room. Her eyes were glassy, but she held her expression otherwise neutral.

Nicolas pulled his attention back to the moment, "What pulled you back out into the field?"

He shook his head, jaw clenching. "More into hiding than into the field. Peter Young negotiated a deal to lighten his sentence. He pinned the blame on me for the missing weapons. Says I hid them to stop the deal. Consequently, now the CIA is looking for me, as is Connor, and the mole."

"Mole?" Payson demanded. She turned abruptly in her chair, worry flickering in her gaze.

"One of our own working both sides. I don't know who it is for sure, but I have a pretty good idea. We suspected there was a mole before I was shot; Peter Young had obtained confidential information and my covers were blown. My real identity, however, has been buried thick since the day I signed on. No way an outsider, or anyone without damn good security clearance, could have tracked me to Seaview. I realized I was being watched when I found the latest model CIA bug in my house in Seaview. Not officially sanctioned, or so I hear."

Scowling, Payson didn't look quite so distant and the glare didn't seem to be at him this time. "I can see why you left so suddenly. An intruder, a bug, a mole, and an accusation against you."

Thrilled with her understanding, Ronan couldn't hide his relief. "Exactly. Even stopping to leave you a note was dangerous, but I couldn't leave without at least telling you." Her restlessness was increasing as she processed everything he had said.

Nicolas watched Ronan scanning the fields as he had every few minutes since he'd awoken this morning, looking for something, someone. "Who is the mole working with on the outside?"

Ronan shook his head, "I'm not positive how everything connects just yet. The mole must be working with Connor Young. One of them killed another agent that helped me capture Peter. Killed around the same time I found the bug, actually."

"I understand why you ran, why you couldn't tell me anything before. I'm glad I know now... but you'll be traced back to me. You need to run. Go far away and hide." Payson was about to flip her lid in panic. She stood from her chair and walked up to the windows, studying the fields as he had. He was glad she understood why he had left, but she needed to understand the danger she was in.

"About that... After I left Seaview, my contact at CIA heard some rumors. She, uh, broke into your apartment and your shop and found several bugs. You were followed." He stood from the table and walked to her. "Looks to be Connor."

She still looked away, her expression determined, angry, plotting. "They were waiting for you to contact me. When I left, they assumed I was coming to you, weren't they?"

"Yes. I would have thought they were planning to use you to get to me, but they could have nabbed you anytime," he replied plainly. "I don't know what they're waiting for."

"They're waiting for you to let something slip about the weapons. How could you be so stupid as to come here? Fall right into their trap?" She turned to him and put her hands on her hips. She may as well shake her finger at him, admonish him like a foolish schoolboy.

His mouth turned up in that devilish half smile, loving her more with every passing moment. "I couldn't risk them grabbing you, holding you hostage, or harming you in any way. So, I got here as soon as I could." He turned and looked to his hosts, deeply apologetic, "I cannot say how truly sorry I am to bring this danger into your lives."

Alain shook his head, speaking more firmly than he had so far, "You came to keep Payson safe, and we do not fear for ourselves. As you are here now, perhaps we can help."

"I have no doubt Connor, or someone, is watching us at this moment. As we're all in this now, again, my sincerest apologies, perhaps we can use this to our advantage," Ronan grinned, grateful things were finally coming together.

Payson glared at Ronan, "I don't think you can walk into an obvious trap, turn around, and hope to trap the trapper."

Smug, he was in full badass mode. "I can."

She rolled her eyes at him. He'd find out soon if Payson still wanted him around after she got to witness professional Ronan. After seeing he was nothing like the spies she was fascinated by in the movies. And a bit different from Ronan the handyman.

28

Payson was furious at his conceited plan. She had no doubt he was as good as he claimed, but this was foolish. "What's your plan? How are you going to turn this around?"

Ronan shrugged innocently, "I'm still working on it. It'll come to me." She wanted to flick that adorable grin off his face. Sometimes she missed his surly self; at least he wasn't walking stupidly into danger when he was cranky all the time. Although, confidence looked damn sexy on him.

Alain stood from the table and started clearing plates. "I agree, he is watching at a minimum. Listening, perhaps."

Ronan nodded as he stepped back to the table and drained the last of his coffee. "I'm counting on it." He carried his and Payson's empty plates to the kitchen.

Nicolas grabbed the remaining dishes and walked toward the kitchen. "Ronan, let's you and I have a chat. Payson, why don't you and Alain do what you came here for? He has some truly spectacular pieces to show you."

Alain nodded, "Excellent, are you ready?"

Ronan followed Nicolas out of the kitchen, leaving Payson with Alain.

"Hang on, I have to use the restroom first." She was peeing constantly; this was not convenient.

After quickly relieving her tiny bladder, she followed Alain through a covered walkway to a stone outbuilding. His gaze was sharp, observing their surroundings as they walked. No longer the warm and friendly host, he was in full soldier mode while they were out in the open.

The walkway led them to an incredible stone outbuilding that must be older than the house. Huge timber beams held up a wooden roof. The stone floors were almost slippery, they were so smooth from years of use. There were several sturdy old tables with items in wooden crates for her to view. The building was somehow cool, light, and airy despite the lack of windows.

As Alain searched the room for signs of intrusion, he told her about the building. "Years ago, my family used this room for preparation of bottling supplies, until the last few decades when we modernized a bit, but Nicolas keeps our methods as traditional as we can." Relaxing again, safe in the windowless outbuilding, Alain pulled the canvas drapes off the crates.

"I hope you find some pieces you like. These are some of my favorites that I pulled from our personal family stores, as well as some from my recent travels." Alain had earmarked a number of amazing pieces, varying from his great-great grandmother's jewelry to vintage lace, a few small furniture items, trinkets.

"These are amazing," Payson remarked as she viewed each piece, taking her time to admire the craftsmanship, try to estimate the period each was from. "Are you sure you want to sell these? This is a truly spectacular collection of family heirlooms."

Sadly, Alain responded, "It is only me remaining. Nicolas and I have no children, and I am the last of my family line. I am hopeful that you can find loving homes for these items. This is why I have asked you to come here to choose from my favorite pieces. I know that you will tell your customers about each piece, so the history will be remembered."

Payson was touched by his generosity. She sold each piece with great care, and it was gratifying to know the love she poured into her work was acknowledged and appreciated. "Of course. I would like to add written descriptions as well, so the story can stay with each item."

Alain beamed. "I can take care of that. Before shipping them over to you, I will add an artful written description for each."

He took the time to describe the many pieces she had selected, which was more than she had anticipated. He told her the details about a silver jewelry box that was his grandmothers. Payson eyed it and decided she would have to set it aside for Maddy for her birthday.

She stopped at a ring with a central green gem set in a simple, yet intricate pattern of interwoven leaves. "This is beautiful, can you tell me about this one?"

Walking closer, he stood at her side, his chiseled face warming with an open smile. "One of my favorites. My great-grandfather brought it back from England for my great-grandmother when he returned from the first World War. He purchased it from the closest jeweler to the docks before he set sail back to France. Didn't want to come home empty-handed, you see, as he had proposed spontaneously the night before he left.

"It was quite the scandal. She was English herself and had run away to France to get an education. Her father had frowned upon her un-la-dylike ambitions and insisted she marry one of his aristocratic friends.

She met my great-grandfather in Paris, and it was love at first sight. Not wanting to lose sight of her dreams, she fought their budding romance at first. Once she realized that he would do anything in his power to support her goals, she agreed to marry him."

"Was she able to pursue her education?" Payson liked her already.

Alain smiled, "Yes, she did. She used her knowledge in botany to improve our crops. Ensured the region produced sustainably. Quite the scientist, she was truly one of a kind."

In the low light of the winery office, Nicolas sketched out the layout of the vineyard. He flipped some music on to muffle their conversation to any potential listeners. Adding details to the map, he pointed out the high ground, outbuildings, paths.

"Potentially, he could hide in many of the outbuildings, and not be found for some time. He cannot have been here more than 24 hours, so he may not yet know which are the least travelled. If it were me, I would want eyes and ears on the main house. There is an old watchtower here, about 500 meters from the house." He sketched out its position, why it would be advantageous.

Ronan nodded, studying the detailed hand-drawn map, "From there, he could see and hear with the right equipment, be protected from the weather. Unlikely to be well-traveled, in the middle of the fields and in disrepair."

Nicolas smiled, clearly enjoying using his training again. "Too far for even a powerful rifle to hit a target inside the house with the stormy weather we've been having, so he'd have to leave to make a move.

Still, this is the spot I would choose, were I him, and my goal were surveillance only. Secluded. From here he can see the entire property. The original watchtower for the area."

Ronan considered, studying the location of the outbuildings around the house. "You're sure Payson and Alain are safe?"

Nicolas pointed out the stone outbuilding on the map. "They won't need to go far from the house, and there is only one entrance into the storeroom. Alain will be on alert and will ensure they don't linger in any open areas."

Considering every potential hiding place, outcomes of any interventions, eliminating any possibility for error, he formed a plan. "I'll make my move at night. Looks to be stormy again tonight, poor visibility."

Nicolas nodded, delineating a path along the map, "If you come from this angle, it will be a bit of a hike, but then you can drop in from behind undetected. The window from that direction is inaccessible, so he won't see you coming."

Ronan stepped back and crossed his arms. He shook his head and laughed at himself. "This is all assuming he is where we think he is hiding, and that he is even there at the time I go looking for him... again assuming that he is even in the area."

Nicolas stood and gave him a manly pat on the back, "Or we could just hide inside like sitting ducks and wait for him to make a move." He laughed and they headed out of the office. "I'll be your lookout. Let's go grab some radios."

After a long day of planning, going over every eventuality, and distracting themselves while they waited, Alain arrived in the large parlor with wine and snacks before dinner. "I find that I've worked up quite an appetite."

As soon as the snacks were on the coffee table, Payson filled up a small plate with fruit and gorgeous fresh vegetables, hard cheeses, dried meats, and a chunk of steaming fresh baguette. The fruit looked amazing; she'd never seen fresh berries as plump and juicy as she had here. Ronan sat down on the couch next to her and tried to steal a piece, but Payson deftly moved the plate out of his reach. "Hey, this is mine."

Enjoying the return of her easy banter, he popped the stolen raspberry in his mouth and reached for the wine instead. "Is this your own?" he asked Nicolas and Alain, studying the label.

"Yes. I will be sure we send a few crates with the shipment of antiques. It is the best in the region." Nicolas held his own glass for Ronan to fill and sat back into the facing couch next to Alain. Ronan smiled, appreciating that his host took such obvious pride in his work.

He turned to hand a glass to Payson. She shook her head, "No, thanks. I'm still jet lagged. The wine would knock me out flat. I'll stick with water. My stomach is still a little off from the traveling anyway." She was babbling again. She only babbled when she was nervous. Ronan felt terrible for bringing her into this stressful situation.

He nodded, leaning back with his glass and pulled her against him, needing to hold her close. "Find some interesting pieces today?"

Payson smiled, enjoying the change in subject. "Yes, Alain has some truly beautiful pieces. Your sister is going to go nuts." Turning to Alain, she told him about Maddy and her weakness for antiques. "I have to invite her over for first dibs whenever I receive one of your shipments."

The foursome enjoyed easy conversation for the next hour, mostly avoiding talking about the elephant in the room, aka the impending mission. Ronan enjoyed talking and laughing with their hosts, but he noted Payson had gone quiet sometime during the evening. Leaning against his shoulder, her eyes drew closed and her breathing slowed. She was sound asleep. Apparently, she hadn't even needed the glass of wine to knock her out.

Looking down at Payson, Ronan placed a soft kiss on her head. He whispered to his hosts, "I hope you don't mind if we miss dinner, but I think we'll call it a night." Ever the gracious hosts, they nodded and rose to clear the snack trays. Ronan lifted Payson into his arms and carried her to their room.

Holding her against him as he fell asleep at her side in the plush bed, listening to the accelerating rainfall, Ronan was absurdly content despite his pre-dawn plans. Wrapped around her, he didn't think he could survive without her. If he couldn't find a way out of this, maybe she would consider hiding with him. Not that he would even consider asking it of her; he wasn't that selfish.

He could see why she'd been wanting to come; her friends were truly amazing people. Generous, kind, and they hadn't even been fazed when he'd told them about the danger he'd brought to their home. At least something had gone his way this week. He could only hope the next steps would go as smoothly.

$$29$$

Night crawled slowly by. The rain came and went, but the sky was dumping buckets by the time Ronan slipped on his black running shoes in the dark bedroom. Behind the horizon yet, the sun was but a dream away. Payson sat up in bed, watching as Ronan sat at the side of the bed to tie his shoes.

Payson wrapped her long limbs around him, trapping him for an extra minute. Whispering softly against his back, she complained, "It's a stupid plan. He shot you with the intent to kill you last time. I'd rather run with you, forever if we have to, than risk him getting you in his sights again."

Ronan gently stroked her arms that were wrapped firmly around him, holding him in place. His voice quiet, the lights still dark, he needed to explain. "This is what I'm good at. The sort of thing I trained my entire life for. Please, trust that I can do this. I am done, ready to settle down. But... if I'm ever to have any peace, I need to find those weapons and prevent them from getting into the hands of someone that will use them."

Her voice still sleepy, she leaned her head against his back, "And I'm to stay here while you're out there? Sleeping soundly in bed like a damsel?"

"Nicolas will be watching the vineyard; Alain will be running security inside the house. Why don't you get dressed and ready, in case we need to run? Be ready to call the police if necessary?"

Resigned, she released him from her iron grip. Ronan turned and kissed her softly, briefly, whispering, "I'll be back. Soon as I can. If you need updates, find Alain. Stay away from the windows."

Ronan stood with his hand on the knob, ready to leave. Dressed in black from head to toe, heading out on a mission, Ronan felt a desperation that he hadn't felt during an op in years. Never had a mission been so vital. Trusting another was never an option, but he couldn't help but place his wholehearted faith in Payson to see this through with him. He was stalling, he knew it, but he wanted to be sure she was ok before he left.

Her emotions raw, she held strong with deliberate posture and voice unwavering as she whispered one final worry, "With no good hiding points for such a wide berth around the house, won't he see you coming?"

Ronan flashed her an arrogant grin, "They never see me coming." He enjoyed the clichéd lines, knowing it would at least make her smile, if not convince her.

Swiftly moving out the door, he dashed silently down the stairs at the same rapid pace. His mind raced a mile a minute, calculating each step, each turn. Driveway clear, he ran straight out the front door without pause, eyes scanning, he circled wide around the outbuildings on the path he'd mapped in his head.

Pitch black, not even the stars were out to light his path. Just as he wanted.

Biting rain soaked him until he was cold to the bone, starkly contrasting the dripping sweat and burning muscles from his sprint around the vineyard. The contradictory sensations drove him faster. Splashing through a puddle at the far side of the vineyard, Ronan rounded the last bend and descended until he could just make out the silhouette of the crumbling watchtower.

Nicolas was right, that's where he would choose to sit and wait if he were watching the house. If he'd timed it right, asshole would be getting some quick shuteye before the household awoke. Ruling out luck, as counting on things to go his way was just asking for trouble, he tucked himself in a cluster of enormous oaks behind the tower. He didn't want to risk being turned into Swiss cheese if naptime was already over.

Watching, waiting for signs of movement, his adrenaline, steady, unrelenting, continued to coarse through his veins. Deep beyond the horizon, a soft purple glow cast the first hint of dawn across the vine-yards. From the upper window, he saw the briefest flash of movement.

Pulling out the high-tech radio Nicolas had given him, he notified Nicolas of his position, speaking quietly, "He's here, in the watchtow-er as expected. I'm in position."

A clipped Parisienne accent returned, "Be ready, I'm running the diversion." On cue, the lights from the next field over flicked on and the loud crack of a single gunshot echoed across the vineyard.

Movement from the tower window. Connor was climbing down from his perch to investigate, or to run. Ronan jumped at the oppor-tunity to get close to the tower without being seen. He sprinted for the tower and waited just outside the exit.

He heard Connor coming out of the tower. With an easy shift of his foot, he conveniently tripped the asshole. Always worked on his brother, why not on a ruthless mercenary?

Despite the slippery mud, merc was back up in seconds, sidearm in hand. He looked pissed, but fortunately disoriented.

Anticipating an attack, Connor aimed for Ronan.

A cheeky smile flashed across Ronan's face; he went on the offensive. Avoiding another gunshot wound, Ronan hit the ground and, with his legs, knocked his opponent back into the mud.

Connor struggled to stand, growling with frustration as he became further drenched and heavy with mud.

Soaked to the skin, Ronan shook the rain and sweat off his brow and heaved on top of the merc as he aimed the pistol.

The move was enough, and Connor recoiled.

That was all he needed. Clenching his fist, Ronan swung out and knocked the gun out of his grip. It flew out of reach.

Ronan knew he was no match to overtake the gigantic man; with a spin, Ronan was knocked off balance and crashed into the ground. Snarling, he ignored the throbbing aches and stood.

Standing face to face, fists in ready position, each got in a few good licks. Asshole threw a hell of a punch. Didn't matter how quick he moved, how hard he hit, the enormous Scot wasn't taking the hint.

Thrown back by a stiff kick to the chest, Ronan felt the wind rushing from his lungs before he even hit the ground. Pissed as hell, he knew when he was outmatched physically. He wouldn't win this one with his fists. Asshole was ridiculously strong. And absurdly fast for someone so big.

Struggling to take a deep breath, fighting the burning in his sternum, he assessed his options. Glancing to his side, he smirked when he saw the bat-shaped board leaning against the stone building. Neither his hand-to-hand combat training nor his intelligence work could have taught him how to hit a perfect home run.

Maybe he should play on a rec league. He flashed to those visions of coaching little league; hell no, he wasn't losing today. Rising slowly, he smiled at his opponent, ignoring the drip of blood tickling its way down from his eyebrow.

Hair plastered to his face from sweat, rain, and caked mud, Connor flicked the sopping locks out of his face. Breaths heaving from exertion, the burly Scot sneered. He should have flattened Ronan with some of the hits he'd made.

Ronan quirked an eyebrow, "If you hadn't already figured it out, I don't stay down."

The sun peaked just over the horizon, illuminating the gloomy sky. Ronan stepped out from the shadow of the tower, letting the bright sunshine warm his back, taking advantage of the light to stun his opponent's vision. Connor threw his body weight, going in for the tackling KO.

Ronan shifted to a perfect at-bat position and swung with full force at the guy's gut. Didn't want to knock him out, let alone kill him, or he wouldn't learn anything.

Connor doubled over from the hit, falling to ground, bracing his hand against his broken ribs as he gasped for air.

Owning the advantage, Ronan hog-tied Connor's extremities and left him on the ground, bleeding and teetering on the edge of consciousness. Crouching closer, Ronan studied his opponent. "Wow, you sure do look like your brother. He sang like a bird; you going to do the same?"

Connor spit a mouthful of blood; the dark, sticky sputum dissipated into the mucky ground. Struggling to pull himself up despite the bindings and bruises, Connor made it to his knees.

No mercy for the guy that had tried to kill him, Ronan blasted him with an uppercut to the jaw. "It took five hours in surgery and a blood transfusion thanks to your bullets, asshole. I have no qualms about shooting you in the fucking face."

With a mocking laugh, Connor sneered, "You Americans are all the same. Think you're in control of a situation. Death would be a blessing; save me from myself."

Ronan was done with the chit-chat. Hoping he'd scared the asshole into believing he was unstable. Testing, he demanded, "Where's your employer? Sent you alone to do the dirty work, did he?" Connor's sneer grew more feral. "I suspect he was hoping one of us would take out the other, leaving just one of us for him to dispose of."

Doubt emerged in his captive's eyes, but he stayed silent. Ronan pushed further, "You didn't think he had any use for you now? You failed to deliver on the weapons, and you failed to deliver on my death... again. Not a very useful mercenary, are you?"

Connor shook his head and quit thrashing against the tightly wrapped bindings, resigned. "Like you, I'm ready to retire. Have a lovely little house in the Caribbean picked out. You help me, I'll help you."

Ronan's eyebrow raised in question, but otherwise he held his body still, refusing to show his hand. "Why would I help you? You tortured children, families, with the biologic weaponry you tried to sell. I'm tracking down those weapons and destroying every last one."

Mirthlessly, Connor laughed, "American," he swore. "That wasn't us. Was made to look like us. Yes, my brother and I facilitated the exchange, for a very good price. But, I'm no psychopath. It was one of your own that led that little demonstration."

Taken aback, Ronan held his face calm, but was seething inside. At this point, he was confident he knew the identity of the mole, but he was waiting for Connor to say it. The fact that their own had unleashed the weapon was new and was more than he could bear.

"Where are the weapons now? I know they didn't make it to the terrorist's base."

Connor lowered his gaze, defeated. "After your man's demonstration, I stashed the weapons in a safe place. Your man lied. Promised us a fortune, not a life of nightmares."

"What do you care?"

"Weapons with revolting effects like that? No scientist would create those for actual use. They're for threats, like the cold war. We're not monsters, just fond of a fat paycheck. Let me go. I'll tell you where the weapons are."

Ronan inhaled deeply, looking around at the rows of early spring vines, feeling the first kiss of dawn and its promise of warmth, renewal. "Give me the weapons, and the identity and location of the mole, and I'll make sure you get a nice deal."

Connor smiled, ignoring the start of swollen bruise on his jaw. "Better yet, I'll help you catch the mole. You destroy the weapons; I'll get you the man behind it all. But I'm not joining my brother in prison or the deal's off."

"Why did you hunt me down, if you already know everything? Why aren't you enjoying your margaritas on the beach already?" Nothing ever came in a nice neat package. Layers and layers of bullshit, as usual.

Running his tongue over his teeth, Connor's cheek bulged, he cussed before continuing. "As much as I hate to admit it, I need your help. I don't have the resources to destroy the weapons without risking releasing that shit into the air. You do. And, call me old fashioned, but I want that asshole to fry."

Silver tongue. Human lie detector. Cold, no-bullshit, no-questions-asked operative. Best of the best. If he were still employed by the CIA, Ronan's next actions would never be sanctioned. Which is why he was so damn good at what he did.

Ronan trusted his instincts, which had been more reliable than any hard facts time and again. "You've got a deal. Tell me his name."

As enraged as Ronan, letting the name pour out like boiling lava meeting turbulent ocean waves, Connor hissed, "You already know. His name is Sharpe."

Fuck. He'd known it for a while now. Since Sharpe blamed him for hiding the weapons. Insisted, really. He began to suspect that Sharpe had been the driving force behind Ronan's retirement. Eager to protect her protégé, Sara hadn't hesitated to pull him out of the field.

30

PAYSON WAITED ANXIOUSLY FOR Ronan's return. Every subtle sound echoed in her mind, each one sounding like a gunshot piercing Ronan's skull. She'd never felt so terrified in her life.

Finally, she knew what the word courage meant. She'd always thought it meant the absence of fear, but today she knew, it wasn't the absence of fear, but more the gumption to keep going. For Ronan, for their future, she would muster up whatever courage she could find. She'd found her optimism, her courage to go on with her life, run her store, and even come here when she'd lost her heart when Ronan had left.

Holding strong, she found Alain in his office, peering through the curtain. From across the hall, she heard Nicolas holler, "Ronan is bringing a guest for breakfast." Payson could hear the ironic smile in his voice. What was he talking about?

She didn't have to wait long to find out. Alain hadn't questioned, but instead quickly fixed a pot of American-style drip coffee and set the kitchen table with fresh croissants, jam, and brie. Coming in through the glass door facing the vineyard was Ronan, bruised and bleeding, along with a slightly more bruised and bleeding giant of a man. The giant's wrists were locked behind his back.

The man from the train. With a few gray hairs in his sideburns teasing his age to be about late thirties, lean build, and dressed in black like Ronan, the 'guest' looked around apprehensively at the cozy setting.

In a thick Scottish brogue, their guest tipped his head in greeting, "I'm sorry to intrude on yer peaceful morning."

Alain, ever the gracious host, eyed Ronan with a puzzled expression while he welcomed the *guest*. "It is not a problem. Would you care for some coffee? Breakfast?" The guest and Ronan sat at the small kitchen table while Alain set out the food he'd prepared and poured coffee for the group.

Soaked to the skin and ignoring the drying blood seeping from the laceration over his eyebrow, Ronan finally made introductions. Looking around, Ronan found his guest to be sedate and not trying to escape or harm anyone. He cut the bindings with the nearby kitchen knife.

Connor took a seat at the table and accepted a steaming cup of coffee.

Ronan asked, "What are the chances he's watching us now?"

Connor took a brief pause to thank Alain, "This is truly excellent coffee," before turning back to Ronan, "Sharpe wouldn't risk himself; he'll want to stay miles away from you. You're the biggest threat to his success."

Ronan raised an eyebrow in question, "Why would he fear me?" He sat across the table from his new friend and picked up his own coffee, leaning back to enjoy the drink.

Payson remained far from the absurd conversation, sitting on the edge of the barstool. Nicolas leaned against the doorway to the kitchen, observing while Alain took a seat at the kitchen table with the others.

Connor tore into his croissant like he hadn't eaten in days. Probably hadn't had much more than protein bars in the past few days, hiding out around the vineyard, tracking Ronan. "For the very reason you and I are having this conversation. As much as he wants your death, he needs those weapons back, or it's his ass on the line. And, he knows either you or I must have the weapons."

"Does Sharpe think you're still working for him?"

"How do you think I found you so easily?"

Payson watched as the huge Scot sat politely in the kitchen. She was surrounded by badasses and none of them seemed to realize this was downright weird. You didn't just have coffee and breakfast with the man that had tried to kill you. And, judging by the blood on his face and shiner forming around his eye, beat the crap out of you a few moments ago. Well, maybe more beat the crap out of each other; both were soaked, muddy, bruised, and bleeding.

Leaning against the breakfast bar, Payson interrupted, "Where's the woman from the train station?"

The entire room swiftly turned their heads toward Payson. Connor shook his head, looking to Ronan, he nodded, "Smart lass, that one." He looked back to Payson, "She should be here momentarily." Payson raised her eyebrow suspiciously. He chuckled, "Peacefully."

Payson let it go for the moment, but she wasn't done grilling him. Ronan may have made a new friend, but she wasn't risking his safety. "Was it Sharpe that ordered you to kill Ronan back in London?"

Connor slowly chewed his croissant, not sure how to answer. He didn't have to. From behind her, the petite blond woman entered from the hallway. Payson about jumped out of her skin, her pulse quickened at the sneaky arrival.

The woman stood in the doorway, ringing her hands in worry. Ronan stared her down, brow scrunched in confusion. "It wasn't Connor. I shot you."

Speechless, Ronan stuttered, "Rose, you...? Why did you try to kill me?... How are you alive?"

A single tear fell down her cheek. She remained frozen in the doorway, knowing she wasn't welcome. "I am truly sorry. I shouldn't blame Sharpe; I should have seen him for what he was. He called me shortly after we parted that night. Said you were a mole, working with the terrorists to get the weapons."

Ronan shook his head, furious. Payson watched as he shut down, leaned back in his chair to distance himself. Staring out the window into the misty morning, he brooded.

Connor rose from his chair. "There, there lass. You were doing your job." He stood behind Rose and rubbed her arms gently, soothingly. Turning to the others, Connor continued for her, "I approached Rose shortly after; I'd been watching all of you for some time. I didn't know where else to turn. She was pretty jaded at being ordered to kill a friend, so she wasn't hard to convince."

They sat silently for a few moments. Payson ached for Ronan. No wonder he wanted out so desperately. Every time he dug further, everything he knew jumbled and turned him inside out. Payson stalked closer to Rose, enjoying her height advantage, despite the fact that the woman could likely kick her ass. "How could you think you could come here?"

Rose looked up so her eyes met Payson's. Filled with tears, Payson didn't know if she could believe the grief. Like Ronan, she was a professional. Trained to manipulate, lie, kill.

"I know I can never win his trust, or yours. But know that I will never forgive myself for not listening to my instincts. For blindly following orders. Well... mostly. I called the paramedics before I even shot him; I... it was the best I could come up with at the time. This whole business, it's bullshit. That's why we faked my death, so I could get the hell away from the lies."

Shaking his head, Ronan finally looked over at Rose, "This is where you and I differ. No matter what intel I dig up, I trust myself first. I just wish I'd followed my instincts about Sharpe sooner." Drawn to him, Payson moved to sit in the chair at his side.

Rose nodded somberly, "I know. There's a reason you're Sara's favorite. Why Sharpe fears you. I know I'll never be able to make up for what I did, but I will do all that I can to help take down Sharpe..."

Done with the chit-chat, Nicolas, from his perch on the barstool, looked to Connor and demanded, "Where did the weapons come from?"

"Where else? Sharpe. Fresh from the lab, All-American Weaponry."

Payson shook her head in disbelief. Taking her hand in his, Ronan nodded, unsurprised. "Part of the reason I wanted out, long before January, was the fucking politics. The shady dealings. I signed on to eliminate threats, not brew violence. If Sharpe obtained those weapons from the US government, then he wasn't alone. Proving it will be the challenge."

Connor nodded, sitting back down and stuffing a piece of brie into his mouth. "We need to pin Sharpe down. Either catch him in the act or nail down a feckin' detailed confession."

Ronan shook his head as he swallowed a final gulp of coffee and set the mug back on the smoothly weathered tabletop. "He's too shrewd; we won't catch him in the act. If he thinks I know where the weapons are, let's let him believe that." Ronan gave a half smile, ego shining bright, "Tell him you've found a way to twist my arm, for me to give him the location of the weapons."

"He'll want to see the weapons himself. After everything we've all worked for, I'm not letting him near those weapons. Nor will he believe you got scared and wanted to give up the weapons to save your own ass."

"Not without a damn good reason, no. Tell him you're holding Payson hostage," he gave her a quick wink and a squeeze of her hand. "If he's been watching me as closely as I suspect, he'll know I'd do anything to keep her safe. But, tell him that I'll only meet with him directly. No more middlemen... no offense."

The scot snorted. "None taken. She's a fine-looking lass, but I'm not so sure he'd believe you'll give up weapons of that magnitude for a woman. I guarantee, he's no romantic."

Alain cleared his throat. "Perhaps you ought to tell him she's pregnant with Ronan's child. If he doesn't understand love, maybe he'll understand fatherhood." Payson tried to hide the blush, but it wasn't possible. Hopefully, Ronan would think it was the idea rather than the truth.

With a wicked grin, Ronan nodded, "That would do it. Payson, mind if I tie you up?"

Sitting in the corner of the most desolate-looking outbuilding on the grounds, Payson pulled and stretched her hands to free herself of the bindings. She rolled around on the ground until dust packed into her clothes and her hair turned into a tangled rat's nest. There, that should do it.

"Honey, I think you're getting a little too into this. I'm really not into the hostage-captor fantasy if that's what you're thinking." Ronan rolled his eyes with a playful smirk.

"Ha ha. I'm making it look convincing. How do I look?"

The ex-merc and the ex-spy stood side-by-side with identical expressions, arms folded, accenting those spectacularly developed biceps. "Lass, you look like hell. Now, try not to smile." Pulling out his phone, Connor snapped a few shots of her looking terrified. "Ya know, she even has a nice glow about her."

Payson laughed off the joke, hoping Ronan wouldn't look too closely and figure out she was pregnant before she was ready to tell him. "Funny. Help me up, I'm hopping in the shower now."

Alain walked in the room, taking in the staged captive scene, he offered, "Please, Payson, we can protect you here."

Ronan nodded in agreement, unmistakably concerned.

Furious, hating feeling cornered, Payson stood with her hands and feet still tied and hopped over to Ronan. "What if Sharpe doesn't believe the hostage story? Or if he decides he needs more than a few photos and a mercenary's word? This is the first place he'll come, putting all three of us in danger. I'm not endangering our hosts any more than I already have. The last place he'll expect to find me is with Ronan. I can go incognito."

With a small laugh, Ronan teased, untying her ropes. "Incognito? You don't exactly blend in with a crowd. Your hair, those fairy green eyes, not to mention your atrocious French accent... he'll recognize you right away."

Huffy, Payson held her head high. "We should be far from here anyway, or he might suspect something. You're supposed to be in hiding to protect me. Remember? You ran away to keep me safe."

Connor nodded. "We need to nail down our story to avoid suspicion. He doesn't know you're here; I've kept that little detail to myself. So, we tell him that I captured yer woman to force ya to tell me where the weapons are. I can't hold her anywhere near here, or I'd risk you tracking us down and getting her back before we learned anything."

"I have a little a safehouse outside of Cork I've used now and again. A good friend, Brody, Irish cop, lives near there. Sharpe's not supposed to know about the house, it's mine not CIA, but I know he does. I was last there a few months before I was shot. Sharpe said a few things he shouldn't have known, stuff Brody and I talked about." Ronan ran his fingers through his hair, closing his eyes in frustration. "Shit, I should have figured it out then. He'd been tracking me already."

Payson stood helplessly, reaching for Ronan but knowing he needed some space to work it out. "I studied abroad in Ireland my last year of high school, not far from Cork. I know just the place we can trap him."

Shaking his head, Ronan's expression tight with worry, he hated the *we* idea. But, she wasn't wrong. As much as Alain and Nicolas could take care of themselves, he didn't want to bring anymore trouble to their doorstep. "Brody would be on board, bring the police to make the arrest. There aren't many others I'd trust to pull this off, and there sure as hell aren't many in CIA we could confidently rely on right now."

Connor put his hands in his pockets and rocked on his heels. "I'd say we have a solid plan. Let's nail down the details."

The rendezvous was in twenty-four hours, at the site Payson had sketched for him in detail. Apparently, she'd worked as a tour guide at an old fort near Kinsale for a few months. Walking Connor and Rose to the front door, Ronan couldn't help but feel like this was going to work. Whatever his reservations, he felt more comfortable counting on Connor to hold up his end of the bargain than he'd ever relied on Sharpe.

Gathering in the small foyer, Ronan asked, "Where are the weapons?"

Connor looked on at the fields out the open front door. "Four clicks away from the south-east Syrian-Iraqi border." He pulled out a map with the precise coordinates written down and handed it to Ronan. "Buried deeply beneath an abandoned steel warehouse." Connor pulled out his phone.

Standing close to his former adversary, Ronan could hear both sides of the conversation. Listening to the agonizing, detailed conversation in which Connor described Payson's fictitious abduction from the vineyard, and Ronan's panic to get her and their unborn child back. Describing how he was holding her in a tower house in the north of France; just far enough to draw them from Alain and Nicolas, but easy distance for a subtle kidnapping. Telling him about the meeting place in Ireland, where the exchange was to happen.

The girl for the weapons. Ronan cringed on hearing his former superior's grating voice through the line, hating that he sniggered at Ronan's broken heart, the description of Payson's terror. At his greedy desperation to find the abhorrent weapons.

Ending the call, Connor turned to Ronan, "This is where we part ways. Get those weapons out of the hands of men with agendas. If you're ever in Barbados... drinks on me."

Ronan shook his head in disbelief. "Enjoy your retirement."

Stepping into the foyer, Rose apologized again. "I'm sorry. For everything. Thank you for hearing me out."

Ronan nudged her, "I'm just glad you're a lousy shot."

It was tough; he'd worked with her a few times and had thought well of her. Still did, but it was hard to forgive when the crime was so personally traumatic. At least she had called the paramedics first; he would have bled out if they hadn't come charging in before he even hit the floor.

She gave him a friendly nudge back. "I don't think I'll ever be able to forgive myself. If there is anything you need, ever, just let me know. If you don't mind though, I'd like to stay dead. Out of the game, indefinitely."

With a warm smile and a nod to Ronan, Connor took Rose's hand in his, "Best of luck to you."

No transportation in sight, the retired mercenary walked down the muddy drive, letting the rain wash away the blood from the fight. The dead spy leaving with him, the ironic pair walking hand-in-hand. Ronan shook his head; this was turning out to be one of the strangest ops of his career.

Nicolas stepped into the foyer, taking a moment to go over things with Ronan. "The plan is sound. I'll be nearby, should he be lying."

"Thanks. Were it just me, I'd go it alone. I can't risk Payson that way. I'll be glad to have her close, but I..."

Nicolas leaned against the doorway with his arms crossed. "Agreed. Alain will stay here to keep our home safe."

31

RONAN PAID THE DOCENT as she flirtatiously handed him a map, revealing the most gorgeous fairy green eyes he'd ever seen as she lowered her glasses. Stepping out onto the cobbled field in the heart of the crumbling star fort of southeast Ireland, Ronan masked his fear. He didn't like having her in the middle of things, but he hadn't been able to let her out of his sight. However this went down, her safety was his priority.

Still cold and damp, few tourists were exploring the park this morning. Guided tours wouldn't start for another hour or so. Playing the tourist himself, he held his map out as he searched the terrain, leisurely making his way to the southernmost rampart. The perfect spot for a confession.

Sitting comfortably on a crenel, he imagined the battles that took place here. Most recently, the fort was returned to Irish hands by the IRA before it became a national park. His thoughts settled on one final battle that must take place in this crumbling failure of a defense.

Across the expanse of green lawn, he saw Sharpe immediately. The asshole approached deliberately, confidently, despite his wide, arthritic gait that resulted from years of jumping out of planes, before being recruited for intelligence work.

Sitting comfortably, looking as relaxed as the gentle breeze that kicked up his neatly trimmed hair, Ronan waited. Studying his adversary.

Sharpe recognized him immediately. His unsurprised expression confirmed that Sharpe had been watching Ronan closely these past months. Officially, Sharpe had never seen Ronan without long hair and a beard, so Ronan would have expected a double take.

Stopping a good ten feet away, Sharpe kept his hands in his pockets. "McAllister, good to see you are looking well in your retirement."

With a sardonic laugh, Ronan said, "I was enjoying my retirement until you decided to ruin it."

Sneering, Sharpe responded, "I made that retirement happen. Gave you a break when you wouldn't die, after all, you did capture Peter Young for me. Had I known you were the one with the answers I needed, yours and Peter's roles would have been reversed."

Raising his eyebrow cynically, Ronan scoffed, "You kept me close a long time before you knew the Youngs didn't have the weapons. How many other agents have you been tracking without approval?"

Sharpe smiled as his own cunning. "You know what they say, keep your friends close and your enemies closer. That's why you couldn't handle this job. The line between friend and enemy is hazy at the best of times."

"Sure. Friends, right. I'd like to know who you consider a friend. Was it the money or politics that drove you to sell the weapons to the terrorists?"

Holding his ground, Sharpe shook his head. "That's not how we're playing this. I've got your girl. Pretty thing too. Feisty. Not showing yet, but I hear she's got a bun in the oven. You sure stayed busy in your retirement. You tell me where the weapons are, and I let her go."

Brow crinkling with regret, Ronan ran a hand over his face, letting his fear show. Wasn't hard; he didn't even have to fake it. Shit, it was scary enough thinking Sharpe could have taken her, but if she had been pregnant, Ronan would be that much more desperate. "I need to know that she's ok."

Sharpe held up his phone that held a picture of Payson. Tied up, mouth gagged. Ronan let Sharpe see his relief on seeing the picture they'd staged. Connor had held up his end of the bargain well, texting the staged photographs of Payson tied up and miserable, moments before Sharpe arrived.

"That do it for you? This was two minutes ago." Sharpe showed him the timestamp on the text.

Ronan nodded weakly. "Where is she?"

"Somewhere safe. Not here. As soon as the weapons are back in my possession, I'll release her." He locked his phone and tucked it neatly back in his coat pocket.

"That wasn't the deal. You give me the girl, and I give you the location of the weapons." Ronan seethed, but remained steady in his position.

Sharpe sneered, "Nice try, McAllister. I'm not letting go of my bargaining chip until I have the weapons in my hands."

"Honestly, there may be a bit of a problem retrieving the weapons. American troops took over the base they're hidden in; just inside the Syrian border." Ronan's face darkened with worry.

Sharpe threw his head back in laughter. "Well that sure worked out in my favor. I'll just call the general and let him know he can start digging; get rid of the middleman. Our own troops can make the drop. Not that they'll know what they're transporting, of course."

Ronan raised his arms in surrender when Sharpe aimed his concealed sidearm directly at him. "Wait. Just, wait. I did everything you asked."

Sharpe shook his head. "I can't leave any witnesses. Eyes only, as I said."

A confused, despondent expression overtook Ronan's face, "How high up does this go? Sara? General Linh?"

Laughing self-righteously, Sharpe countered, "Maybe you're not as bright as she always said. Sara's too strait-laced for under the table deals. Keeps her nose awfully clean for a former spook. I'm here so General Linh can keep his nose clean, no official military involvement. You don't think they would just hand over dangerous biological weaponry, with the power to wipe out millions, to little old me? My idea, my deal, my fat promotion on the way, but this is a hell of a lot bigger than me."

"Tell me Sharpe, are you planning to shoot me *here*? Or, are we going somewhere less public?" Ronan held his hands in the air. Sharpe rolled his eyes. "I'm just trying to plan ahead. First tour of the day starts soon, and I'd sure hate for my bloody corpse to be part of it. Might add a nice new ghost story to add to the tour though."

Ronan kept his hands in the air, face neutral. Distracting his adversary from the stealthy goddess sneaking through the fort, swiftly getting closer and closer. Not part of the plan, but damn, she was a natural. He should have known after the rousing game of laser tag.

Sharpe continued, quite pleased with himself, "Why don't you just stand up, so you'll fall backwards. It will take days, minimum, before anyone notices. It's a pretty big drop. Silencer might reduce my accuracy a bit, so hold still for me." Asshole was enjoying himself.

From the grassy rise behind the inner rampart on which Sharpe stood, Ronan saw a wooden hurley swing round and knock Sharpe smack dab in the knee. His howl of painful disbelief was rather gratifying.

Ronan didn't hesitate, he took advantage of the distraction and dove the few steps towards Sharpe and nailed him with a stiff jab to the nose.

Blood pouring from his nostrils, limping on his injured leg, Sharpe pulled his gun from his large coat pocket and swung around toward the newcomer.

After her brilliant swing of the hurley, Payson had ducked below the rampart, out of sight. Smart.

Kicking Sharpe firmly in the backside, Ronan dove after his tumbling form as the asshole crashed the ten or more feet to the next level down where Payson hid.

Sharpe struggled to stand, holding the new gash on his forehead, conscious but disoriented. It was clear he understood when his gaze landed on Payson, gripping the hurley in preparation to smack him again, smiling mockingly at him.

Shaking his head with a superior smile, Ronan taunted, "You know, you should really be careful who you trust in this business." Ronan finished him with a solid right hook, knocking him out cold.

Payson flew into his arms. "It's over, right?" Sirens wailed in the background; the fort notably empty around them as the area was secured.

Ronan climbed back up the wall and picked up his phone. "Sara, you got all that?"

He heard a woo-hoo from the other end of the line. "Sure did, every word. You better believe I'll be making some calls. Chasing this all the way up. We've got the weapons too; they're on the way to be destroyed.

Apparently, they'd been stolen from a test facility. American, but they hadn't been approved for use. I've got a few calls in to ensure they never are."

Another voice echoed through the line, thick Irish accent, "Nice work Ronan. I hope that's the sound of our fine police force approaching in the background."

Ronan smiled, "That's them. Thanks, Brody. I trust he'll be locked up securely until he can be extradited?"

"Absolutely. We'll lock him in our most secure facility."

Ronan ended the conference call. In the distance, he watched as Nicolas gave him a friendly salute, and made his exit before the police arrived. Seconds later, Irish police came running into the fort.

"I thought you were going to wait in the gift shop?" Taking her hand in his, he led her away from the chaotic scene once he was sure Sharpe was in cuffs and in custody.

Payson leaned into him. "I couldn't let you have all the fun. Besides, I haven't been hurling since high school."

Hand in hand, ignoring the steady influx of police all around, they slowly toured the fort. "When we get home, how about a few rounds at the batting cages instead?"

"It's a date."

Ronan sighed, starting to feel a sense of relief. "I'll have to go back to Langley for a few weeks, at least. I'll be drowning in paperwork for a while."

Pulling back, Payson looked up at him with a playful grin. "Don't take too long. I've got work for you to do."

32

WALKING CONFIDENTLY ACROSS THE airport, Payson saw Maddy waving madly at her. "You're home. And you're safe. Where's my elusive brother this time?"

Reaching her friend, Payson tossed her backpack, trusting Maddy to catch it and carry it to the car. "It's good to be home. He should be home soon. He's stuck at work for another few weeks. They're making him teach an ethics class."

Maddy threw her head back in laughter. "Oh, that's fantastic. I'll bet he loves that."

Walking arm in arm, they chatted and laughed. Hoisting herself into Maddy's jeep, Maddy stared at her friend's belly. "Are you starting to show?"

Shaking her head in adamant denial, Payson defended herself, "I've just been eating out a lot; belly pooches happen when travelling. I'm not that far along."

Pulling out of the parking spot, Maddy rolled her eyes. "Maybe. What did Ronan say, is he thrilled?"

"Uh... well. He doesn't know yet." She'd meant to tell him, but there hadn't been a time that felt right.

Swerving into the next lane, barely missing an airport shuttle that was trying to pass, Maddy was shocked. "How have you not told him? He's going to notice pretty soon."

Payson sighed. "When was I going to tell him? When he was sneaking out to capture the mercenary? Stopping an illegal weapons deal? Capturing a traitor?"

Maddy begrudgingly agreed. "Good point. But you have to tell him soon. I haven't told anyone, well, except Chase of course, but no one else knows and it's driving me crazy. You know I hate keeping secrets. Mom's going to freak."

"For twins, you and Ronan sure don't have much in common, do you?" she joked. "Besides, I haven't even seen the doctor yet. I'm calling as soon as I get home." Payson nodded, resolving to make it official.

Maddy reached into Payson's purse and grabbed her phone. She thrusted the phone into her friend's face. "Call, now. And please tell me you're taking a prenatal vitamin."

Payson rolled her eyes. "Of course I am, it's great for hair and nails. Ok, I'll call." She wanted to wait until Ronan was back so they could go together, but the nurse midwife she preferred had an opening and wanted her in for an ultrasound to confirm her due date.

Due date? What was she getting herself into?

Another fucking interrogation. This time from the Deputy Director of the CIA. Hiding his wandering imagination, he struggled to pay attention to his interrogation.

Three weeks. Three weeks since he'd last held Payson in his arms. All he could think about was getting back to her. Getting back home.

He'd been quarantined, not allowed to contact anyone outside of Langley while they completed the investigation and decided whether they wanted to arrest him or promote him. The lack of contact was heart-breaking; he couldn't imagine Payson would be pleased with him when he got back after not hearing from him for so long, again. Maybe she'd shoot him one of those spectacular death-glares she was so adept at. At least this time she knew where he was and why.

No, I don't know where Connor Young is. Yes, I had heard he was the one who shot me.

No, I don't know who Sharpe's contact within the terrorist organization was.

Yes, I know I was working without the permission of the US government in collaborating with a known mercenary, and when I recorded the confession of a higher ranking operative.

Finally,

No, thank you for the offer, but I'm finished working for the government.

Would she think it was too soon if he proposed when he got home? Before they'd left, Alain had pulled him into his office. Gave him a gorgeous leaf-patterned ring with an emerald in the center, perfectly matching Payson's eyes. Alain told him the story behind it, and that Payson had seen it and fallen in love with it. Must be worth a fortune; he'd tried to argue, but Alain told him to get moving and ask her. And to invite him to the wedding.

He had another few days left before he could go home, and he still had to teach the fucking ethics seminar. Sara had managed to ensure he continued to receive his sorry-you-nearly-died income and was left alone for the rest of his life, but only on the condition he teach the damn ethics seminar.

Sara popped into his temporary office and sat on the cursory cheap plastic chair across the desk. "You did good."

Ronan nodded, "I'm ready to get out of this mess. Why didn't you warn me about the dirty politics involved all those years ago?"

She leaned back and crossed her legs, looking out the window at the grounds. Collecting her thoughts. Finally, she brought her attention back to him, "Do you know why I hired you? On the spot?"

The corner of his mouth turned up in the devilish smile he knew turned Payson to mush. "Because you thought I was so clever."

She snorted indelicately. "Maybe because *you* thought you were so clever. No, really, I hired you because I saw something in you. I saw this intensity, this determination to do the right thing, no matter what. We need that... more than another clever smartass."

Sara rose from her chair and smoothed her charcoal gray suit. Extending her hand across the desk, she took his hand, "Are you sure you won't stay here and work with me? No more undercover work, I promise."

Ronan shook his head with a laugh and met her handshake. "Not for all the money in all the world. I found a better job back home."

"You take care, Ronan. Call me if you need anything, really."

"Thanks Sara. For everything."

Sara headed out the door, out of his life. All the shit he'd been through, he had to admit... he'd had a lot of crazy experiences. Had fulfilled the goals of his youth.

Now, to fulfill the dreams of his adulthood.

Ronan couldn't wipe the smile from his face. He had waited near-ly four long weeks to return home. Swinging his backpack over his shoulder, he swaggered across the line signifying that he was now outside of the secured area. Payson watched and rolled her eyes at his arrogance. Stopping a few inches in front of her, he looked down and grinned at her.

She rested her hand on his cheek, rough with stubble. "Don't you ever shave?" She tsked and stood on her tiptoes to reach him.

Gripping her waist, he pulled her up against him. Ignoring the crowds, the busy airport surrounding them, he fell into the kiss, pour-ing all of his love in the meeting of their lips. Breathless, she pulled away with an adorably shy smile.

"I thought you liked the beard?" He teased, pulling her hand into his and letting her lead him out of the airport. She rolled her eyes as they reached the parking garage. Her keys held in her hand, she stood back and watched as he tried to guess which car was hers.

Looking down at the baby blue 1964 and a half mustang, he laughed out loud. "Why don't you just bite the bullet and buy an Aston Martin?"

Unlocking the doors, she laughed with him. "Hey, this was my father's car, and my favorite antique. It was only in one Bond movie."

They hopped in the car, top down with the heat blasting to combat the blue-skied chill of the first sunny day of spring. She revved up the lion's roar of an engine and tore out of the garage. The car moved like it was fresh out of the shop. "Who's your mechanic?" he ran his hands along the dash as he admired the car.

She serenely replied, "I am."

"Really? You've never shown any interest in cars." The woman had a ridiculous number of layers. Held more secrets than he did.

"I'm not interested in cars, exactly. Just antiques, which extends to beauties like this one. My dad was hugely into cars, and I spent a lot of time under hoods with him. Since before I was old enough to even walk. He collected old cars; each of us kept one when he died. I don't have a garage since moving to Seaview, so I go to my older sister's place at every opportunity and work on this bad boy."

"With her moving to Denver, maybe we'll have to buy a house with a good-sized shop, for automotive repair and carpentry. Do your sisters maintain their own cars, too?"

"No. Cara was too young to learn and Jen to prissy to care. They keep theirs stored and drive newer cars. If they have any issues, I fix them."

As they merged onto the expressway, the wind was too loud for conversation. Ronan didn't mind, he relaxed and enjoyed the moment. Patting the little box in his pocket, he felt increasingly impatient. He wanted to time it just right, but he wasn't sure he could wait much longer.

They arrived back in town at dusk. Without asking, she drove him straight to her apartment. Half of his belongings were there anyway. Following her up the stairs, he felt a wave of excitement, of anxiety as they returned home, heart thumping frantically in his chest.

She flipped on the lights when they got inside, and dashed in to use the bathroom as soon as they walked in. That's ok, he could wait. Tossing his backpack and shoes under the entry table, he moved into the living room and lit a fire. For good measure, he laid her big soft throw blanket on the floor in front of the fireplace and laid down to wait.

Walking out of the bathroom, she spotted him camped out on the carpet. "Planning a romantic evening in front of the fire?"

He sat up and raised his eyebrows suggestively, "You game?"

Standing above him, she crossed her arms. "Are you ever going to leave without telling me again?"

Sitting up on one knee, he swore, "Never." He pulled the ring out of his pocket. "Payson, you're stuck with me. I love you so much. I've done a lot of soul searching over the past year. Trying to make my way along the broken path I'd been stuck on. The moment I met you, the path changed. You are everything I want. Will you marry me?"

"Shit." Tears started pouring down her face.

"Honey, did you just say *shit*?" He slowly rose from his kneeling position and pulled her against him. She let him in, let him hold her in his arms.

"I cried so damn much while you were gone. I said *shit* because I'm out of tissue."

He couldn't help but laugh. "Please say that was a yes?"

Thankfully, she laughed with him. "Yes, that's a yes. Yes, I want to marry you." Head buried against his chest, she laughed again, shedding a few more tears. "I waited my entire life for you. I love you."

He pulled back and looked down at her, wiping the tears from her wet cheeks. She smiled up at him and laughed again. "Hang on." And she ran to the bathroom. Presumably to get a tissue. Was she...? He heard the unmistakable sound of retching, a flush, teeth brushing, nose blowing, then she came back to him.

"Payson, did you just... vomit?" he cocked his head at her like a puzzled dog.

"Uh, Ronan. I, uh...," wringing her hands nervously, she took the long way around the living room but finally made it to him and sat down next to him in front of the fire. Taking a collect-your-thoughts pause, she finally, calmly announced, "I'm pregnant."

The ground suddenly fell from beneath him and he was plummeting, fast. Rubbing his chest, he soothed the new, unfamiliar ache that was developing. "Shit," he managed to say.

Quickly correcting himself, he laughed, "Sorry, I mean... wow, shit... what... how...?" Then he laughed. And laughed some more. "Wow, shit," he watched her waiting, nervous, hopeful. "I'm not sure any path is going to be as exciting as this one."

He lunged for her and pulled her into his arms, tilting her head back and kissing her deeply. Lips locked onto hers, he pulled her down on the blanket next to him and they made love until the sun rose.

The End

Carrie Thorne is the author of kick-ass romance novels, specializing in white-hot chemistry, healthy relationships, and a mix of action and dreamily falling in love. Whether it's a sinuous flow down a lazy river or evil bad dudes hot on heels, Carrie's stories will draw you in and ruin your sleep. Happily ever afters are for everyone, and kindness is everything.

She's also an introvert who loves people, travel, fitness, video games, food, and is a true Pacific Northwesterner who lives for rain and outdoors and trees and mountains and ocean, and... she's a total dork. At home, she's lucky to have two creative and confident kids, a witty veteran husband she fell at-first-sight for, and a tiny pup snuggled at her side. In addition to writing romance, Carrie has been a nurse practitioner, a Martian and Earthling geologist, a banker, and she is usually elbow-deep in a DIY project in which she bit off more than she could chew.

Where is she now? Depends on the weather. Cozied up by the fire with a steaming mug of black coffee, or stretched out on the hammock with a frothy IPA in the shade of her forest. Either way, she's working on the next great love story to conquer your TBR list.

www.CarrieThorne.com